PRAISE FOR
Up from the Blue

"A haunting tale of the terrible ways in which we fail each other; of the whys, the what ifs, and the what nows. This is not a book you'll soon forget."
—Sara Gruen, #1 *New York Times* bestselling author of
At the Water's Edge and *Water for Elephants*

"*Up from the Blue* deftly portrays a family with contradictions we can all relate to—it's beautiful and maddening, hopeful and condemning, simple, yet like a knot that takes a lifetime to untangle. You will love it completely, even as it hurts you . . . it's a heartbreaking, rewarding story that still haunts me."
—Jamie Ford, *New York Times* bestselling author of
Hotel on the Corner of Bitter and Sweet

"[An] elegant debut. . . . Henderson's fascinating novel fearlessly examines the complexities of depression, romantic and filial love, and motherhood. Beautiful, funny, sad, and complicated, Tillie's quest to understand her complex, troubled family is filled with lush descriptions of painfully emotional moments."
—*Publishers Weekly* (starred review)

"Haunting and unsettling, *Up from the Blue*'s real alchemy is the way it uncovers the stories that alternately save us and keep us from our real truths. Incandescently written, this is a stunning debut with heart."

—Caroline Leavitt, author of *Girls in Trouble* and *Pictures of You*

"*Up from the Blue* is a heart-wrenching, tender story with a mystery that kept my pulse racing. What a joy to discover Tillie Harris, the most memorable, charming, and plucky narrator in fiction since Scout Finch."

—Jessica Anya Blau, author of *The Summer of Naked Swim Parties*

THE
Flicker
OF
Old Dreams

Also by Susan Henderson

Up from the Blue

THE
Flicker
OF
Old Dreams

A NOVEL

Susan Henderson

HARPER

An Imprint of HarperCollinsPublishers

THE FLICKER OF OLD DREAMS. Copyright © 2018 by Susan Henderson. All rights reserved. Printed in the United States of America. No part of this book may be used or reproduced in any manner whatsoever without written permission except in the case of brief quotations embodied in critical articles and reviews. For information, address HarperCollins Publishers, 195 Broadway, New York, NY 10007.

HarperCollins books may be purchased for educational, business, or sales promotional use. For information, please email the Special Markets Department at SPsales@harpercollins.com.

FIRST EDITION

Library of Congress Cataloging-in-Publication Data has been applied for.

ISBN 978-0-06-283407-2 (library edition)
ISBN 978-0-06-268670-1 (pbk.)

18 19 20 21 22   LSC   10 9 8 7 6 5 4 3 2 1

Dedicated to Esther J. Scherlie Adams of Winnett, Montana

The world is growing less familiar, less yours, day by day.

—ANAND GIRIDHARADAS

THE
Flicker
OF
Old Dreams

Prologue

MOST WHO PASS THIS stretch of highway don't notice there's a town here at all. The drivers' eyes glaze over the flat, yellow land of Central Montana that goes on and on. The only landmark tall enough to see from the road is the abandoned grain elevator. But just as the gray wooden tower comes into view, the AM radio tends to lose its signal. The drivers look down to fiddle with the dial, and there goes the town of Petroleum.

When I was a kid, I could stand on the porch and listen to the grain elevator pounding like a heart. *Pop,* I had asked my father, *do we have the same heart? Because when it beats,* and I touched my chest, *I feel it right here.* He tugged gently on my ponytail. *Mary, Mary, Mary,* he said. *What an interesting little person you are.*

Before the summer when misfortune struck, one day was like another. Tractors and sprinklers clattered to life on the nearby ranches early each morning. As soon as the first speckles of sunlight reached our lawn and the empty lot beside it, I'd tramp through the weeds. Toads and jackrabbits seemed to pop out of nowhere if you stomped your foot hard enough.

At five, I was too young for boys, but I'd begun to notice them. They looked entirely different when they were out of school, smiling, squinty eyed, and the color of baked beans, except for the redheads, whose freckles multiplied like magic. These boys were beautiful and scabbed, riding bikes past our house and over the train tracks, letting their pool-wet hair dry in the sun.

In the distance, black splotches of cattle moseyed across pastures, the air sweet with manure. From our porch, I liked to watch tractors divide the land into squares. Week after week, I'd look for changes—the deep brown of turned earth sprouting green, the green rows growing chest-high. If they stayed green, I knew it was timothy hay that would be made into rectangles and thrown from the beds of pickups for cattle to eat. If they changed to gold, it was wheat, which was mowed and threshed, then came to town in trucks brimming with kernels to be weighed and dumped through the grated floor of the grain elevator.

The gray tower stood tall and straight in those years when the train still pulled into Petroleum every weekday afternoon, the final stop on the Milwaukee Road line. Children listened for the blare of the horn, and the rattles and clangs as it came over one last valley to collect our wheat. If I could beg a penny off my father, I'd chase behind the other kids to meet the train.

They weren't unkind to me, not yet, but I was peculiar to them. Almost all these kids were the sons or daughters of ranchers. Even if one parent was a shopkeeper, schoolteacher, postman, or waitress, the other likely worked on a ranch. No one but my father and me lived in the funeral home.

We crowded near the coins we placed on the tracks, most of us wearing dirty T-shirts, cutoff jeans, and oversized cowboy boots, the uniform of kids who got the bulk of their clothes from the free bin at school.

"Stand back," the conductor would yell out his window, and I would hold my cheeks to keep them from vibrating. After the train rolled away, we gathered our flattened coins, still warm, while mothers straightened pictures on the walls of their homes. I didn't have a mother so ours hung crooked.

The train continued on to the gray tower. We were supposed to keep our distance as grain poured from a spout into the hopper car, but I liked to get close enough to hear the rain of kernels and inhale the dust that powdered my arms. By the time I looked away from that fantastic spray of wheat, the other children would be halfway through the field. And I stood apart.

I have always stood apart, off to the side or in the row behind or looking on from my yard as I did that late July afternoon when so much was about to change. I knelt with my trowel beneath the single tree on our property, digging a hole. My collection of Barbies and Matchbox cars shone in the sun. I had enough to share in case anyone wanted to join me.

The dolls were too big for the cars so I had to hold them, face-down, on the roofs as I drove them around the tree roots, toward the deep hole. In my mind, the black Matchbox was a hearse like my father's, and I could imagine the mournful singing of hymns, the quiet coughs, and the unwrapping of hard candies.

"There, there, rest in peace," I said. I covered a doll with dirt, placed a rock over the grave, and drove the little cars away.

It would have been a day like any other if not for the sound that turned our heads toward the gray tower. It's a terrifying thing to hear grown-ups cry out like children. I stood with a tiny car in my hand, and soon a rush of neighbors moved toward the grain elevator. When my father hurried out of our house and told me there had been an accident, I knew something had gone very wrong. It's almost never good news when people call my father for help.

"Be a good girl, Mary," he told me. "Stay right here until a sitter comes for you."

I dug up my muddy-haired doll and started my game again as I watched my father run like he never did before or since.

I was not alone very long before a teenager from the neighborhood came to look after me. She chewed her nails and looked toward the commotion the whole time.

"It's Eddie," other teenagers called to her as they sprinted past our house. "It's Eddie Golden."

And without a word, she grabbed my hand and we ran together, my shoulder and elbow and wrist feeling as if they might separate. My feet tripped over each other but I had to keep up. We ran until we were standing in a crowd of somber neighbors. The great building itself was quiet, but the crowd hummed with worries and pleas. Many wore their work uniforms—waitresses in aprons, K–12 teachers in dress shoes, ranchers in dirty boots and gloves.

I wriggled my sweaty fingers free of the sitter's and pushed toward the front, where a half circle of girls sobbed quietly and said the name Eddie again and again. I tried to place where I'd heard his name before. Another girl came running as she pulled a crimson jersey over her tank top. Her friends touched the name GOLDEN on the back of it and cried louder.

"Oh, him," I said to the girls as I moved closer, because of course I knew who Eddie Golden was now that I saw the basketball jersey. He'd taken the Petroleum Oilers to the county championship the year before, when he was a senior. He was the only one I ever saw on the court with a beard.

The girls closed their circle and called toward the gray tower, "We love you, Eddie!"

When I wormed my way around them, I came to the side of the train, where it would normally stop to catch the wheat. I squeezed between freight cars, followed the piercing buzz of chain saws and men shouting with strained and testy voices.

"Give me a shovel or a bucket, goddamnit!"

"You see I'm busy cutting? We need to made this hole bigger."

No one seemed to be working together. Some focused on breaking open the wall, but couldn't agree how or where to cut through it, while others tried to manage the grain that exploded out of the hole.

"Saw's overheated. Fuck this."

The man looked around like someone might lend a hand, but everyone stayed quiet.

"Mary, where'd you go?" The sitter grabbed my wrist hard. "I've been . . ."

She stopped to look where I had been looking, where all of us had been looking, and her grip went soft. There, in the jagged square they'd cut in the side of the building hung Eddie's yellow work boots. If you could shut out all the hurrying and shouting, if you could shut out the endless wailing high up in the tower, you'd hear the grain dropping all around Eddie.

I felt a tug on the back of my T-shirt, up by the neck.

"This is not what I'm paying you for," my father said to the sitter. "Take her home."

All that walk back, I listened to the drone of voices and the awful crying that wouldn't stop. And if I closed my eyes, there were Eddie's yellow boots.

We stood at the edge of my lawn, watching others as they flowed to and from the gray tower. I kept one foot on the grass, the other in the road.

"What happened?" the sitter asked whenever another teen passed our house.

A boy stopped to answer her.

"Eddie Golden fell in the grain," he said, distracted, looking toward the ever-growing crowd.

"I heard he went under," said a second boy, and he shook the other's hand. "Hey, man."

"Hey. I'm just heading up. My dad's already there with his chain saw."

"What's he cutting?"

"They're trying to break through the wall of that storage bin."

"What happened?" the sitter asked again.

Like most boys in town, they knew plenty about the work that went on at the elevator, how the grain was pouring into the hopper, as usual, and then it just stopped.

"The wheat gums together," said the first. "When the weather's been wet. It happens all the time."

The second boy looked at the sitter and explained, "That's when you have to send someone up to the storage bin."

"They sent Eddie and his younger brother."

"The younger brother, too?" he said. "What's he, twelve?"

"Nah. Fourteen. Just skinny."

"They went up to do what?" the sitter asked.

"Just walk out onto the grain," said the first boy. "Break up the clumps. It's easy work."

"How do you know so much?" she asked.

"I had that job a couple summers ago," he said. "The pay is shit. If it's your first job, they don't pay the full wage."

I imagined the scene that day and for years after: the two standing at the top of the hot and dusty grain bin. Eddie tall and capable with his dark, thick beard and athletic build; the younger brother slight, his hands still baby soft, complaining of the heat.

"You guys talking about the accident?" asked a third boy. "I was up there a while. I just came back for my camera."

He aimed it at the sitter and clicked.

"Don't," she said, covering her face.

There had never been so many kids standing on our lawn at once when there was not a funeral service inside. The first two ignored the new boy, describing how the younger brother harnessed up and climbed through the hatchway.

"And then he just stood on top of the wheat, kicking at one clump of grain."

"Like this," said the boy with the camera, and he kicked his foot in slow motion, like he was the laziest guy in the world. "Eddie's yelling at him to put some muscle into it."

"How do you know?" the sitter asked.

"I told you. I was up there," he said.

He aimed his camera at her again.

"I said, don't."

I'd been standing with one foot in the road but moved back onto my lawn.

"So, before anyone interrupts again . . ." the first boy said.

"Who's interrupting? I can't tell the story too?"

"No one asked you to tell it."

"I'm the only one who was even there," he said. He looked at the girl. "The boss, he goes running up to the tower, asking what's taking so long. So Eddie gets out there on the wheat. And he's stomping hard, breaking up the clumps."

"He should have worn a harness."

"Yeah. No shit."

"These pockets in the wheat, you don't see 'em. They can just collapse under you."

"You can be gone in seconds. Sucked under fifty tons of grain, man."

"I heard him bawling," said the sitter.

"No. That was the younger brother. The kid in the harness."

"The lazy one I told you about. The one who kicked like this," and he gently kicked the sitter's foot.

"I heard him too," I said. "Just crying and crying."

"He was dangling at the top of that storage bin."

"He's still there. You hear 'im?"

We all looked nervously toward the grain elevator.

"Did they save Eddie?" the sitter asked.

The boy with the camera bent over, laughing. "Save him?"

"They're trying to dig him out," said the first. "That's what my dad's been doing up there."

"Imagine it, man, all that grain going up your nose."

"You can hold your breath."

"I don't think so, man."

"We should get up there."

As the two walked toward the tower, I thought of how Eddie's feet hung through that square they'd cut out of the wall.

"Wait up," said the boy with the camera, hustling. "My dad has a shift tomorrow morning. I wonder if they'll give him the day off?"

Late that night, my father and the men who'd stayed until the end came back to our house, so sweaty the room steamed. There were five of them, covered in dust from the wheat: Pop, the doctor, the sheriff, the manager of the grain elevator, and the father who'd hurried up there with his chain saw. I made a joke about the stink in the room but no one laughed. They just sat around our kitchen table, hands trembling, pouring drinks. The babysitter, anxious to go home, shooed me toward my room, but I only went as far as the stairs.

"What killed me was all those girls telling us, 'Hurry, hurry.'"

"And that goddamned whimpering."

I tiptoed closer.

My father's face looked deflated, as if air had been let out of it until only the creases and folds remained. What these men understood the moment they reached the scene was that there was never the chance of a rescue. They knew, as they started up their chain saws, that Eddie had already suffocated. It had taken three hours to recover his body, three hours of cutting through the wall and shoveling away grain. Once the star of his high school basketball team, the guy cracking jokes during breaks at work, here was the version of Eddie Golden they'd always remember, his nose and mouth plugged with wheat.

"Have anything stronger, Allen?" the manager asked my father.

Sweat dripped down the backs of my knees. Sometimes the room was silent, the house hot with breath, and only the sound of glasses clunking against the wooden table. Other times the men talked over each other, telling their stories until all the parts fit together.

After Eddie's death, his mother asked to have a photo taken with both her boys. She'd failed to take pictures of them as young men—life had simply become one of rushing to finish chores, rushing down the highway to do errands, rushing home to make dinner—and she needed to remember Eddie as he looked that morning. His dark eyebrows, the full beard that couldn't hide his near-constant grin, the strong body like his father's. She needed to remember them all together, even if that image was hardly true.

The three wore their most formal clothing and posed as if Eddie, eyes closed and slumped between them, were still alive. This is what I would think of all that night and for many nights after with an awful, secret thrill. Mrs. Golden and her younger son argued about whether or not to smile. The look on their faces—though it's only a story now; no one I know has ever laid eyes on the photo—is said to be the glassy-eyed look of shock. And no one would mistake the younger boy's tight lips or the mother's exposed teeth as smiles.

The day after the accident, the men who worked at the grain elevator stayed busy at the site. The grain had to be thrown out because it had been sitting in there with Dead Eddie and all the sawdust from cutting a hole wide enough to retrieve his body. Spoiled grain piled near the opening where they'd pulled him out, and flies buzzed around it and laid their eggs.

I wandered close to the gray tower, an ice cream cone dripping to my elbow, and watched the grown men argue. Some calculated the losses from that day—wheat they'd grown and cut and would have shipped to the flour mills and breweries. Those numbers showed in their jaws, clenched and twitching. When the train pulled in at its usual time, these men spoke for a long while at the engineer's cab with hands in their pockets.

I thought I was the only kid too curious to stay away, but noticed a number of us standing behind trucks or along the tracks.

"She'll know something," a boy said, tipping his chin toward me.

He called me over to a cluster of older kids, probably nine- or ten-year-olds, sitting together on the rail. They didn't stop their talking as they made a space for me beside the only other girl, and I sat politely, with hands clasped.

"We saw the younger brother walking home afterward. His face was covered in snot."

"I wanted to spit on him. All that whining. Jesus."

"I hear Eddie looked pretty bad. He got real hot in there."

"Tell us what you know," the girl said to me.

They had not heard the details of the family photo. They had not heard of Mr. Golden's outburst at our house, when he told my father that his younger son could not attend the service. His wife, either, if she complained. We feasted on this story as it passed from child to child, each adding grisly details overheard or simply imagined as we lay in bed, too jittery to sleep.

We sat with our legs touching, the rail heating up with the sun. I'd never felt such a sense of belonging.

Over the days that followed, as the gray tower stayed silent, men still drove their trucks to work in the morning and parked. In a little while, they drove away again. The spilled grain began to sprout, and the funeral attended by all those sobbing teenage girls came and went. But nothing returned to normal.

I was only vaguely aware of the strangers who'd come to our town with their clean shirts and clipboards (the county inspector, contractors, people from the railroad and insurance companies), all collecting information, and with each visit, stealing a little more hope that work would resume. The men who grew wheat on the ranches seemed to understand right away, as they did not meet the eyes of the men they knew so well at the grain elevator. Because they would still grow wheat. They would just drive it farther to other towns and other men.

The beating heart of Petroleum had stopped. And as word spread that it would not be revived, that the elevator would be closed from that day forward, its workers stripped out levers and dials. They cut out the little buckets that used to carry the kernels, scoop by scoop, to the top of the tower and tip them into the storage bins.

Mr. Purvis, the plant manager, was the last to give up on the place, dressing each day for work (jeans and a button-up) and carrying his black lunch bucket. He'd just sit there in his office as we peeked through the window. The day he finally cleared out, lugging one large box of papers to his truck, a desk fan jammed under his arm, he wouldn't let anyone help.

It wasn't long before the kids took over the grain elevator. We found Mr. Purvis's office, the walls fireproofed with tin, and the only thing pinned there was a NO SMOKING sign and a calendar with a different naked lady for every month. We explored the maze of wooden rooms and shafts, the place full of floor sweepings and rats, echoing as we climbed the rusted ladders. There in the dark, we played a game called Eddie.

We stood in a circle and held hands—girls I hoped would

one day play dolls with me, boys with calloused fingers whose touch felt electric. I thrived on the sound of our breath together, amplified inside those walls, the dusty air drying the backs of our mouths.

We played with the savagery of children who'd learned not to burden adults with our fears. We shouted at one another at the volume many of us knew in our homes.

"Do your job, you weakling!" the one playing Eddie might shout as he stomped into the center of the circle, where the younger brother kicked his feet at the clumps of grain like he didn't care a thing about this kind of work.

Everyone understood Eddie's rage, how laziness in a town like this had consequences. We felt it then, the town spiraling around us, though we knew nothing about insurance hikes or the shiny metal elevators of bigger towns. Whether the accident was directly to blame or only seemed so, it marked the year the grain elevator shut down, the year the train no longer stopped in Petroleum.

We played the game for hours each day. When the one playing Eddie jabbed his stick at the ground, the children all screamed and fell on him. This was the part of the game when injuries happened, boys and girls crushing each other, pushing sod into noses and mouths. The youngest, not yet invited to play, cheered from the sidelines, full throated.

Whoever played the younger brother cried like a baby while the rest pointed fingers and chanted, "Sissy, sissy, look what you've done."

I loved all this touching, though many complained my hands were clammy. I even loved the pushing and tackling, the scrapes and bruises it left. I believed this was friendship. I believed it would last.

From this frenzied scrum, we eventually emerged with hoarse voices and sweaty hair to reenact our favorite scene. The game always ended with a family photo. Everyone wanted to be Dead Eddie, slumped with his head at a tilt.

For the men who had carried proud titles like manager, elevator operator, grain merchandiser, and industrial mechanic, the days no longer had structure. You'd see them in the diner or leaning against the outside of a building, not sure how to spend their time. Something hard had grown into their faces, and you could follow it down their tight jaws to the raised cords on their necks, and you just knew the tension kept going. They'd become rigid, like that tightness would never get itself unclenched.

They often stood clustered in town, demanding the dignity of work. You'd overhear their grumbling. They needed to do something with their hands. They needed something to fill the hours, something to talk about when they went home at the end of the day. Many developed strange ticks—rubbing their hands together and forgetting to stop, looking hard off to nowhere and not hearing if someone spoke to them. Whenever I saw these men in town, I'd walk way around them as I would a hot stove. By summer's end, many had taken jobs as handymen, bartenders, short-order cooks, janitors, whatever was available—changes they probably thought were temporary.

1

I STEP ONTO THE PORCH with a bucket of hot, soapy water, slip on long rubber gloves, and set to cleaning the plastic apron I wear for embalmings, laying it flat and then, on hands and knees, scrubbing with a sponge. It's still mild for January, which worries many of us about how much snow we might get before winter is through. The worst blizzard in our history came after one of these mild spells.

Neighborhood kids, coats thrown aside, ride their bikes in the last light of day, jumping the old train tracks covered in mud and the stubble of dead grass. I scratch at the dried lumps, soak them again, as coyotes howl in the distance. I look across the wide open land, bleached of color, to see if I can spot them.

This has been my view all my life. Thirty years in this town. This house. Sometimes it feels like thirty years wearing this same ponytail at the nape of my neck, trying to keep my hair from blowing in the constant prairie wind. I turn the bucket over for the first rinse, then go inside to wash my hands and refill it.

When I come back out, I see my father's hearse pull off the highway. We've always called it a hearse because of how we use it. A traditional one couldn't function out here on the rough dirt roads, often slopped in snow or the sticky mud we call gumbo. Pop's hearse is just a black pickup with a hard cap over the bed. He keeps a three-by-five-foot American flag mounted on the antenna, and I follow it through town.

I splash clean water over the apron and hang it over the rail to dry. Wiping my hands on my jeans, I meet my father when he pulls into the driveway.

"Did you hear the news?" he asks as he steps out.

"No."

I'm used to being out of the loop—part of the stigma of living in this house. Father and daughter. Funeral director and embalmer.

"Younger brother's come back to Petroleum," he says, jingling his keys. "That's what people are saying anyway."

I can't help but look to the old grain elevator. That gray tower is still the defining monument of Petroleum, even now as it buckles in the middle, several boards stripped from those outer walls, exposing its skeleton.

"What's he come back for?"

"To spend time with his mom, I guess," Pop says. "I don't think she has long."

"Have you seen him?"

He shakes his head. Jingles his keys again. "I've got to get our guest inside," he says.

"Need a hand?"

"Nope. But check the mail, if you could. See if we got anything to deposit."

I wrap my scarf higher over my chin and set out for the post office. Strange how I'd just been thinking of the accident, almost like I'd heard someone humming the song from our old game. *Sissy, sissy.* I look for signs of the younger brother, can't help looking for a fourteen-year-old because it's all he's ever been to me.

Anyone who doesn't live here stands out right away. Except for hunting season, when strangers visit with elk chained to the beds of trucks, the only outsiders we see are the high school basketball teams, here for a game, or the occasional stray driver who pulls off the highway, looking for gas or a bite to eat. We can only accommodate the bite to eat.

I listen to the stamp of my boots against the cold ground. I like to walk these dirt roads when it's just me, nothing but my footsteps and the swish of my parka. Our town has no streetlights, no traffic lights, so as soon as the sun sets, the houses and shops look like black cutouts against indigo, everything leaning south, away from the wind. I close my eyes against the dust. You can do this in a town as small as ours, walk in the middle of the street with your eyes shut.

At the post office, I unlock the box marked Crampton. Every family name on the brass doors is deeply familiar. There are 182 residents of Petroleum. We all keep track of the latest number.

Those who've heard of Petroleum are often surprised it's still here. The town is primarily known for what it no longer has: oil. In its heyday, when the pumps drew black fuel from the ground, the population spiked to almost two thousand. But many were only passing through, here to make a quick buck and then move along when the wells ran dry.

Most who stayed are scattered over miles of cattle country. About a third of us live in town. I recognize all of them by sight even if we've never spoken. Everyone has to stop here if they want their mail, though some don't.

Pop will be upset to see more bills but no checks. I peek through other windows, always curious about magazine subscriptions and package slips.

Back out in the night air, I push the hair from my face with a glove, but the wind swipes it right back. There's a good number of coyotes out now, and if you know where to look, you can see the glow of their eyes moving closer to town. A mother shouts her child's name across the dark. Then come more names and the sound of a bell as children are called home for the night. They begin to run and ride their bikes, shadows with coats tucked under their arms.

It's not long before I hear those thin tires and boys' voices behind me. I pick up speed, but not enough to show fear. My home is just around the corner, the outline of the chimney distinct from here.

The voices hush but the sound of pedaling and the rattle of bicycle chains draws nearer. I'm used to the nicknames: Scary Mary, Bloody Mary.

The first boy rides past. Two more follow, rocks spitting beneath the tires. The one in front circles around me, so close I feel the handlebars brush my sleeve. I hear his gruff breathing and then the word *"Freak!"* said in a joyous whisper.

I don't even turn my head as he speeds off. The other two pedal after him, laughing as they go.

I remember every name I've been called. Sometimes they are shouted, but most often they're said in a whisper. Words to be remembered even when you're apart, lying alone in the dark. My first instinct is to hate the person who has whispered the insult and to think, *It's not true!* But then I ask, *Is it?*

By the time I get home, the words have settled inside like stones. Like I've ingested them and they've become a part of me—*freak, weirdo, spinster*—clacking together with each step. I cross my yellow lawn. Crampton Funeral Home, like all the other buildings, leans to the south. Its steps are chipped, its gray clapboard faded, and the flooring on the porch squeaks so much, you can hear people at the front door before they ring the bell.

My fingers grab the knob, and I am glad to be inside the foyer, barely lit with a small lamp on the table. I toss the mail beside our vase of plastic flowers and stacks of bereavement pamphlets, then turn around quickly, thinking I hear more laughter. I shut the door hard enough to cause the lamp to flicker.

"Mary, is that you?"

"I'm home, Pop."

He's got the TV turned way up.

"Mr. Mosley's downstairs," he shouts.

This is the sound of my father in his pajamas. When he takes off his suit at the end of the day—earlier, if he can get away with it—it's as if the role he's been playing falls away with the costume. The energetic businessman rumpled on the floor. And beneath that suit: a sweaty, slouched man, so exhausted he can't even make it to his bed.

This time of the evening, he sits in his recliner with a whiskey. He likes to choose a show that'll rile him up, shouting at someone on the screen who can assume the blame for everything that's not going right in his life. All day he is polite, even-keeled. But now he can let go. Rage. Fall apart. Things he won't do in public.

I hang my coat in the hall closet, gloves tucked in the pockets. On my way downstairs, I pass the door to my father's office, his desk covered with invoices, the carpet strewn with more pages, snack wrappers, and discarded clothes, including the suit he wore today. How tired he gets just living his life. I turn off his desk lamp and head to the basement workroom, where I'll spend the evening with Mr. Mosley.

I like my world in the basement with its alphabetized shelves and sharpened instruments, every surface wiped clean, every bottle lined up with sides touching, labels facing forward, the temperature a perpetual sixty-five degrees.

The dead come to me vulnerable, sharing their stories and secrets. *Here is my scar. Touch it. Here is the roll of fat I always hid under that big sweater, and now you see. This is the person I've kept private, afraid of what people would think. Here I am, all of me. Scarred, flabby, covered in bedsores. Please be kind.*

When a body comes to our funeral home, it comes draped in a white sheet. The sheets begin clean, but soon, they carry the essence of the one who died, first in silhouette, the contour of the nose, a valley or mountain at the stomach, the feet turned slightly in or out, the bumps of shoulders, breasts, chin. Before I move the sheet aside, I study this landscape. At first glance, it is like a field covered in fresh snow. Then the details become more visible. Just as a field of snow, upon closer inspection, shows signs of the life that has tramped through it, so will the sheet show something beyond its surface. There are smears and drips, a spot of blood from where the IV was removed, a stain from loose bowels not thoroughly wiped, the sticky smear of saliva, the gray shadow of one final sweat.

I pull back the sheet and welcome Mr. Mosley to the bright white silence of my workroom, take his cold hand and hold it gently in my own. His face, neck, and hands are red and toughened from years of working in sun and cold and wind. The rest of him is quite pale, soft. I don't often get to know my neighbors until we meet this way, and that is the case with Mr. Mosley. His wrecked body lies on the stainless steel table—a faucet near his head, a drain near his feet—and there is much to do. But first this. His hand.

Here is the man, nothing to hide behind. No sheet or uniform or name tag. This is the man without his possessions, with chores left undone, with mistakes he can't make right, with nothing more he can prove.

I'm right here, I tell him.

It is what I have longed for my whole life. Perhaps everyone longs for this. Just to be and to have someone stay near. He does not complain that my hands are clammy. There is no pressure to be charming or clever. We are simply here, together in this quiet.

Even if I didn't know Mr. Mosley was a rancher, I'd be able to tell by the missing tips of two fingers (probably jammed in machinery), and the scars from hooves, horns, ropes, and amateur sewing. I trace the bruises on his face down to the fatal gash where his ribs were crushed when the tractor overturned.

My mind is at work now, taking a mental inventory of the damage: broken collarbone and ribs, crushed chest, fractured hip. There's not enough time for a major restoration, and his family can't afford it anyway. I imagine the chest rebuilt and stuffed, his bruises masked with concealer. This will not be my finest work, not when they want Mr. Mosley back tomorrow evening, the only time all the relatives are able to gather. But I will make it happen, even if I have to work through the night.

"Don't make him fancy," his family wrote in the note my father left for me. "Don't send him back in makeup and a monkey suit."

They want to see the man they knew, in his checked flannel and a clean pair of jeans. But I want to protect them from reminders of his last moments—the buildup of mucus in his lungs, the coughing up of blood, the struggle for his last breath. I tighten the waterproof apron around my waist, secure the paper mask over my nose and mouth. I want to provide his family with a face they aren't afraid to kiss good-bye.

Water streams from the faucet for his final bath. A moment to wash and say good-bye to this skin that has held his soul. This skin he has probably loved and hated and mistaken for who he was. I notice the scabbed elbows, hands nicked and calloused. A man made of the same nature as this land: rugged, persevering, wind carved. I rinse the dust and dried blood from his hair, run a soapy sponge from head to foot, honoring what of this man will and will not last. I bend and flex his limbs to keep them from stiffening.

I work without music, appreciating the clang of tools, the whir of machines, and the silences in between. Occasionally, the sound of the TV, two flights up, and my father's outbursts drift through the house. I know he drinks too much, but I'm glad he has this time to let off a little steam.

After rinsing and wringing out the sponge, I wipe Mr. Mosley's behind and insert three cotton balls into the rectum. Every orifice, if not plugged up tight, can leak when he's on display for his loved ones. My first embalming job, I forgot some steps, and the old woman foamed at the mouth and nose during visiting hours. Ever since, I've followed a precise sequence. Abrasions I fill with lime—Pop prefers bleach—then seal with soft wax. I spray disinfectant over the tongue, palate, clouded eyes and huge pupils. When people ask me what I do at my job, I've learned they don't really want to know.

Secretly I think of myself as an artist. Drawing was my obsession in high school and, briefly, I dreamed I could make a career of it. My mind, my hands have always wanted to create art. Embalming is not completely separate from that impulse. My job is a study of the human form, its beauty and vulnerability. I take pleasure in choosing each tool and color, in making a clean stitch, in positioning the body to create a portrait.

I touch Mr. Mosley's face. All this time it has been without expression, but not for long. The family has supplied a picture of him standing in a field of cattle beside his tractor, perhaps the same one that crushed him. He has a handsome, sun-toughened face and does not seem to smile but rather tucks in his lips. His eyes reveal more—a playful squint as if he hopes to get into mischief. I wonder who was on the other side of the camera and what happened after the photo was taken. I place oval-shaped plastic caps over the eyeballs so they won't appear sunken as the body dehydrates. I sew the lids shut.

As I close the mouth, running wax string through the lower and upper gums, then the nostrils, I imagine Mr. Mosley earlier in the week, climbing into the cab of his tractor, maybe sitting awhile with his feet up, drinking coffee, having the morning to himself.

What I hope for each body that comes to me is to add something that gives a surprise burst of life. I pad the mouth with cotton to get the expression right—a man who holds his breath, who finishes his work even if his hands are cut and his joints are sore. I pull the string a little tighter, causing the jaw and lips to close very naturally. Two small knots, and there he is, the man in the photo. Satisfied, I seal my work with Super Glue.

2

THE SMALL WINDOWS NEAR the basement ceiling rattle, but something persistent about the noise causes me to freeze. What if the boys have returned and flung their bikes aside so they can drop into the window wells and press their faces to the glass? They do this sometimes. I only have to show my face and off they go, whooping, clapping one another's hands. It used to be my peers who did this. Now it's the children of my peers.

When the banging becomes more forceful, I climb the counter below the windows.

"Leave us alone!" I shout.

But even as I slap at the glass, I remember their words that have become a part of me. Why else would they treat me this way unless there's something strange or repulsive that they see? The outrage drains from my arms. I search again for their bikes, their smug faces, so they can have their laugh, get it over with, and go away.

All I see is a stick, pinned on one end, and striking our house whenever the wind blows it. No boys. No teasing, at least not tonight.

Trash cans tumble through the dark, dusty streets. The sky is filled with twirling plastic bags, bits of roof tile, tarps set free to billow through town like phantoms. And then I see it. The shiny pickup in Doris Golden's driveway, brake lights on. I can't see the plates well, only that they're not Montana. It has to be the younger brother.

The brake lights go dark, and I press my forehead against the cold glass to see the man who steps out. Only his shadow at first. I still remember the day we heard he'd quit school and skipped town. The playground erupted in cheers.

As my eyes adjust, his form separates gradually from the night sky. His leather jacket looks silly. No one here wears a thing like that. He walks closer to a light hanging above the side door of his mother's house. His dark curls fall almost to his collar—the kind of hair I've only seen on TV. For a moment he turns, looking directly at me, no change in his expression. And I realize I am completely exposed in this bright window. I imagine my face alarmed and washed out under the fluorescent lights.

Slinking down from the counter, I strip off the latex gloves and rub my fingers together, trying to work the nerves out of them when the doorbell rings.

I know who is ringing the bell because I made the mistake of catching his eye. I've called him to me like a stray dog that I looked at for too long. The younger brother waits on the other side of this dark stained door. Upstairs, the TV continues to drone, but my father is likely passed out by now.

I twist the knob and feel, even as the door groans open, that Pop would insist I keep it closed. Wind slips inside, running through our front hallway. And there he is—the town's disgrace—thin, even in a leather jacket, its black skin buttery and creased. His wavy hair, streaked with gray, blows to one side of his head. Funny to see him grown when I've thought of him all my life as a fourteen-year-old.

"I saw someone at the window," he says with no trace of the local accent. "I'll be needing your services before too long. For my mother. I don't know what I need to do to get started except come here, I guess."

The entryway is almost completely dark except for a soft blue glow from the upstairs den.

"I'm Robert Golden," he says, wiping his hair back in place.

He extends a hand much too smooth for the men in this town. All I can think of is that awful crying up in the gray tower. He stands there a moment longer before withdrawing his hand into his pocket.

"My mother. She's not well," he says. "Doris Golden. She lives just over there."

He points into the dark.

"I know where Doris lives," I say.

"Are you one of the Cramptons?" he asks.

What a funny thing, in a town this size, for someone not to know all about you.

"I'm Mary Crampton," I say. "The embalmer."

Another gust blows inside, knocking the brochures to the floor. *Funeral Planning Made Easy, Sad Isn't Bad, Prepaid Peace of Mind.* Robert Golden should read that last one, but it's too late at night to remember the introductory speech I'm supposed to give. I've never had a knack for talking with those who need our services. It's fair to say I'm not a people person. Pop usually meets with clients so I can stay in the basement.

"I'll help you pick them up," he says.

I pull the door shut behind me as a response to his offer so that now, quite unintentionally, we are standing too close together on the front porch. My eyes sting under the glare of the naked bulb.

"Oh, there," he says. "The light helps. Now I can see you."

His smile lifts on only one side of his mouth as if the muscle hasn't fully developed.

Wind elbows between us, rocking us onto our heels. My cheeks feel hot. A wisp of hair falls across my face, and I tuck it behind my ear. Then, remembering that my ears are weird, how they curl too hard at the top, I swipe my hair back down so it hangs flat against the side of my face.

For most of my adult life, I've tried to make myself invisible, but suddenly I'm aware of my physical presence. I'm an ordinary woman. My hair is brown, but not a brown that would inspire a name like chestnut or milk chocolate. It's more the color of a brown couch cushion that's sat too long beside a sunny window and faded to something you could only describe as drab. My eyes are hazel, but most wouldn't know because I look at my shoes if others are around. You wouldn't call me fat or thin or tall or short or curvy or flat. I'm what you might call unremarkable in my ponytail and grocery store makeup.

"So you'd like to set up services for Doris?" I ask, folding my arms.

"Yes," he says. "I think so. I've never had to do anything like this before."

We are shouting over the wind.

"I don't know how much longer she has," he says. "I just want these last days to go peacefully."

Across the street, a rusted sign over the Petroleum Hotel

bangs back and forth. The building is plain as a sugar cube, with an unadorned window for each of the six rooms. It's no-frills living in this inn that was built to serve hunters. No television in any room, and a single toilet and shower down the hall. Much of the year, as now, it's empty, the rooms on the top floor dark. The only one there is the owner, an old man who lives on the first floor through a door behind the welcome desk.

"I'll get you the forms," I say. And remembering the mess in my father's office, how it may not even be possible to get to the file cabinet, I add, "Tomorrow, when I'm not in the middle of a job."

"I've interrupted your work," he says. "I'm sorry."

Wind shoves my shoulder back toward the house, and we hear a loud crash, then a barking dog. Across the street, a light snaps on in the hotel lobby, the owner's face glowing at the front window. He looks to the rusted hotel sign, finally ripped from its hinge. But when he steps outside to have a better look, it is our porch that interests him. He doesn't even pretend not to stare.

"I should head back to my ma's place," Robert says. "Mary Crampton, did you say?"

He looks as if he might try to shake my hand again, but decides against it, turning down the steps. I say nothing as Robert Golden walks into the black, debris dancing along the ground under the moonlight. He's an odd man for these parts. His clothes are out of place. He walks too fast. I want to keep watching until he's gone, but the wind has forced my eyes shut.

Back inside, I hold the knob for some time, letting my nerves quiet down. I think of "the younger brother," said like a curse in this town. Then I think of the man at my door with his crooked smile, hair blowing to one side. Right now I feel, well, I don't know what I feel. I only know I haven't let go of the doorknob.

I bend down to gather the pamphlets that had scattered across the floor when I remember Mr. Mosley. I still have work to finish tonight.

Hurrying downstairs, I slip on gloves, then squeeze my fingers open and shut to calm my nerves. I search the tray of tools until my fingers relax around the metal handle I need. I inhale, exhale, then draw the scalpel down Mr. Mosley's neck.

My hand disappears, sliding through dark and slippery passages. My fingers know the way, feeling the dense muscle, soft knots of fat, until they locate the thick, white carotid artery. I tie it off with string and attach a tube to the free end. I do the same for the jugular vein, then, using my elbow, flip a switch.

Embalming fluid the color of pink lemonade pumps through Mr. Mosley's arteries via one tube while blood leaves his body out another. Red streams and jellylike clumps gurgle down the drain. Right away, his skin becomes firmer, his face appears to blush. As the machine hums and clicks, I massage his arms and legs to break up clots and help distribute the fluid. Already he looks like the man he must have been earlier in the week. I wonder how his life measured up against his dreams. Or if he still had dreams. Some of us have let ours go.

3

I STAND AT MY BEDROOM window, dressed for the day, and look out on my town at dawn. Outside, the dry creek bed flows with plastic grocery bags. More garbage collects along the barbed-wire fences and metal windbreaks. Soon all the neighbors will be out, picking up the trash and tending to vacant properties or the whole place looks like a dump.

Robert Golden's truck sits in the driveway across the street and it's hard to know what his return to Petroleum means. I don't expect many to make him feel welcome. And maybe that doesn't matter; visitors never stay long. Most take a look at this place and these miles and miles of treeless prairie and see a whole lot of nothing.

But look, how could you see nothing while you stare at this fluid painting in the sky? Watch it deepen to a muddy purple, so everything beneath it seems to glow. And closer, hidden among the pale grass and tiny shrubs and pincushion cactuses and patches of snow, see the mule deer, almost the same color as their surroundings, and elk wearing their winter coats?

I turn my head toward a sudden flap of wings. Crows and snow geese holler, *Morning. Morning! Get up!* And the town begins to awaken.

I like the view from here, where I feel in harmony with these early risers, stoics, and hard workers. The beautiful boys from my childhood have grown into men in flannel and work boots. So many redheads, so many named after trees and horses. Colt. Trotter. Ash. Birch.

Fathers and sons pile into trucks with thermoses and packed lunches. Sometimes I wave as they head out to the local ranches, but mostly not. I understand that our relationship is this, watching each other go about our lives, needing each other's businesses to survive if we are to survive. And mostly, sharing a love of this land that is not for everyone.

Out here, you are never separate from the weather or wildlife. Open your door in the morning and there are tracks of bobcats and coyotes that walked through your garden while you slept. Some fear being flung so far into nature without a nearby hospital, firehouse, or cell-phone tower. You have to be willing to look after yourself, scrub out your own wounds and sew them up with fishing line. There are plenty in town with impressive scars, limps, missing fingers, glass eyes.

And yet, some of us can't bear to leave this place. We like waking to the call of geese, and dwelling among more animals than people. At night, there are no streetlights, no lights on this expanse of highway. When you stand out on the prairie, you can open or shut your eyes and it's just as black.

But this is as much as we share. I don't pretend to have any illusions. I know we'll get along easiest when I see them on the embalming table.

Two more trucks head toward the highway as the sun pushes higher and color bursts beneath the clouds—salmon pink, egg-yolk gold. The air comes alive with the rumble of machinery and the bawling and bleating and clucking of animals waiting to be fed and let out to roam.

I hear the swish of boots through the weeds as neighbors begin to pick up trash. Women with scarves tied under their chins, men holding caps in place, squint into the wind with crosshatched faces and hair that never looks brushed. It's time to wake my father.

I clomp down the hallway in untied boots and find Pop in the recliner under a blanket. From this angle, he has more scalp than hair, his skin freckled and shiny. He looks older when he sleeps, mouth slack, cheek squished into the side of the chair.

When I look closely at my father's face, it is like a map of the journey he won't talk about. I like the lines by his eyes that I imagine come from my mother making him smile. I like the nick under his chin from a ski accident he had on their honeymoon. I like the turned front tooth that makes him look a little happier than he actually is.

It seems, for my whole life, I've wanted to know the side he keeps hidden. Does he cry, and if so, about what? And when he fishes, quietly as you're supposed to, casting out again and again, where does his mind travel?

I straighten a stack of magazines on the table beside him, mostly expired TV schedules, and make gentle noises to let him know I'm here.

Pop is something of a local celebrity with his television ad that has run unchanged for a decade. But this is not the man the community sees—not with his oily hair, what's left of it, the stained undershirt, the checkered pajama bottoms with rice stuck to them.

"Morning," I say, finally, and pat his leg. "Come on, Pop. Time to get up."

I open the blinds to let in the sun as he moves a bit in his chair.

"Come on, time to get a move on. Everyone's outside cleaning up from the storm."

"I'm up. I'm up," he says, struggling to open his eyes.

He tries to stand too quickly. The remote control falls from his lap, and then the blanket. He seems embarrassed that I've bent down to help untangle it from his ankles.

"Did you hear the wind last night?" I ask.

"I must have had the TV up too loud."

"Well, everyone's getting to work out there," I say. "You didn't hear the wind?"

I'm making a point. I do it this way, never directly. I can't make the words in my head come out of my mouth: *You could talk to someone instead of making yourself pass out. You could talk to me.* Instead, I fold the blanket as he reaches out to the chair for balance.

"I could use a quick shower," he says.

"Are you feeling all right?" I ask.

"I'm just fine."

He's never been one to talk about his troubles. Not about losing Mom, not about the tragic stories we absorb in our line of work. He fusses about money but never says he's afraid. Ask how he's doing, he's always fine.

"I'll meet you outside," he calls, as he closes the door.

I hear the sweep of the shower curtain. The faucet squeaks and water rumbles through the pipes. I remember when my father used to sing in the shower.

As I walk down our driveway, I hope no one says hello. Our trash can has rolled to the bumper of Pop's hearse, spilling its contents. Most of the garbage has caught under the back wheel. I reach for a page of newspaper covered in grease stains—fried potatoes I cooked earlier in the week.

"Mary, can you give me a hand?"

I look up to find Fritz Berg, owner of the Petroleum Hotel, who stared so long at our porch last night. He stands across the street, leaning on his cane. His clothes, all variations of blue, look two sizes too big. I cross the street, suddenly aware of the greasy newsprint on my hands.

"That was a lot of wind," he calls.

"Yes."

My voice comes out weird and high—I get nervous around most people—and my shoulders rise in embarrassment.

"Any damage at your place?" he asks.

"No."

"Well, I've got a problem here," he says.

"Yes. I see."

We both look up to the hinge, where the hotel sign has ripped from the pole. Then we follow the long drop that left it at his feet.

"Do you have gloves?" he asks.

I pull the pair from my pocket and put them on as I walk across the lawn. Up close, the sign is bigger than I would have guessed. The metal is so corroded, it's hardly readable.

"Don't know if you can use it again," I say.

"Oh, we don't need a sign," he says. "Who doesn't know this is the hotel? I just want it off my property."

It's heavy enough to have dented the ground.

"Try to pick up that end," he says.

I lift it to my knees, but I doubt the two of us could haul it anywhere.

"I saw that guy with the long hair on your porch last night," he says. "I was worried I'd have to come over and drag him away."

"He just needed some paperwork," I say.

"You know who he is?"

"Yes."

"He should know better than to pay a visit so late at night."

"I'm usually up late," I say.

"Well, I don't trust him," Fritz says. "Guy's gone for decades. Comes back just in time to collect his mother's money."

I set the rusted metal back on the ground.

"What did you think of his outfit?" he asks. "Strange, wasn't it?"

"I guess."

I hear the front door to my house shut, and I'm relieved to see Pop. He's wearing what we both refer to as his happy suit— the green one he used in the commercial where he famously said, "Don't be afraid to stop by Cramptons'—this is a happy place."

There is only one other funeral home reasonably close to Petroleum, and Pop fights hard for this small pool of customers. He believes that what people see of you during your off-hours, as you go about your business, is how they decide whether, in a time of need, they can rely on you.

Pop raises a hand. "Fritz," he says.

And Fritz answers, "Allen."

My father crosses the street as the businessman with an easy smile and firm handshake. The men stare at the sign.

"I'd like to put it in the Dumpster," Fritz says.

"Then that's what we'll do."

He puts on his gloves and crouches beside it, the green fabric of his suit straining.

"Quite a wind last night," Pop says.

He's good at using the information I give him.

"Kept me up most of the night," Fritz says. "That and seeing the younger brother on your porch."

"What's this?"

"He wants to start making plans for his mother," I say, turning to Pop. "He needed the preplanning package."

"I'm surprised you didn't mention this to me."

"I still need to drop the papers off."

"Let me handle it," Pop says.

"I don't mind."

"Let me handle it," he says sharply.

"He's right," Fritz says. "Why have a thing to do with him if you don't need to?"

He sets his cane on the lawn. Now that there are three of us, we lift. The nearest Dumpster is behind our house, so we cross the street in shuffling steps, Fritz grimacing whenever he puts weight on the weak hip. Pop and I try to hold our ends high to take the burden.

As we grunt and huff to the middle of the street, I see Robert leave his mother's side door.

Pop lifts his chin. "First time I've seen him grown up," he says.

"Who?" Fritz asks, looking over his shoulder, then he cries out. "Oh, goddamnit! I've got to put my end down."

We lower the sign and Fritz grabs one of his wrists and squeezes.

"Are you hurt?" Pop asks.

Fritz stares at his glove. A metal sliver has cut through it.

Robert drives slowly past.

"Hey!" Fritz shouts. "Can't you see!"

"He wasn't going to hit us," I say.

Fritz takes off his glove and examines his finger.

Pop leans over for a look. "Any metal in there?"

"I don't know. If there is, I ought to send him the medical bill."

"You need a doctor?" Pop asks.

"No, I don't have time for that."

Our town has never had a hospital, but until three years ago, we had a doctor who could treat a mild snake bite, manage diabetes, and at least stabilize a broken bone before sending you on a two hour drive to get proper help. Most don't bother about the little stuff anymore.

"I don't know how that guy can show his face here again," Fritz says as if Robert had inserted the metal splinter himself.

"Well," says Pop, "he ought to say good-bye to his mother."

We help Fritz to our lawn and set him down gently, adjusting our grip each time we see him wince.

"Comes all the way here," Fritz says. "And he can't pick up a piece of trash or wait for people to get out of the road before he practically runs them over."

I sit beside him.

"And look at that," he says.

The curtains open to the Goldens' living room, and there is Doris, setting up her easel, tubes in her nose to help her breathe.

Most neighbors cover their windows in tinfoil and towels to insulate during the cold weather, but Doris needs the light to paint.

"You say he's here to look after his mother," Fritz says. "But he's left her all alone."

"I'm sure she's all right painting by herself," Pop says.

"All I know is Doris has been through enough."

"She has indeed."

Fritz studies his palm.

"Can I get you some tweezers?" Pop asks.

"I've almost got it."

Pop stands up, dusts off the seat of his pants, and walks toward the sign in the road.

"I'll help," I say.

"Nope. I'll just drag it."

This is the image my father loves. The man from the commercial right there in the road helping an elderly neighbor. The kind of man you'd like to do business with. He needs but won't accept my help, so I simply watch Doris in her window.

Pop has told me about her hobby, how she's very taken with the former president, the cute one, as she calls him, who paints self-portraits. Inspired by him, Mrs. Golden bought art supplies.

"I've never understood that hobby," Fritz says. "She showed me some of her paintings and they didn't look anything like her. If you want a picture of yourself, it'll come out better with a camera."

"Maybe she likes the feel of a paintbrush in her hands."

"I just don't see the point of it," he says. "We all have mirrors."

I watch my father, face reddening, as he hauls the sign closer.

"Well, I guess it doesn't matter anymore," I say. "Now she paints by numbers."

Fritz nods his head slowly as if this idea makes better sense. There's no staring at a blank canvas, no wondering what color to choose or where to put it. It's all there for you: one, two, three.

I'm sorry Doris gave up on her self-portraits. She would make a great subject for a painting with her long nose that tilts hard to the right and her pale green housedress covered with daisies. I notice the resemblance now, how Robert has the same delicate features, the long, narrow nose, though his mother's looks Old World with a bulge you only see from the side and a crook you only see from the front. They share long slender fingers, a slim frame. I know from the game Eddie that the younger brother was derided for being small boned. Boys here are praised for being tall, broad shouldered, with a toughness about them.

The sign gouges the road as Pop walks backward, heaving it over the curb so forcefully he nearly slips. Once he lets it go, he straightens again, face moist. There's a rust stain on one of the pant legs.

"Well," he says, as if he isn't struggling to catch his breath, "let's get you up on your feet."

My father links arms with Fritz at the elbow, and I do the same. I'm glad he stopped talking. Sometimes, the more people talk, the more removed I feel. It's early morning and I'm already tired of the day.

We walk Fritz to his side of the street. Pop hands him his cane and then pulls a large plastic bag from each pocket. I take one and we set off through town, Pop a little winded but walking with his only-in-public posture. I turn to look at the rusted sign lying across the lawn, our problem now.

4

WE LIVE BELOW A flat-topped wall of sandstone, known as the rimrocks. Its beige hillside is painted with a giant letter *P,* fifteen feet tall. Pop and I set out toward Main Street, the one paved road in town. None of the streets have signs or official names; there are just a shared set of reference points: Main Street, Church Street, Railroad Street, Crick Road, Rimrock Lane, and our street, Crooked Hill Road, which most would recognize as crooked but not a hill.

Just about everyone who hasn't already left for work is out picking up after the storm, not concerned with whose trash or whose property it is. They simply pick up each piece as they come to it. We wave or nod as we pass. Sometimes my hair blows so completely over my face that the person I'm acknowledging is a mystery to me.

In ten minutes you can pass every building in town—small, abandoned homes beside lived-in homes, trailers up on cinder blocks, everything leaning away from the wind. From one street to the next are yellowed signs that say FOR SALE BY OWNER, but there are no buyers.

The storefronts are clustered in one block. You can count the surviving businesses on your fingers, even if, like many here, you have fewer than five on each hand. Several stores are padlocked, their windows murky, and paint so faded only an idea of the original color remains. What you can read of the old signs reminds you that our town once had a First Security Bank, Jim's Feed and Farm Supply, and Northwest Hardware & Ranch. Both pumps have been removed from the old gas station, the holes filled with cement.

We're used to the rumor that Petroleum will be a ghost town before long. This doubt in our future comes most regularly from the town of Agate (or Maggot, as the kids from Petroleum High School call it when the teams compete). Two hours to the west, Agate boasts a forest of ponderosa pines, an Albertson's grocery, a Wagon Wheel drive-through, and a movie theater that shows two films at a time.

Their students love to tease ours because so few go on to college. But how many kids from Agate know how to work tractors, buck rakes, graders, and D-8 Cats? How many can whitewash barns, set up irrigation systems, run traplines, lift hay bales, pull calves, split wood, and budget the feeding and grazing of livestock even with all the surprises in the weather? When you work on a ranch, one day you're a veterinarian, the next a construction worker, the next a mechanic, fixing tractors and plows and loaders because you don't have time to wait for someone to come out and do it for you.

Sometimes, you'll overhear a kid from Agate, here for a basketball game, suggest, "Let's find a good place to smoke." It can be hard to tell which houses are empty and which are still lived in, and I have to admit there is some delight in watching one of those kids walk up to a building half swallowed by the earth, press his face to the window, only to find the family who lives there staring back. We are still here, their stares tell him. The message is the same when, each spring, the high school students climb to the giant letter *P* and give it a fresh coat of white paint. We are still here.

I grab a handful of newspaper pages that have collected along the fence outside the municipal pool. Pop stretches for a plastic bag caught in a tree when he spots Mr. Vinter unlocking his grocery store.

"Make sure you wave," my father whispers to me. "These are all future customers."

My father gives a hearty *good morning*. He moves through town with the pride of a businessman providing a crucial service. He gained a lot of respect for taking over the town's funeral home after the previous owner died. Until then, he had worked at the hardware store. But he and the older residents remembered the days when Petroleum didn't have a funeral home, when families from this and surrounding rural communities struggled to get their dead to the nearest mortician while the body was still in good shape.

Many tried carting bodies curled into backseats or covered with tarps in the open beds of pickups. They packed them in ice, sometimes frozen vegetables. In good weather, the trip to the nearest funeral home took a couple of hours. The body, once embalmed, then had to make that same trip back. Many, unwilling to make this journey, opted to host viewings of dead loved ones in their homes, but found that the logistics of keeping a body fresh and presentable interfered with their first order of business, mourning.

My father stepped in, to the relief and surprise of many. He'd never imagined himself as a funeral director, but why not? From the stories I've gathered, he and my mother had almost a sense of humor about what they were taking on, howling as they cleaned the equipment that had been left in the basement and sold to them for cheap. He kept his day job, and for two years studied in the evening and apprenticed at the Agate funeral home on weekends. By the end, he was licensed with a skill no one else had or wanted.

As we turn onto Church Street, I hear the crackle and nattering of a radio show. Only two stations have signals that reach all the way to town—talk radio, which airs the livestock auctions, and all-request country music. Pastor Lundy, who lives and preaches in the A-frame church, turns up the volume at the first strums of an acoustic guitar.

"Morning, Cramptons," he calls.

He lifts a bucket of ash and carries it to the far side of the lawn, where he tips it over. A wagon on his porch is filled with white patties of dried manure, a cheap alternative to firewood. The cow chips are quick-burning and the fine ash gets all over the drapes, but it's a source of fuel that won't likely run out. We all have to make an extra effort during these tough times— adding a little water to the milk, a little vegetable oil to the gasoline. Everyone gets by as they can.

My father talks with him awhile about last night's wind and how much they both like the George Strait song playing on the radio.

"How is work with your patients, Mary?" the pastor asks.

"We don't actually call them patients when they're dead," I say, squeezing the trash bag closed.

"Mary," my father says quietly.

"I've got to finish up Mr. Mosley when I get home," I say, trying, for my father's sake, to chat a bit longer. "I think I'll have to pad his chest with something so he doesn't look so flat in his shirt."

"His burial's today?" the pastor asks, his fingers drumming against the bucket.

"This evening," I say. "On his ranch."

Pop whispers, "Come closer, Mary. Don't stay way back there."

But I've never enjoyed socializing. I don't know why Pop insists I have more of these throwaway conversations when they only make the day feel slow and interrupted. I step on a cardboard box, pretending not to hear, then move on to the deserted lot next door.

This yard alone will fill my trash bag. Not only is there garbage everywhere, but there's a mattress that's been sitting right in the middle of the lawn for years, like the family couldn't leave fast enough. No one bothered to move it.

Sometimes I think of the town the way I think of Mr. Mosley pumped full of pink fluid. We want to fool ourselves. Pretend that our community is thriving. For all the effort neighbors put into keeping up the town, it seems that one roof tile and windowpane at a time is not worth replacing. Piece by piece, Petroleum is crumbling away. Even the asphalt on our town's one paved road is cracked, full of shallow craters, and will soon return to dirt.

I spot a couple of plastic grocery bags and head toward them, but lose my footing when one boot sinks into the ground. Damn gophers.

Through my pant leg, I feel the cold, damp walls of the hole. I put my hands out to push myself up and notice a funny smell and the bones of a mouse. Just as my heart starts to race, I feel my father and the pastor hauling me away from the hole, their gloved hands squeezing hard under my armpits.

"Back up a little more before you put her down," says Pop.

"I should have known those rattlers would come back," the pastor says.

Staring back at where I'd fallen, I realize how close I've come to waking a den of drowsy snakes.

"I tried flushing that hole out with ammonia last year," the pastor says. "I'll get someone on it this time."

"Are you all right, Mary?" Pop asks.

I'm thinking of the rattlers, how they wrap themselves into one big ball to keep warm.

"My armpits are gonna hurt awhile," I say.

"Then you're all right."

He helps me up as the school bus chugs past. Some say the obese driver everyone knows as Slim looks like another species, with his thick neck and lashless eyes. His hair is in patches as if he's cut it himself, simply grabbing handfuls and scissoring where he can reach. It's his job to drive students from outlying towns, who leave home while it's dark and return when it's dark again. Ours is the closest school for them, despite the long trek.

These towns in our county depend on the services each offers—Breadroot for its ranchers' co-op; Kestrel for its two-room medical clinic, though it's been closed since Doctor Fischer died; Lewis Gap, a town of only nineteen people, for its sheepherders; and Petroleum, the largest, for our hotel, post office, K–12 school, and funeral home.

This is how our cluster of communities is able to function so far from the bigger towns—we share basic services. And borrowing students from these surrounding towns allows Petroleum to have enough bodies for a basketball team and a senior class.

At the sound of the school bell, children walk from houses and trailers and alleys, wearing jeans, scuffed cowboy boots, and hand-me-down coats. They take their time, kicking at the dirt road. As my father tells them good morning, I wonder which of the boys rode their bikes so close last night.

"My bag's full," I tell Pop once they've passed.

He raises his to show me he's run out of room, too. We lumber back, fat trash bags knocking against our legs.

"I wish you'd talk more with the neighbors," he says. "Maybe not so much about work, but other things, the weather."

"Pop, sometimes . . ."

"I know what you're going to say."

"Do you?"

"I'm overprotective," he says. "I can't help it. I've always had to do the work of two."

He's speaking of my mother, who died giving birth to me.

"I'm thirty," I remind him.

I stop in the road. His trash bag rustles as he takes a long breath.

"Come on," he says. "I've got something in the oven."

We both look at the broken hotel sign on our lawn as we walk up the driveway. I wonder if it will be like the mattress or, on another street, the rusted stove where we all played pretend when we were young.

We take the bags to the Dumpster behind the house. Hoist them in. When we open our back door, the timer is already beeping. Pop washes his hands, then pulls a tin of muffins from the oven. The steam smells of brown sugar and cinnamon.

Pop takes off his jacket, loosens his tie, lets his posture wilt. He can use his regular voice and stop sounding so happy now. He removes two muffins from the pan but stays there at the counter.

My mother has followed us into the house. My mother is the name I've given his grief. She was gone long before I knew what death was so, for me, she is an abstract loss, a game of guessing at the life I might have lived.

My mother is a collection of stories and inanimate objects. She is a wedding ring in my father's bedside drawer, a rosehips-flavored tea bag in the back of our kitchen cupboard that we both refuse to use or throw out. She is a picture of someone standing on the rims too far away to see. She is a book underlined only to page seven. She is a pair of burnt rosebushes in the yard that Pop won't dig up. She is the line between his eyebrows, the groove where his smile would be. She is a feeling in the gut I can't name or move.

It is my father's grief that we both suffer. I think of my parents in Doctor Fischer's two-room clinic in what even people from Petroleum would call the tiny town of Kestrel. I'm certain Pop never imagined that he would come home with only me. That he would suddenly have to figure out every single thing without a partner. He'd never even held a baby before, not a living one. You can see it in our first photo together, taken weeks after he had buried my mother; still his elbows poked out awkwardly and I did not nestle into the crook of his arm.

"Are you all right, Pop?"

"I'm fine."

He opens a cupboard, a drawer, his back turned. We don't talk about these burdens we carry. Maybe because there are no easy words for them and nothing we could do even if we found the words. Pop rinses his hands again and then comes to the table, carrying a small plate for each of us. The muffins are burned on the bottom, but it gives them more flavor.

Here, where we sit most mornings with the windows covered in tinfoil (he likes to save on bills, too), I break open a muffin and let the steam warm my chin. Pop opens the newspaper, but he does not read. He does not eat.

He has noticed the stain on the leg of his suit. He curls over it, making himself smaller. His thin wisps of hair flop forward as he scrubs at it.

"You're sure you're all right?"

"I'm fine," he says. "It's the stain."

Today his grief feels unfair. A way to stop me from telling him I'm not a child. That he doesn't need to fix me. That shallow talk with our neighbors will not make me happier. But how can we have such a frank conversation when he has brought my mother into the room? When he's folded over himself?

I stand up to get the butter and a knife. Let him work on the stain.

5

A MORTICIAN IS AN ILLUSIONIST. The goal is to cushion reality, slow down how fast the hurt seeps in. Cuts are filled, the gray pallor painted over. Lips moistened with tinted cream. Hair washed and combed but not overly styled. The embalmer's threads and glue and brushstrokes must be invisible so that when a family looks into the face of a loved one for the last time, there is no sign of illness, injury, or suffering. The grieving can pretend that their loved ones are merely sleeping. That they will hear you when you bend over to whisper all you had meant to say.

We need these illusions. Need to pretend the funeral will bring comfort. Closure. We need friends and family members saying, *We've got you. You won't slip away into a black hole of grief. You won't. Look at the body again. See? No signs that he suffered.*

But don't linger too long. Don't touch the skin if you hope it will be warm and supple. Don't rub your hand against the cheek or you will find makeup on your fingers and a smell, like lard, that you will try but not be able to forget.

Mr. Mosley is due back at his family ranch in an hour. I've stuffed the chest cavity with cotton batting from the roll my father used to mend the couch in our parlor. Both our projects have come out lumpy and uneven. And I'm afraid this is as good as Mr. Mosley is going to look.

Beneath his clothes, he's wearing plastic coveralls from neck to feet because there was too much of a risk that he'd leak. After the struggle to get him into his jeans, the tough work is over. I fit his checkered flannel shirt over the rustling plastic. With a quick look over my shoulder, I snip off a button and place it in my pocket. It's a silly habit, but I can't help myself. Later I'll put it in the shoe box I keep under my bed, where I've saved a button (or if necessary, a snap) from each who've spent their final hours with me.

One last check—remove lint from his sleeve, position hands just above his belt—and he is ready.

We have two ramps in the basement, one to get bodies and caskets in and out of the driveway and the other to get them into our parlor. The gurney rattles out the basement door and into my van. The hearse is no good for this job because the Mosleys didn't want a casket, and only the van has locks in back to keep the gurney from sliding around. After fastening the final lock, I bend over Mr. Mosley and whisper good-bye. I think his family will be happy with the look on his face—his mouth a stoic line, his cheeks still windburned, except where I shaved his thick stubble. There, his skin is smooth and pale.

I start the van, knowing I'll have to keep the heat off so Mr. Mosley will arrive at the ranch in good shape. I feel the engine's temperamental chugging before it quits. It does this reliably in cold weather—maybe because I've been saving money by skipping checkups. Eventually I'll have a mechanic see what the frequent stalling is about, but for now, I know a temporary trick: turn off the radio and lights, then wait.

I pull the sleeves of my sweater over my hands and tap out a tune on the steering wheel to keep from trying again too soon. Then I remember the papers I'd meant to deliver to Robert Golden. I unbuckle my seat belt. I'll have to make this quick. But, just as I'm about to open the door, the sheriff pulls in beside me with his white Ford—a fully loaded special service vehicle—the blue and red lights off.

Sheriff Petersen gets out of his truck and moves around the front of it in his beige uniform, Smokey Bear hat, and the one monstrous orthopedic shoe he wears to even out the length of his legs. He waits by my window while I roll down the glass.

Pop's told me the story a dozen times, how Pete, as he has always called him, shortening his last name as if it's his first, had been born in the breech position, and in the process dislocated his hip. Consequently, his right leg is three inches longer than the left. Even with the thick-heeled shoe and tall lift inside it, he has a distinct limp, leaning toward the shorter, weighted leg.

I feel a kinship with him over our difficult births, how they each changed the course of our lives.

"Need a jump?" he asks.

"No," I say. "It always starts eventually."

"You've got to keep it looked after, Button."

"I know, I know."

I wonder about the nickname for the first time, wonder if he knows about the buttons, or if, as I've always assumed until now, it's just one of those names you give to people you've known from the beginning.

"Headed out to the Mosley ranch?"

I nod. "I did the best I could with him. He came to me in pretty bad shape."

"Rolled his tractor, I hear," Pete says. "His wife's having a hard time of it."

Pete knows all the families in his jurisdiction, from here to Agate. We stay a little longer, done with talk. At last, he taps his hand on the window frame.

"You must be getting cold," he says.

We each smile, close lipped. As I close the window, Pete limps up the back steps to meet Pop in the kitchen, where they gossip like schoolboys.

I pump the gas and turn the key again. This time, the engine starts. I beep my horn at Pete, who pauses on the top step. He tips his hat—his jaw jutting out and up as if everything in that difficult birth got moved out of place.

It's twilight—the blue hour—the town silhouetted against the sky when everything seems to glow. The dirt road outside the funeral home snakes back to the paved one of Main Street. Some neighbors acknowledge my van as it goes by, standing still as Mr. Mosley passes through town one last time. I turn at the gray tower of the grain elevator.

Highway 200, with its deep barrow ditches on either side of the road, crosses the entire state. When you're on it for too long, it can play tricks on your eyes. You start to see curves and obstructions that aren't there, shimmering water where the road is dry. Once I pulled over for a hitchhiker only to discover I was alone. Every day the road is littered with the carcasses of rabbits and pheasants, the only sign that trucks have driven through at all.

The few houses along the way sit in fields of dried and flattened wheat. There are skeletons of barns, pens without animals, unrepaired fences. Out here, only a couple years after a home is vacated, you can't tell anyone ever lived on the land. Nature grabs it back, kicks down what doesn't belong—house, barn, or fence—spreads its pale stubble and cactus and greasewood along its low hills again.

When I pass another truck, likely the last I'll see tonight, the driver lifts two fingers from the steering wheel in the familiar, local wave. Just out of town, I pass the old rodeo grounds and scattered ranches, some lit up, some long dark, with wooden signs above the entrances showing the names of local cattle brands: P HALF CIRCLE, BAR F, RAFTER T. And soon, save the long stretch of telephone poles and wires, you see nothing at all made by human hands.

Under the blue glow, mule deer and elk come out to feed. You can imagine what would happen if your vehicle broke down in this prairie—how very long you would walk before you met another human or even evidence of one; and how little this land could sustain you—not a berry to pick, no water to quench your thirst, so few trees for shade. In the relentless quiet, you are reminded how small you are against this vast space, utterly dependent on the strength of your own body and your own thoughts. Petroleum is no place for the weak.

As I near the Mosley ranch, I see the shock of black Angus against all these muted colors, then worn-out machinery and trucks with hoods propped open. I assume the busted tractor is what crushed the man I've gotten to know over the past two days. I think of him in back, eyes sewn shut, hands crossed one over the other, dressed in his checked shirt and jeans. They didn't send shoes.

At the cattle guard, I hop out of my van to unlock the gate.

Two blond dogs bark and trot my way. I keep my door open as I drive through, hop out again to close the gate, then drive slowly toward a man in overalls, waving his arms for me. I notice a hay wagon waiting in the field for Mr. Mosley.

Family and friends slowly approach, walking silently toward me, from the house, the barn, the field, stepping over cow patties and spilled grain. They are casually dressed, many in rubber boots.

The man in overalls helps me open the back of the van. Those who are ready to receive the body step forward. Others turn away or hold the heads of young children to their hips. I pull Mr. Mosley gently from the van, helped by men whose backs are likely sore from a lifetime of shoveling, pitching, lifting, falling. Someone in this crowd of mourners discovered the accident. Or maybe he was there and saw it happen, the tractor on too steep an embankment, pinning Mr. Mosley underneath. Someone here may have put the machine in reverse, hearing the last plea for help. Someone loosened the collar and felt for a pulse. Someone told his wife and children. Someone called the funeral home. Someone walked through the stiff grass the next morning in order to believe it happened and to view the now hallowed ground. As the family and friends come closer, there are quiet, muffled gasps. No one is ever ready to see a loved one this way, to feel his weight but see no sign of his spirit. To see the bare feet and wish they hadn't.

Together we carry Mr. Mosley to the back of the large wagon. His plastic coveralls crinkle as we lay him on a bed of hay for one last ride across his land, one last night in the cold, open air.

When I return to my van, a man pulls me aside.

"The payment's going to be tough," he says. "But we can pay in elk meat. It'll be fair."

He tucks his hands into his pockets.

"I'll have my father work it out with you," I say.

At regular intervals, my father calls the clients who haven't paid their bills. Then the bargaining begins. Some offer old cars that don't work but have engines worth something. Some offer free goods from their gardens. In most cases, Pop takes what they propose as a fair exchange. It's the way of people around here; you make it work.

I hand the man a plastic grocery bag and he looks inside to find Mr. Mosley's watch and glasses. He nods, then squeezes the top of the bag closed in his fist.

"Join us if you like," he says.

"I'll watch from here."

I sit on the rear bumper of my van as the family gathers, bats swooping, dogs barking. The hayride begins with a young boy out front, carrying a lantern. And so Mr. Mosley rides beneath the great sky, family and friends walking beside him, not making a noise except to shout occasionally for the dogs to be quiet. The hope is that he might experience this moment, a last blast of color in the west, black in the east, pinpricks of stars overhead. This is their parting gift to him—the smell of earth and cattle, the steady crunch of wagon wheels against dry stalks, the jingle of dog tags.

One woman—the wife, I assume—has withdrawn from the crowd, hand pressed against her mouth. She bends over, hands on knees, lips moving. She waves away all who come close to offer comfort. Perhaps their last night together was one of silence, of one back turned toward the other, each waiting for an explanation or an apology. Pop said once that relationships are more often like old houses—the place where you want to live, but an ongoing project—something always leaking, peeling away, breaking down. The woman stays there, bent, talking, talking, talking into the wind.

The others continue their slow march, figures more and more in shadow, following the blurred orange of the lantern. Slowly, the wife straightens and begins to walk toward the hay wagon, still paces behind, but soon they will all arrive at the hole they've dug.

6

I WAS FIVE WHEN I saw my first dead body. Pop had always kept a Do Not Disturb sign on the door to the embalming room. And beneath it, because I needed reminders for what the words meant, he'd drawn a frowning girl. It was a sign that told me, *No, Mary. Not now, Mary. I'm working, Mary.*

I sat, as I often did, on the steps, staring at the large swinging doors where he disappeared for hours. Most times I'd listen to the sounds of whirring machines, rolling wheels, drawers opening and closing. But this time the room on the other side of the sign was quiet.

I scrunched the fabric of my nightgown in my fists, and slid, step by step, to the bottom, needing to hear the noise of my father working. Since the accident I was frightened by the quiet. Stories of Dead Eddie and playing the game were fun when I was with other kids, but alone, all that was left were the dark stairwells, the rats, and the memory of those yellow work boots.

I hadn't made a conscious decision to disobey the sign. I was simply outside of the swinging doors and then I was inside, the room cold, the shiny floor tiles continuing up the walls. I couldn't take my eye off the metal table in the center of the room or the heaping mound on top of it, draped in a sheet.

I set my foot inside the perfect square of one tile and let the other land beside it. A strange and powerful scent drew me deeper into the room. A scent I'd known all my life from my father's hands.

At any time I could run back through the swinging doors and up the stairs to the part of the house I knew. That is what I thought as I began to skate, zigzagging around the edge of the room, my slippers making a shushing sound across the floor.

Oh, but the feeling of skating through the shiny room where I wasn't allowed, the feeling of my impulses triumphing over the sign—it all thumped through me like a song turned up loud in Pop's hearse. I skated with my arms out to the sides. I skated round and round the table, near the great lump, then away toward the white cabinets, near the shiny tools, then away toward the wall.

When I finally stopped, I saw up close what I had tried to convince myself I could not possibly have seen: a foot. A bare foot—waxy, the color of an unpeeled potato, a Yukon gold like we grew in our garden. Right away I thought of questions I was in no hurry to answer: Why was there a foot lying on the table? Who did it belong to? And what else was under that sheet?

I let the white cloth brush against my arm, but that was all. Water gurgled through a pipe along the ceiling, and the swinging doors suddenly seemed very far away. When the room quieted again, I heard my name, just a whisper. "Mary." I looked to the toe as if it had spoken to me. The voice grew louder—"Mary"—and when I turned to run, it was right into my father.

What relief to fall into his arms, my cheek against his plastic apron. He bent down, the plastic crinkling, until we were at eye level. I felt the warm weight of his thumb on the tip of my nose, his indication that I was in trouble but not very much. I was now safe to lower my shoulders, to breathe out. Because this was why I had come downstairs: to find him. To ask if it was time for breakfast and if I could have the pink cereal.

Still holding my shoulders, he leaned back as if to see me more fully, inspecting me the way he might if I'd fallen off my bike.

"Pop?"

"Yes, Mary, what is it?"

I wanted to ask about breakfast, but a different question pushed it out of the way.

"Tell me, Mary. What?"

I looked into his face, dented and nicked from a rough-and-tumble boyhood, worry lines between his brows as he waited for me to speak.

"I wanted to know, can I touch the foot?"

A smile formed. His new smile that showed the sorrow and the strain he'd absorbed that tragic summer.

"Well," he said and paused a long while. "I don't see why not." His smile became an unsure laugh.

"No," he said as if finishing an argument in his head. "No reason at all."

He took my hand and we moved closer to the table. But I pulled back, not so sure anymore.

"It's all right," he said. "This fella won't wake up."

Slowly I reached forward, first with my whole hand but then with only my pointer finger. And I touched the foot—prodding the heel, then the fat pad closer to the top, and finally the very bendable big toe. It felt like a trout we'd caught and kept in the cooler. I broke out into giggles, hysterical nonstop giggles.

When I could breathe again, my question felt squeezed tight. "Is there only a foot under there?"

"No, Mary. There's more."

He pulled the sheet upward to expose a yellow, bruised slab I only recognized as a leg when I noticed the coiled hairs. This time, laughter exploded through my closed mouth, the sound strange and wet. I poked my finger into the doughy flesh, allowing my mind to connect this leg, this foot to my father's work. Maybe this was someone he would help bury.

"Is there a hand?" I asked.

I kept my poking finger extended, as if to keep it far from the rest of me. Pop was already reaching beneath the sheet. When he lifted the wrist, the dull yellow fingers curled forward. Though he held it still for me, I would not touch it.

The hand, somehow, made me understand that the body had once been a living thing. This was a hand like Pop's, something that held a mug of coffee in the morning, that petted my hair when I was close by and being a nuisance. I shook my head fiercely and stepped back from the table, losing a slipper, the shock of cold tile rocketing through my foot.

It was after midnight when Pop and I sat at the kitchen table eating pink cereal.

"Just because you're hungry," he told me, "doesn't mean it's morning."

The room felt unfamiliar with its black windows, and the

heat set low for the night. I prodded at my cereal, watching the pink slip away into the milk. I had never noticed it doing that in the daytime, maybe had never eaten it slowly enough to discover that the thin pink coating was a trick, as if nothing in my world was what I'd thought.

I let my spoon sink into the bowl.

"Maybe it's time to call it a day," Pop said.

He took my hand and helped me from the table. He guided me through the darkened first floor, past the clouded mirror and plastic flowers. I watched my wool slippers climb each step to my room.

Death was starting to mean something more concrete to me. It meant the troubling change in our town's grown-ups, who forgot to ask where you were during the day or how you got so dusty. It meant angry men standing against buildings with nothing to do. It meant the foot you touched in the basement could have belonged to someone like Eddie.

I remained silent as Pop kissed my forehead good night and closed my door.

I was glad to be under the covers again, my father's footsteps creaking down the hallway to his room. But as I lay there with the night-light casting my walls in orange, I felt alert to every shadow in the room, every noise, and through the bedroom wall, a woman's voice, sharp with disapproval.

"You're just coming to bed?"

Many of these women over the years tried to sneak in and out of my father's bedroom without my noticing. His status as a widower attracted caretaker types, who longed to nurture him. I don't remember all the women but Bernice, whose voice I heard that night, was starting to feel permanent. Pop's answer was soft-spoken, contrite. If he'd ever had an excuse for working into the night, forgetting time, forgetting his latest girlfriend, he'd already used it up.

I heard only murmuring, laughter, more murmuring. Then Bernice snapped, "Touched a foot?"

Pop finally raised his voice, arguing that I'd soon get used to it.

And Bernice practically shouted the question that would come to define my place in Petroleum, "Do you understand what a strange child she'll be if this becomes normal to her?"

After that night, I couldn't forget the body in our basement, two stories below my bed, one story below our kitchen table. I began to notice the rhythm of the work that went on in our household. The phone call. The arrival of the body beneath a sheet. Pop's late nights in the basement. The house filling with old men in suits, hunched like crows, old women trembling in pretty hats. The sound of ladies weeping in my father's arms and his soothing voice, how he sounded like he did on the commercial.

Maybe he felt relief finally showing me his workspace, ending the trickery to hide it all those years. To my father, this was honorable, tender work. A part of his life, a reality of our home.

"You've forgotten that death is rare and traumatic for most people," Bernice told him. "You might want to keep it that way for Mary."

Their relationship was serious enough that she occasionally tidied up our house and kept an eye on me as Pop worked. She cleaned in knee-length dresses and my father's mucking boots, which she liked to wear because they were several sizes bigger than her feet and she could step into them even if her hands were full, moving from room to room with rags and sprays and handfuls of the various things we had dirtied.

She dusted around us while I sat beside Pop on the sofa, choosing casket fabric from the fat three-ring binder. I loved to touch the swatches of taffeta (though customers always chose polyester). My favorite colors were named after flowers: buttercup, orchid, peony, magnolia. I loved to open the tackle box, where he kept makeup. He let me paint thick, putty-colored grease on the back of my hand.

Bernice helped wash it off. She scrubbed too hard. Later, she scrubbed the house with bleach and sprayed with Lysol to cover up what she called the "smell of death." Afterward, she lay down in a dark room, complaining of headaches she believed were from the formaldehyde and my father believed were from the cleaning products.

The problem with dating my father was that you also had to take on his business and me. If he had ever fretted about whether a woman could learn to love his mood swings, his drinking, his habit of going to work early and finishing late, this set of baggage (our home and me) was the hardest sell.

Bernice came into my room one day, wearing my father's boots and carrying a stack of folded clothes. She sat on the bed, holding the laundry, and watched me at play.

"I washed an outfit you might want to wear for school," she said. "I added a bow to it. Would you like to see?"

But I was like my father; it was hard to break my attention when I was at work.

I folded sheets of tinfoil into shiny metal beds and placed my plastic dolls on them. I whispered words like *Glory* and *Our Little Angel,* then draped them head to foot in Kleenex. I played wearing latex gloves, powdery inside, loose on my hands. I heard Bernice draw a breath. I looked up to see her mouth open as if to speak. I peeled off a long piece of tinfoil to make a second metal bed. Bernice closed her mouth, hugging the stack of clothes to her chest. And I could feel the shame of the strange child I'd become.

7

USUALLY THE FIRST PERSON downstairs in the morning starts the coffee. But today, still in his pajamas, his hair unwashed, Pop stares at a table littered with paperwork and bills.

"Oh," he says. "I didn't see you there."

He gets up, opens the can of coffee beside the sink, scoops out two heaping spoonfuls.

"Did you even sleep?" I ask.

"Little bit."

While he pours water into the back of the coffeemaker, I look for a space at the table where we might eat breakfast.

Much of his paperwork has to do with making death official: starting a file to get a death certificate, submitting a notice to the newspaper, canceling Social Security benefits. He keeps prospective budgets for customers trying to decide on caskets, flowers, music. But I also see a list of our clients who haven't paid their bills, and I know Pop has a grueling day ahead filled with delicate bargaining that will cause financial harm to both the client and to us.

"Did you use all the cotton batting?" he asks as he flicks a switch to start the coffee.

"I did," I say. "For Mr. Mosley. Is that all right?"

"I just wasn't expecting you'd use all of it," he says. "I had plans to fix a chair."

"I didn't know," I say.

He sits at the table.

"I'm just trying to get all the numbers right."

I can see him doing calculations in his head. Always, as my father works the numbers, I see his anxiety about being the next business to fail. The uncertainty of tomorrow, a resignation to the general direction we're all headed in this town.

"Things will turn around," I tell him.

We say things like this from time to time. Whoever is feeling down, the other chimes in with optimism. Usually we at least pretend to perk up, but Pop just stares at the mess.

I look for a place to sit—my usual chair is piled with papers—so I take the spare next to his. I can't put my elbows on the table, and Pop is so close I hear him swallow.

"I haven't given any thought to breakfast," he says. "I'm sorry."

"I can put something together."

Then we both turn toward the front door because someone has just walked across the squeaky board on our porch.

"I'm not ready to see anyone just yet," Pop says.

The doorbell rings.

"What do you want me to say?"

"Say I'm in the shower," he says. "Get a phone number."

The doorknob turns and footsteps enter the foyer.

"Hello?" a man calls.

"Hello?" I answer, looking into the hallway and seeing Robert Golden.

Pop whispers, "Send him along."

"I didn't know if I was supposed to walk right in like I would at any place of business," he says. "I hope I did this right."

"It's fine," I say.

"Send him on," Pop whispers.

"My father's in the . . ."

"Oh, Mr. Crampton, hello," Robert says, peering into the kitchen.

He extends his hand.

Pop stands, reluctant, and shakes it.

"Coffee?" I ask Robert, pouring.

"No, thanks."

The room feels smaller, hotter with Robert in the doorway and Pop bristling in the corner.

"I came to pick up those papers," he says. "Preplanning forms?"

I set the cup on the table, embarrassed I'd forgotten to take care of this.

"I'll drop by this afternoon," Pop says, stepping in front of me. "We can go through all the arrangements then."

"To be honest," Robert says, "I waited for the papers all yesterday. My mother is dying. I don't have endless time here."

"I'll get them right away," I say.

"Mary."

It's all my father says, and when I turn to face him, my hip rams the corner of the table, knocking over the cup of coffee.

"Sorry, sorry," I say. "Someone pass me the paper towels."

"Here." Robert rushes in with a dish towel, everyone trying to reach the table at once. I stretch past my father, finally spotting the roll of towels.

"Mary, let it go!" he shouts. "Can I have a little space in my kitchen, please?"

I rarely hear him yell like this and never in front of a customer. The papers soak up the coffee.

"This obviously isn't a good time," Robert says. "But I'd like the papers by this afternoon."

He lets himself out and the door clicks shut. I can't stand to look at my father or all this smeared ink.

"I wasn't ready for company," he says.

"He's right that he doesn't have endless time," I say. "Let me grab those papers."

"No."

"Pop, is there some problem I should know about?"

"I don't want him to fill out any paperwork."

"What?"

"I took care of it a long time ago," he says, trying to pat everything dry. "I planned the whole service and secured speakers, singers, everyone who will be involved."

It's not unusual for my father to plan services for widows and people who are without local family.

"I see how that makes things awkward," I say.

"No one expected Doris's son to return," he says. "And to be honest, I know her needs better than he does."

"Well, now that he's back, I guess you'll have to cancel those arrangements."

"It's complicated, honey," he says.

"No, it's not," I say. "He's next of kin. This is his right."

My father grows quiet. He tries so hard to keep our business afloat, tries every way he knows to keep our customers and potential customers happy.

"He's a bad memory for this town," he says, carefully choosing his words. "I think our neighbors will feel relieved the less involved he is."

"We have to do what's right for the customer," I say.

"We have to do what's right for the town."

"I won't do anything unprofessional, Pop."

"Let me handle it, then. It's really a matter of making strong suggestions to him. Things will go better if we don't disrupt the plans."

If my father could see himself right now, hair slick with grease, the agonized look in his eyes as he leans helplessly over the drenched papers, I'm not sure he'd trust himself to make a rational decision.

"He asked for my help," I say.

"And I'm going to step in," he says.

"Pop, don't. Don't treat me like a kid who's not allowed to let go of your hand."

He dabs the papers with the towel again.

"Listen," he says. "How about we get breakfast at the Pipeline?"

"I'm okay waiting till your work is done," I say. "We can eat here."

"No," he says. "Look at the mess I've made of this table."

He picks up one of the dry papers with his hurried writing, like thought spasms, going up the side of the page.

"All right," I say. "We can go as soon as you're dressed."

"Why don't you head up there and save me a seat?" he says. "A few of these folks are early risers, and I can get some calls out of the way."

"Pop, I can wait. We'll walk up together."

"No," he says. "Give me a few minutes by myself. Anyway, it's good for you to get out of the house. Talk with the neighbors."

I fetch my coat, my hip throbbing where I smacked it against the table. I hear my father's first phone call, his cautious request for payment, the clear resistance on the other end. And I know, after the call, his best efforts will put us a little further in debt.

I zip my coat, and then, because it feels right, I wind my way through the obstacle course of his office and choose a handful of papers from the file cabinet. My father, seeing them in my hands as I leave out the back door, covers the mouthpiece on the phone.

"That's a girl," he says. "Might as well get it done."

8

ONE GREAT THING ABOUT covering your windows with tin-foil is the surprise you find when you open the door to last night's moon and this morning's sun hanging together in the sky. As I walk toward the road, I see Robert in his driveway, inspecting the side of his truck.

"Hey," I say. "That wasn't my father's best side you saw this morning."

I reach into the bag slung over my shoulder and grab the pre-planning papers.

"Thank you," he says as I hand them over, though there's still a touch of prickliness to his voice.

And now I see what Robert had been inspecting so intensely—the long, deep gouge on the side of his truck.

"I'm sorry," I say.

"People can be so petty when it's not a time for pettiness."

"I'm close with the sheriff," I say. "I'll mention it to him."

"I don't have a lot of time left with my ma," he says. "I can't waste it arguing about the paint on my truck."

"How's she doing?" I ask.

"She's tired," he says. "Short of breath if she does too much. It's worse if she lies down."

"My pop says she wasn't a smoker."

"Just bad luck," he says.

"I knew her a little from when she worked at the school."

"Was she a good teacher?"

"I didn't take chorus," I say. "But I'd see her at all the holiday performances."

"Shame she can't sing anymore," he says. "She tries. But she doesn't like how her voice has changed."

"You took off work for this?"

"I don't want her to die alone."

"I'm sorry," I say again. "About your mom and the truck."

From his driveway I can see into the backyard. For many years, Doris would be out there, throwing grain to her chickens, the yard in constant motion. All day they clucked and left their droppings across the yard.

In the end, they were too much work for her, but the yard is still a maze of wire mesh. Beyond the unused hutch, I see something I hadn't noticed before: a little tree house is built into the gnarled crabapple, still standing after so many years.

Robert looks at the papers in his hand. "I ought to get started on these," he says and offers a half smile.

"Yeah, I have to get going, too."

The preplanning forms I gave Robert don't appear controversial: Who should take custody of the body? Where will the body be buried? How will the ceremony be conducted? Who will be invited? Who will make a speech? But Pop always cautions me how quickly simple decisions can turn contentious in our business. Family members are often surprised by their feelings of jealousy and entitlement, weighing who was most loved and who carried the greatest burden.

As I near the diner, men slouch against the wall nearest the stairs—letting you know they're available for any odd jobs. Sometimes they're old men. Sometimes they're my age and younger. My father likes to stop and talk with them.

He tells me that, in their hearts, all these years later, so many of these men remain train conductors, grain elevator operators, gas station attendants, oil drillers. But what becomes of them when there are no trains, no grain elevators, no gas stations, no oil wells? The jobs they had, the skills that defined their worth are gone. Perhaps they lie in bed at night and ask of dark ceilings, *Who am I now?* The question rubs against who they once were and the fear of being irrelevant. Set aside. Lost.

I don't have my father's urge to talk with these men. Still, I try to smile as I pass the lowered caps, taut mouths and chins. They look up to see who's here, if there's an offer of work, then look down again, most chewing something . . . gum, tobacco, cheek.

The Pipeline Diner is the social hub of Petroleum and the only place to eat in town. It's even the nightlife scene here. At 8 P.M., they turn off the overhead lights and turn on strings of colored bulbs, converting the diner to a bar. You can still order hotcakes, but after hours you can have them with whiskey.

Pop has encouraged me to join the late-night crowd at the Pipeline. Join anything. Get out of the basement. Make friends. He brings it up casually, as if it's not something that nags at him. But I've overheard his phone calls, asking the person on the other end, *Did I cause this? Will she always be alone?*

The sign for the Pipeline groans on metal chains with each push of the wind. I pull open the door. The diner is warm and smells of bacon and mud, and most seats by the window are filled. One wall displays the local cattle brands, seared right into the wood.

I feel the stones clack as I step inside, and when others look up, I wonder if they've heard them too.

"Mary, what a nice surprise."

So Martha Rudd has this morning's shift. This may be why Pop suggested coming to the diner. She steps behind the counter to pour juice into a pitcher and holds up one finger to say, *Be with you in a minute.*

Pop has a soft spot for waitresses. His own mother worked as a waitress here, before she moved on to assisted living in Agate. Pop and Martha seem to have gotten together a couple of weeks ago. At first their conversations were the same as he'd have with anybody in town. Then, he started bringing up her name for no reason and I'd notice her lingering behind our house.

I grab a stool at the counter, take off my coat, set it on the seat to my right, gloves and shoulder bag on the seat to my left. Someone may still ask to sit beside me but, at least now, they'll think twice.

Martha reaches for a place setting. "Why don't you take that sunny table by the window?" she suggests.

I wonder if she and Pop have been talking about me, *Why is it so hard for her? It's like she tries not to make friends.*

Martha hangs up my coat as I move toward the new table. I sit among three extra chairs as if I'm waiting for friends. Maybe an old classmate, who used to ring my doorbell for kicks, will take a seat and we can have a good laugh about our school days.

I come across people I'd gone to school with all the time.

They're polite. They've grown up. We say hello and nod. Sometimes we share a sentence or two about the weather. But it's not until they come to me draped in a sheet that our guards drop. This past year, I embalmed Jenny Johnson, one of my high school classmates, and we never got along so well as the day I fixed her hair with rollers and painted her nails crimson, like the school's colors.

"If you'd like a stack of hotcakes," Martha says, pouring me coffee, "you'd better place an order quick. We're running out."

"Sure," I say, trying to act casual, except my voice sounds like someone's squeezing my throat.

I study our ad on the paper placemat. I hate sitting alone in public. Pop's words are in my head. *Don't just sit there. Don't look down. Don't wait for other people to speak to you.* The don'ts are the only things I can think of. *Don't share your private thoughts. They're private for a reason. Don't talk about work. Don't ever talk about work. And try not to look bored.*

I know he gives this advice because he loves me. I hear in his words a desperate plea, *Be like them so they'll include you.* It's exhausting. I have to think before I speak, smile when I don't feel like it.

A man sits at the next table, takes off his hat, and sets it down like a centerpiece. I wonder if he remembers when we went on a school trip to a nearby ranch to study the constellations. Our class lay in the back of a pickup and drove through the pasture. But my memory was the boy's boot pressed against mine, his fingers gently sweeping my arm. Boys only reached out to me in secret—a note slipped through my locker, a touch in the dark.

He and I are the same age, but he has the lined face and rough hands of someone who works outdoors. As he looks over my shoulder and out the window, I see no memory in his eyes of lying together in the bed of that pickup, as if I'd imagined it all.

Once I thought of leaving Petroleum. I imagined a world where people didn't already have an impression of me. I could be anything, maybe try my hand at art. I'd even collected brochures from colleges in faraway cities, a secret I shared only with my art teacher, who had shepherded me through all twelve years.

Paging through those catalogs, I glimpsed a bigger world— dense canopies of trees, students of all sizes and colors with outrageous clothes and hairstyles. Nothing like the people of our town. The world beyond Petroleum seemed to follow a completely different set of rules.

I applied to two colleges. The first turned me down, and as for the one that accepted me, I didn't have the nerve to ask my father to help pay. I felt ashamed for acting so selfishly. Who was I to think I deserved such an extravagant life? Besides, art, when I thought about it, wasn't a realistic pursuit. What can art even do? It just sits there.

In the end, it was easier to stay put. I'd developed an expertise in my work, and staying in Petroleum allowed me to keep an eye on my father. After a while, my dream of being an artist seemed so far in the past, it was as if it belonged to someone else. Though sometimes at night, I would sweat, just thinking of the life I might have lived. What if I had gone away? Where would I be? What would I be doing?

Martha brings out an order of hotcakes. "More coffee?" she asks.

I shake my head no. Now that I've switched seats, I'm conscious of the sound of chewing and the fork scraping my plate.

The door opens, and before I see my father, I recognize the tune he likes to whistle. Pop turns to each table.

"Gentlemen. Good morning."

"Allen," Martha says. "I didn't know you'd be here."

Pop gives his weird, too-big smile that shows his top gums.

He and Martha are friendly, but carefully so, because the fact that she's married to Tim Rudd complicates everything. Tim, like all the other men here except for my father, is a rancher.

Pop takes the seat across from me and I smell cologne.

"Take care of everything?" he asks.

"Yes," I say and push my menu to his side. "Did you get your calls done?"

"Some," he says. "And I ran into Fritz. His hand's just fine."

"Good."

I'd forgotten about his hand.

"I saw the obituary you wrote in yesterday's paper," Martha tells Pop, stopping with the coffeepot. "You're a very good writer."

"I thank you for the compliment," he says in a voice that sounds too formal for breakfast.

"Was it a nice service for Mr. Mosley?" she asks, setting out another placemat and flatware.

She seems to know we refer to the dead by their formal names.

"Yes," I say. "They gave him a ride through the ranch in a hay wagon before they buried him."

Men at other tables have turned their ears or chairs toward us as we talk about Mr. Mosley. His story is theirs in many ways. Every day walking, climbing, chasing, riding, lifting, falling. Muscles cramping. Blisters opening. Knees, shoulders, back, and hip clicking. And they walk it off. No break because it's the weekend, no break because of the weather.

These men think of the year in terms of the rancher's four

seasons: calving, branding, haying, and shipping. They don't clock hours but simply work until the work is done, with the financial payoff several pages away on the calendar. On the big payday, after the ranchers have returned from the shipping pens and sold their steer calves to feedlots and auctioned half their heifers and pocketed the earnings for a year's work, the whole town celebrates.

"Nice man," she says. "I hope he enjoyed his ride."

"You've always got a cheerful outlook," Pop says.

He nods to me as if to say, *Isn't she so cheerful?*

"You knew him well?" Pop asks her. "Mr. Mosley?"

"Sure. Our families drew elk tags last fall so we got to do some hunting together," she says. "And, of course, Tim would see him at the cattle auctions."

I watch to see if my father stiffens at the mention of her husband.

"I almost forgot to order," Pop says.

"We're out of hotcakes and blueberry muffins," she says.

"In that case, an omelet and bacon."

"And no toast," she says, smiling.

She strikes me as too meek to stray, but maybe it only takes being lonely.

A man at the far end of the counter picks a piece of straw out of his shirt collar and sets it beside his plate. When Martha comes closer, he says, "I could use some aspirin, if you've got any."

Lots of customers come here sore. A shelf behind the counter is stocked with medicine. Some days the whole place smells like BENGAY. Martha passes him a bottle. Like Mr. Mosley, I imagine this man has calloused hands and swollen knuckles. I listen to pills clatter into his palm.

"Anyone else?" she calls, holding up the bottle.

"Sure, I could use some over here."

"Here, too."

To ask for this is as much as they will speak about their pain. One rancher after another swallows a few pills, then hunches over his plate again, grateful, it seems, for a time when he doesn't have to move or think.

I swirl a wedge of hotcake into syrup. I've been looking out the window over Pop's shoulder, and now I see a black pickup go by. A wild beating begins in my chest as I recognize the deep scratch down the side of it. My foot taps from nerves. I wonder if Doris is in the truck with him. If Robert's coming or going.

"See who just went past?" someone asks.

"The guy coming back here is like giving us the middle finger."

"Coincidence he comes back now. Only time he's bothered to see her all these years."

"Probably wants to make off with her money and furniture."

"That money was going to go to the school."

"What's this?"

"I heard she was going to give her life savings to the school. And this one's come to take it all."

Over the years, Robert's role in the accident has grown. The boy with the lazy work ethic has become someone who rejects this culture, who thinks he's better than we are, who willfully destroyed this town.

"Bought himself a fancy truck. You see it?"

"Probably drives an automatic."

"It's money he should have given to Petroleum."

You can hear something old and sour rising like bile, the loss that has never eased, the disgust aimed at Robert.

"Did you know someone scratched the side of his truck?" I ask Pop.

"This isn't the place, Mary."

"You should tell Pete next time he stops by."

"Leave it be," Pop says. "It doesn't concern us."

"Even if he's our customer?" I ask.

"He isn't, really," Pop says. "I thought we had an understanding."

My father looks at his omelet. And I pretend to read the ads on the place mat again. I have a neck ache from staring at this place mat.

9

WE PUT ON OUR coats, then Martha hands my father a Styrofoam container of leftovers. But I see that she snuck a slice of cherry pie into it, along with a little folded-up note that partially sticks out the side. Pop's thumb fidgets with it as we leave.

"Good day, gentlemen," my father says when we pass the men slouched against the wall.

He stops to shake their hands, and the men answer, "Allen" or "Crampton," caps still low on their heads.

Sometimes Pop will hire one of them to unblock a sink or fix a leak. Then the guy leans against the diner wall again, waiting for the next job. Pop's attention to them is as close as he gets to saying he's scared of becoming the next guy leaning against that wall.

It's not as if those with jobs aren't struggling. I know Pop is. And I can imagine Vinter sitting over bills for his grocery store, wondering what changes to make so the numbers come out black instead of red. Even the ranchers we sat near at breakfast are hurting, despite constant work. Supplies cost more, and folks try to save money by letting go of hired hands, keeping more of the profit in the family. But the extra work can be brutal. And there are new regulations about grazing, about environmental preservation that make the job more complicated. As a child, I viewed those sprawling fields as simple squares of brown and green and gold, but I knew nothing about blight, or early sprouting, or the trouble birds can give a crop.

"Pop, did you hear all that talk about Doris having some secret stash of money?"

"I have no idea what Doris does or doesn't have," he says.

"They talk about it as if the money's owed to them," I say. "If there even is money."

"I heard," he says.

"Well, that's just dumb," I say. "She doesn't live like someone who has money. And even if she gives some to the school, it's not going to change anyone's life."

"Don't call it dumb, Mary."

"But it is."

"It's not dumb," he says. "It's hope."

"It's dumb if it's false hope. If there's not a bit of it that's true."

"Nothing's dumb if it helps you look forward to the next day," he says.

The wind has picked up. The metal clip on the school flag clanks against the pole. On the ground are scattered bits of roof tile and shutters that didn't get cleaned up yesterday. I think of all those men and their dumb hope. Maybe, despite what they know of the economy, they dream of a revival in Petroleum—a feeling of relevance, a place where the train might stop again.

• • •

When we pass Doris's, Pop asks, "You didn't have any trouble when you dropped off those papers?"

"No trouble," I say.

"You told him we can handle all the arrangements ourselves, right?"

"Yes," I say.

I have to look away because Pop once told me I scrunch my mouth to the side when I lie.

"Good," he says. "Keeps things simple."

At some point I'll have to break the news to him. When he's in a better mood. When I've thought of how to say it.

"Did you ever notice the tree house in Doris's backyard?" I ask him.

"Is it still standing?"

"Yeah," I say. "I mean, it's missing boards, but there's definitely a tree house back there. There's even a little rain boot hanging from it."

"That was from an old pulley system," he says. "It used a rain boot, filled with rocks as a counterweight, for lifting things up to the window. Doris told me she used to send sandwiches up there."

"Pretty good place for the brothers to play," I say.

Pop's thumb moves back and forth over the edge of that little note as if he has to maintain contact with it.

"I think Robert built it," Pop says. "He was the only one who used that old fort."

"Robert? Really?"

"Oh yeah. He'd climb into Dumpsters and haul stuff back to the tree house. An old clock, printer, bicycle part, you name it."

"And do what?"

"Take it apart," he says. "And then he'd use the motors and valves and springs and pumps and drums and rims and circuit boards and metal bars to make any number of inventions that didn't work. You'd hear the tantrums from our porch."

"They must have thought he was an engineer in the making."

"I think it worried his father," Pop says. "He was always shouting for him to get down from that tree. Everyone was out playing ball or climbing on tractors, and his father didn't want Robert staying to himself."

I try to imagine a young Robert inside the little fort, so determined and frustrated. Who goes by Robert except on their birth and death certificates? How lonely a boy must be to never get a nickname. Didn't anyone think to call him Robbie or Bob? There's something about his aloneness and the way people formed an impression of him—*this person's not like us*—that pulls at me. I know what it's like when a town has made up its mind about you.

We step over the sign on our way to the front door.

"Wonder how long that will be on our lawn?" I ask.

"Dunno," he says. "I probably won't get to it today."

When I look at him, I see he's finally eased that note out of the container and has it pressed tight in his hand as if it'll help him look forward to the next day.

10

For days, as the temperature has dropped, our basement empty of bodies, there has been too much time at the kitchen table. Every so often I'll hear Pop wander from room to room and then sigh as he settles back into one chair or another. I put my hand on top of the saltshaker, turn it, turn it once again, and let it go. It will continue like this all day. The agitated quiet. The sky dark by four o'clock. Without work, we are irritable. Pacing, sitting, standing, staring at the tinfoil on the window, and drinking too many cups of coffee.

Pop walks into the kitchen. He picks up the phone, looks at me, then places it back on the receiver. Clearly, he was about to call Martha, and now I've ruined it. When he takes a seat, I pass him sections of the newspaper I've already read. He shuffles through the stack, then opts to read the backside of the section I'm holding. And now I feel pressure to read faster.

I give up and toss the whole paper to his side of the table.

"More toast?" I ask, standing up.

"Sure."

We've been eating all morning. Something to do. I press two slices into the toaster.

"I'm thinking of renting out the parlor for bingo nights or AA meetings," he says.

"Are you kidding me?"

"It would bring in a little extra money," he says. "We need to do something."

We come to this crossroads regularly—these periods of no income. Though we serve all the small ranching communities outside of Agate, death comes when it comes. There's nothing you can, or would want to do, to hurry it.

"You want people in our house all the time?"

He stares at the phone. The toast seems to be taking forever.

"I did some cleaning in the basement," I say.

He doesn't ask what I cleaned so I tell him I scrubbed every surface and poured Drāno down the sinks.

I butter the toast and bring it to the table.

"I organized cupboards, too. Shower caps, gloves, flower stands, embalming fluids."

The clock on the wall ticks. I don't always hear it, but when work is slow, it's like someone turned up the sound. I take a bite and wonder if I'm full.

"Oh, and I finally organized the boxes of unclaimed cremains," I say.

In every community, there are always the lost and unloved: transients, prisoners, and elderly who die alone on the prairie.

"I organized them by the dates they passed," I say, catching my father glance at the phone again.

"You should really get out of the house more," he says.

"Fine," I say. "I'll go for a walk."

I'm in such a rush to leave the house, I'm already down the street before I slip my arms through the sleeves of my coat. I zip it closed, sure my father's already dialing Martha.

I know it hasn't been easy for him to find a partner. I can feel the heartache in his phone calls to her, how much he needs someone who thinks of him during the day.

I pause for a moment when I see cigarette butts at the bottom of the Goldens' driveway. I guess Robert's a smoker. At least he knows better than to do it near someone with lung cancer.

Wind blows my hair into knots as I reach the road that leads up to the rimrocks. This has always been my favorite place in Petroleum. Sometimes I climb to the top to watch the sun rise and animals forage for food, although my goal this morning is just to put some distance between me and home.

When a truck grumbles up the road, I move to the right to let it pass. But it pulls alongside me, and when I turn to look, the window lowers.

"Hey," Robert says. "How's work?"

"A little slow right now."

"Lucky for your neighbors," he says.

He seems pleased with this attempt at humor.

"Actually, I have some questions about the papers you gave me last week," he says. "I tried to call, but I can't seem to get a signal."

He pulls a cell phone from his pocket to show me, and I can't help but laugh.

"It'll take a while," I say.

His eyes squint and a smile lifts on one side. "Are you trying to tell me I'll never get a signal?"

I can't stop laughing. "Closest cell tower's in Agate."

I brush my hair behind one ear, forgetting, then sweep it forward again.

"What kinds of questions do you have?" I ask.

He unlocks the door on my side.

"Here, hop in," he says. "I have so many questions, I'm not even sure where to start."

I look around before I open the door.

"Don't worry, no one will see," he says. "I know how people talk around here."

"Let them talk," I say, glad there's no one around to see me climb onto the cold seat.

"I'm surprised," he says.

"That I don't live my life based on what other people think of me?" I shrug and close the door. "So what if they get mad. I don't think there's an emotion I can't shut out."

I'd meant to sound tough and unconcerned but, instead, feel I've exposed where I'm most fragile.

"Where should we go?" he asks, rolling up my window.

"Not sure."

"I'll just wing it, then," he says and turns the truck around.

I've been with two men—that's two more than my neighbors would presume. One was more a boy than a man. I was still in high school, and he was a benched basketball player from a rival team. We kissed and touched and traded phone numbers. His number, when I finally tried it, rang a pizza shop in Agate. The other was more recent, a man who visited Petroleum for a hunting trip. We had hurried sex in the open bed of his pickup when anyone standing on the rims could have looked down and seen us.

I don't like to remember the shame afterward, allowing such

rushed hands on me, mistaking his glazed eyes for affection. But I do like remembering the rush of blood through my body, the feeling I have now, along with a tingling of misgivings.

I hear the click of the blinker, and Robert turns onto the highway.

I feel daring as I watch the town disappear behind us, listening to the songs playing through the car speakers. This is music you don't hear on the local stations—more drums and keyboard, darker lyrics, bass pounding through the seat.

It's funny to watch out the window with a different soundtrack. I can't make the music and scenery fit together. We've been conditioned to reject the world beyond Petroleum, the world most of us only know from TV. Immoral, garish, crowded. Different from us.

"Too loud?" he asks.

"What?"

"The music. Is it too loud?"

"No," I say. "No."

But he lowers it, anyway.

"What's it like growing up in a funeral home?" Robert asks.

I turn so my knee rests on the seat, noticing, even as I do it, that it isn't like me to make myself so comfortable.

"No one's ever asked me that before."

"You're kidding me?"

"No," I say.

"Did you hang out at funerals as a kid?"

"I wasn't allowed till I was eleven or twelve," I say. "I had to stay in my room."

Standing at my bedroom window I'd watch the mourners file into the house in dark clothing. Truck doors opened and closed. Footsteps of formal shoes clicked on the porch and then inside, moving from hardwood floors to carpets. Sometimes there was a piano playing, and always a series of hymns and amens.

"I was under strict orders to keep quiet," I said.

I often skated along the hardwood floors in my socks, trying to avoid the one patch of rough wood that was sure to snag a thread loose.

"Sometimes I'd tiptoe downstairs and sneak off with a handful of cookies or a can of Shasta. If my father caught me, he'd let me sit on a chair in the very back of the parlor, and I'd watch the ladies' hats with the fake flowers and dotted veils on them."

After the last guests left the house, I'd charge up and down the stairs, run in circles through the parlor room, weave in and out of the folding chairs, shrieking, needing to expend all the energy and noise that had been restrained, as if I were a spring needing to uncoil.

"And you like this work?" he asks. "Now that you're allowed in on the action?"

"It's a steady job," I say.

"So that means you like it or don't like it?"

This isn't the kind of conversation I'm used to, and it bothers me that I can't simply say yes, I like my job.

I don't not like it. It's just that I didn't really choose it.

It was more that this business was a part of my home. It was comfortable, second nature. I read the pamphlets and played with the makeup. I knew the tools. I watched how my father used them. I followed him around until his work became my play. And my world moved more and more into the shiny white-tiled basement. How else was I going to spend my time?

"Isn't there a lake out here somewhere?" he asks. "I'm remembering a lake."

"I can show you."

I know every bit of this road. Soon, there will be the leaning barbed-wire fence that begins and ends for no reason, and then, lit up silver by the sun, the two white memorial crosses at the highway's bend—a warning to slow down, to pay attention, to stay in your lane—although all of us instinctively take our eyes off the road.

"Want me to keep on the highway like this?" he asks.

"Yes," I say, daring now to watch his profile as he drives. "I'll tell you when to turn. It's a while yet."

I still can't get over the idea that this man is the grown-up fourteen-year-old who has whimpered so long in my imagination. He must be almost forty.

He points out a hawk overhead.

"You see it?" he asks.

There are the rumors. Things I'm supposed to believe about Robert. And then, I don't know.

"You're going to take the next turn," I say.

I grab the door grip when he takes a right at too much speed, maybe assuming the asphalt would continue. The truck rocks over the uneven earth.

"Now this way," I say and point to something that looks even less like a road, just faint tire tracks through stubbly white grass.

"Right," he says. "Now I remember."

He takes the turn slow this time.

From here, you wouldn't know there's a lake anywhere nearby. The illusion in Petroleum and the surrounding towns is that everything is visible—your eye believes it can see for miles in every direction—when much is, in fact, hidden in the folds and pockets of these low hills. The eye sees miles of yellow and sage, but right under your nose are trailer homes, cabins, black cattle, and the muddy school bus that disappears and reappears from nowhere, like a ghost on wheels.

We reach the wooden sign, faded and chipped, announcing BRINE LAKE. A row of gray, splintered fishing shanties line the bank. Long ago, visitors would rent these shanties and carry them onto the ice so they could take breaks from the cold and fish a little longer. When Robert shuts off the engine, I can still feel music thump in my ears.

"Ready to answer a whole lot of questions?" he asks.

He sets the parking brake.

"Paperwork's in the glove compartment," he says. "Go ahead. Open it up."

This is not what my father wants, but my fingers find the papers and touch Robert's cramped handwriting, the depressions and tiny tears made by the pen. I'm quiet for some time, noticing all of Robert's mistakes and the sections he left blank.

"Okay, so you've circled cremation and casket. Maybe we should start there."

"Yes," he says. "I realize doing both will be tricky."

He starts to chuckle, and then realizing we are actually speaking about his mother and her death, he quiets.

"The price shocks everyone," I say. "But, really, no one around here cremates."

This is a line I say so often, it no longer feels like a lie. Cremation is the most reliable way to put a funeral home out of business, and it's always a touchy subject for Pop, since he does the bookkeeping. The cost of the casket and the restoration is where we make our money. No one's trying to profit from death, he likes to remind me, but this is a business.

Robert has questions about caskets and liners, grave markers, and the difference between a visitation and a memorial service.

"First one includes the dead person. Second doesn't."

"Clothing selection?" he asks.

"What she'll wear in the casket."

"Memorial displays?"

"Usually a photo to set out on the table," I say. "Sometimes people include more, a Purple Heart or some other medal. But it's usually a photo."

"And I have to locate all these documents?" he asks.

"Yeah, that part's a pain," I say. "Birth certificate, marriage license, Social Security, will, property deeds."

"I hadn't wanted to talk to my ma about this stuff, but I guess I'll have to."

He inhales for a very long time.

"Okay if I take a break from this for a couple minutes?"

"Sure," I say. "It's a lot to take in."

"I shouldn't have waited till she was so sick to talk about these things with her."

"For a while, everyone said she was getting better," I say. "I heard she had a tumor removed."

"She did," he says. "And then more masses grew in the lining of her lung. They went back in and took out the whole lobe. Cancer returned."

"There wasn't any more she could do?"

"I guess they could have done more," he says. "But she was tired of getting her hopes up. Tired of the long trips back and forth to Agate, the chemo, her fear every time the phone rang that it would be more bad news. She asked the doctor to stop treatment."

"She gave up?"

"She didn't see it as giving up," he says. "When her life just became about being comfortable and painting, she felt like it was her own again."

"She's decided to die?"

"Or decided to live," he says. "It depends on how you look at it."

"So there's nothing you can do for her?"

"The other day I took her to Agate so the doctor could drain fluid out of her lung," he says. "And she has a couple of oxygen machines at home now. Those help. But mostly all I can do is set up the humidifier. Make sure she has pillows behind her to help control the wheezing. I buy her magazines and paints. Do some laundry. Watch TV with her."

"Sounds kind of nice," I say. "I mean your time together."

"I don't want to make it sound better than it is," he says. "We sit together and watch TV because, if we didn't, we would notice how much we don't talk. I've been away a long time. We're still learning how to be together."

I look at the papers again.

"At least this next page is pretty straightforward," I say.

But Robert admits knowing little to nothing about her taste in music, the names of her closest friends, or her favorite lines from scripture.

"We've written so many letters over the years," he says. "And I met her in Agate for doctor appointments, if I could, not to mention for meals and birthdays. You'd think I'd know more about her."

"I didn't realize you'd stayed in touch," I say.

"She was always sending clippings from the local paper and

the school newsletter after she'd read them, with little bits circled and underlined," he says. "She sent recipes, though I don't cook, and advice columns, though I didn't have time for them. But I appreciated how, when she read the paper, she was thinking of me."

It begins to snow. Not much, but we both stop to watch the little stars fall on the windshield and melt apart.

"We're better with letters," he says. "You can take a break for five minutes or a day, and there's no awkward silence or struggle to find things to discuss."

I nod. Though he's also making my father's point, that he's not the best person to plan Doris's service.

I smooth the papers, realizing we're done. He still has to fill out most of the answers, but I think the confusion is cleared up.

"Have I answered all your questions?"

"Yeah," he says. "I guess I have work to do."

I put the papers back in the glove box. He turns the key and music flows through the speakers again. Soon we'll be back in town and our time together will be over.

"Robert?"

It's the first I've called him by his name. He turns down the volume.

"Can we walk down by the lake for just a bit?" I ask. "I used to come here as a child. I'd love to see it before it freezes over."

"Sure, we could do that," he says and cuts the engine.

We step over the knotted ground. The few trees bend over the water, and there is a frayed rope from a tire swing, the tire long gone. Robert squats down and shows me the oil and salty brine—runoff from the old oil wells that have gotten into the soil.

"See the salt scarring on the shore, the lack of any growth nearby?" he asks. "You can bet it seeped into the water, too."

I see what he's pointing at, but my father has assured me it's nothing to worry about. More of the outside world trying to assert its will in decisions we can make for ourselves.

11

POP TOOK ME ICE fishing on this lake in one of his many attempts to find an activity we could enjoy together. We went out at dawn, parked beside the edge of the lake, and built a fire on the shore so we could warm up quickly with hot chocolate on our return. I skated out on the ice in rubber boots, holding a candy bar in one mitten and my father's hand in the other. He promised I could eat the chocolate if I sat perfectly still on an overturned bucket while he drilled the hole.

When he was done, still breathing hard from turning the handle of the auger and kicking the slush away from the opening, he let me lie on my stomach and look into the dark hole. It blew its cold breath into my face, and I slid my mittens along the thick icy sides around the hole that my father said proved I was safe from falling in. I, however, knew all along that I was safe because he was there. He dropped his line into the hole and I dropped my wrapper after it. He popped me on the head to remind me not to litter but in a nice way that made me show him my chocolate-covered teeth.

Out on the ice at dawn, you can hear everything, every sniff of a runny nose, every rustle of snow pants, the whir of the fishing pole's reel, the sound of opening a second candy bar, the one you snuck that was supposed to be his. Pop relished this time outdoors in the dead of winter when a man who liked to be busy could escape his cabin fever. But for me, it was endless waiting, frozen fingers despite the mittens, and a lot of effort for something we could buy at Vinter's grocery.

There was one fish that day. The pole bent and tugged, and Pop stood, reeling at intervals. He wouldn't let the fish get away. Near the end, he put the pole in my hands, instructed me not to move, and then bent on his knees over the hole. He reached in to get the fish, a rainbow trout, his arm wet to the elbow. I had to give up my seat for the fish. The cold and boredom were suddenly too much to bear. As we walked back to the fire, he told me if I wanted to become a good fisherman, I'd better learn not to fidget. My constant singing and kicking the bucket had scared away all but that single trout.

I always wondered if my father was disappointed I never took to fishing. How we've never found an activity to do together besides work.

"You're quiet," Robert says. "Did I lose you?"

"My father used to take me fishing here," I say, like it was something we did a lot.

A great gust of wind awakens geese on the lake, sending them running along the water, trumpeting and squawking until they alight. We track the birds as they fly overhead in the dotted sky, their heavy black-tipped wings flapping, their hysterical chorus sending a vibration we can feel below.

"We have a lot of snow geese in Seattle," he says, his skin growing red with cold. "That's where I live."

"I've never been farther than Agate," I say. "What made you choose Seattle?"

He pauses a long while and flicks the zipper of his jacket up and down.

"I went out there at fourteen," he says. "Took the bus and stayed with a distant aunt."

And I realize he's going to tell me about running away from Petroleum, when I'd wondered what another part of the world looks like. What I believed I had asked is, *Have you seen oceans? Tall buildings? Trains that still run?*

"Worked on getting my GED while she taught me about laundry, bills, and job hunting."

"Who? Your aunt?"

This is not the conversation I wanted to have. Why does everything have to circle back to the accident?

"People are nice there," he says. "Never had my car keyed. Never had people smoking in my driveway while they stared at the house."

His face twists so hideously, I wonder if he's bitten his tongue.

"I thought when I came back to stay with my ma, maybe enough time had passed." He stops, his mouth twisting again. "It doesn't matter. Good thing I'm not here for long."

I wait for the feeling to pass, the sting that I'm included in his disappointment. The whole idea of being together here leaves me trembling with old wounds. The strange girl burying dolls, the brush of handlebars, the word *Freak*. I should have stayed in the basement and spent the day cleaning my tools and lining them up on the tray in an order that makes everything right. I stare hard at a family of wrens as the wind pushes them across the lake.

"You haven't liked any part of being here?" I ask.

"Obviously I don't want to hurry this time with my ma," Robert says. "But as for the rest, I really can't leave this place fast enough."

He looks up now.

"Mary," he says. "You're crying."

He reaches out as if he'll touch me and then doesn't.

I turn my head and furiously wipe at the tears.

"Did I do this?" he asks.

I keep my back turned.

"I didn't realize you hated every person you met here," I say.

"I wasn't talking about you, Mary."

He sits down on a rock and motions for me to sit as well.

"You're easy to be around. One of the few."

He finds a flat rock to skip.

"Well, that's a first," I say, my voice in a knot.

He raises one eyebrow as if to tell me he's serious.

"We don't quite fit here, do we?" he says, reaching for another rock and brushing it clean of snow. "Sometimes that's a lonely place to be, and yet, you don't really want to be on the inside, either, where you feel pressure to be someone you're not."

He has identified something I've felt but never put into words. That feeling of being most alone in company, the frustration of trying so hard to enjoy fishing, hunting, and basketball, when I just can't. I've lived in Petroleum my whole life, but somehow I feel like an outsider.

"This town wants you to be as it's always been and do as it's always done," he says. "But what if that's not what makes you happy?"

He throws another rock, and I feel the flicker of old dreams. The haunting of what I'd given up. The feel of a good, graphite pencil in my hand, the memory of a girl I sat beside year after year in art, who said my drawings were pretty. For some number of weeks, we talked about how we wanted to become artists, how we'd open an art gallery on Main Street. She moved away before we graduated, and I wonder if she still draws, if she opened an art gallery somewhere else.

Robert passes me a good flat rock, which I cup in both hands.

"Go on, show me what you got," he says.

I give it a sideways toss and we count the number of skips. It hurts, what he's said. I don't know what happened to that girl who dreamed such impractical things. As we reach for the next rocks, I long for our hands to touch.

Though it's too cold to sit by the lake for so long, we name all the wildlife we see—yellow perch, northern pike, waterfowl, ring-necked pheasants, mule deer, snow geese. Then, for a long while, there is no more talk, just the plink of rocks into the water.

In the quiet, I think of Robert's crooked smile, his flashes of temper, and the way he nearly wiped my tears. I pause each image, turning him like a prism. Something about how different he is both frightens me and draws me to him. When we've thrown all the flat rocks from the pile, I know it's time to head back.

"I've had a nice time," I tell him.

Though this is not true. Nice does not at all describe the time we shared today. I feel shaken. Exposed. Awake.

12

ROBERT AND I DRIVE back past ranches so far off the highway you won't see the roads leading to them unless you already know where they are.

"Do you live near the ocean?" I ask.

My question probably sounds like it's come out of nowhere, but I've been thinking it since he first mentioned Seattle.

"Not too far," he says. "I can see the Sound from my office. If I open the window, the salt air comes in, which is so nice but can mess up the computers."

Salt air.

I've never heard of such a thing, and my brain conjures images until I notice we are passing the rodeo grounds. Up ahead is the grain elevator set against the beige rimrocks.

"Mind dropping me off here?" I ask.

"Along the highway?"

I can't hide my cowardice.

He stops the truck and asks, "Are you sure?"

All that bravado when I first got into his truck, now he knows it was just an act. Once my boots touch the ground, I whisper an apology, but I don't, can't, look at him. I look instead toward cattle, wandering the pastures, snow sprinkled on their backs. Many are already pregnant, ranchers trying to get a jump on the market. Robert drives on and takes the turn at the gray tower.

I walk into the wind, my coat tight against my body like someone's pulling it from behind. I try to at least enjoy the smell of hay, the chatter of livestock, the jolt of crisp air in my nostrils. But mostly, I feel guilt for how I treated Robert.

My face is numb from the wind by the time I turn off the highway. As the sky dims, I notice coats and bikes scattered across the frozen grass outside the grain elevator. And then I hear it, the old game we used to play. Children who weren't even born at the time of the accident, and they're in there, singing.

"Sissy, sissy."

I see them through the gaping hole where the sliding doors have rotted off. They hold hands and march in a circle, wind in their hair. I watch their colored shirts as they spin and laugh and tackle each other.

When I was cast in the younger brother's role in childhood games of Eddie, my chest used to tighten with shame. I would have rather played anyone else. I would rather play the grain; that was one of the parts you could play, just lie down stiff and let kids step on you.

Time doesn't seem to dull the old prejudices. They just become unconscious, reflexive, fact. I pass Robert's truck, long cooled off in the driveway. Did he hear the song, too? Would he have known they were singing about him?

I turn back toward the kids playing in the fading light. I imagine them inside those dark passageways—frayed ropes hanging from the old pulleys, gears and cranks rusted in place, motors quiet. A couple of teenagers have climbed to the top of the tower to sit in the window, cigarettes glowing.

When I walk through the door, I smell my father's cooking, my eyes still watering from the cold. I see we've received our payment from the Mosleys, the kitchen table dark red with elk meat. My father has begun the task of chopping it into meal-sized portions and placing it into plastic bags. The meat takes up the whole table—some of it bagged, some sliced on the cutting board, and a giant hunk of carcass needing to be butchered. A cooked steak sits in the frying pan, the grease still clear.

"Is that you?" my father calls down the stairs.

"Yeah, Pop."

"Dinner's on the stove," he says. "Grab a plate and come to the den. I have the TV trays set up."

Now that work has slowed—no bodies since Mr. Mosley—Pop sits too much, over the bookkeeping, in front of the TV, and dialing Martha in the fleeting hours between her shifts, each word buzzing with fear, paranoia, ecstasy.

"Get you a beer?" I call.

"If you've got a free hand."

Climbing the stairs, I feel the careful balance performed by my hands, but also by the expression on my face, trying to hide my nervousness for the lies I've told and will tell again.

I find Pop in the recliner, gnawing on a bone. I set the beer on his tray and take the armchair. He begins wiping his hands on a paper napkin, using a touch of beer to help clean off the grease.

"What are we watching?" I ask.

"It's that singing competition," he says, eyes on the TV.

I think of the singing inside the gray tower, how many emotions are swirling through our town. I pick up my knife and fork and pretend I'm not someone who got dropped off on the highway, not someone who spent the day walking Robert through the very paperwork I promised not to give him.

"You were gone most of the day," Pop says, passing me the saltshaker.

"I spent some time with a man I like," I tell him, shocked I said it so straightforward, or at all.

Pop sits up tall. "Well, this is some good news," he says. "Do I know him?"

And now the conversation feels intrusive. I shouldn't have shared this private news, this overstated description of my day, as if I'd been on a date. Pop stares at me, awaiting the mystery man's name.

"We drove around, that's all. I don't think it was even a date."

"I wasn't trying to pry," he says. "I'm just interested in who you spend your time with."

But is he interested, or only when my choices and feelings line up with his? I can't remember the last time I talked to someone without faking an interest or feeling bored, and I won't let my father take this joy from me.

A singer belts out a song we don't know, voice full of power, face contorted, fists clenched, but the music strangely devoid of emotion.

"I'm going to keep him to myself for a bit. But I'll tell you that we drove out to Brine Lake, and I told him about ice fishing with you."

"If you call eating chocolate and kicking your heels into a bucket fishing," he says, laughing.

"I do." I smile.

Sometimes I feel like we get along best when I tell only pieces of the truth.

The heat turns on, causing a great rattling noise as if men with hammers are in the basement and in the walls, banging on pipes.

"Maybe you and I can go out there with our poles sometime," he says.

"Maybe, yeah."

Pop draws on his beer and turns the sound back up when he sees a singer wearing a cowboy hat. "Finally a song I know," he says, his grin slow and satisfied.

"He has a nice voice," I say.

"I hope this one wins," Pop says. "You can vote by telephone, but it costs money."

Though I am staring at the TV, I'm thinking of the little rain boot hanging from the old battered tree house. I'm thinking of the pile of flat rocks, the dark smell of the leather jacket, the glee of children singing, *Sissy, sissy.*

Pop looks over at my plate. "Like your steak?"

I take another bite and enjoy the tender meat, its spill of sweet juices, the faint taste of sage that I know is from the elk's diet and nothing Pop added from a spice jar.

"Yeah, it's good," I say.

"I'm glad." He adjusts the pillow behind his back. "I hope you don't get sick of it too soon."

We can't use elk to pay the bills or fix my van, but the meat is good and will last most of the year if we're careful. The show is almost over, the singers lined up onstage to see who will go on to the next round. I saw at another piece of meat so mindlessly that, once it's cut, I continue sawing into the plate.

"You told him about ice fishing?" Pop asks, muting the TV.

He laughs, more to himself than to me. But I have drifted back to the feel of the smooth rocks, the sound of their plunking, and how everything looked sprinkled with sugar.

"You don't seem like yourself today," Pop says, moving his tray to the side so he can kick out the footrest on the recliner.

And I'm not. I feel tingly and in flux. "It's just this lull in work," I say because this is what we do. We only let each other get so close.

13

NORMALLY, I'M AN EARLY riser, but today I stay under the covers as the sun reaches my bed. My fingers mindlessly stroke the quilt. My limbs feel heavy. I fiddle with a loose thread in the stitching and feel a weird fluttering in my chest that makes me want to stay very still so it doesn't go away.

In my mind, I'm back at Brine Lake, skipping rocks, but I've edited that day—no more awkwardness or friction. Robert places a flat rock in my hand. This time his touch lingers. He wipes my tears, hair blowing all about his face. Has it already been a week?

I make the mistake of opening my eyes, and the lake is gone. I see only my bedroom. The clock showing it's past noon. The too-bright stretch of sun along the floor.

How foolish to believe he might see me as I see him. I know the danger of overconfidence, feeling as if you belong, as if you're wanted, walking into that old trap. I feel, even lying here in my bed, the pinch of my old mustard-yellow one-piece, the bottom nubby from its previous owner. A barrette held the straps together so they wouldn't slip off my shoulders. With one hand, I tugged at the fabric whenever it exposed a cheek, while trying to keep up with my father's brisk pace.

Pop, distracted with a case neighbors still talk about, walked me to the municipal pool, telling me I could swim as long as I wanted on that hot afternoon. He'd hurriedly changed out of his embalming clothes and into a blue suit just for that brief walk, pumping my hand in his, something I'd experienced many times as a kid and had learned it meant he was thinking hard.

The body in his workroom was the victim of a rappelling accident, a badly tied rope, and a fall that smashed one side of the climber's head. Pop used newspaper to reconstruct the skull like a papier-mâché project, but I didn't know it holding his hand at age six, that summer after kindergarten. I stepped carefully on the dirt road, my feet still tender.

He took me inside the gates of the pool, the powerful smell of chlorine in the air. Kids bobbed up and down in the water, their shouts echoing.

"Do you see anyone you know?" he asked, careful not to step too close to the water. A splash of chlorine could stain his suit.

I studied the wet heads as they appeared and disappeared.

"I don't know," I said, and then, "Yes. That one."

I pointed to the girl I'd sat with on the train track the previous summer.

"Good," he said. "When you're done swimming, just walk home."

He handed me the towel he'd been carrying. It looked like an American flag. My father turned to exit when the teenage lifeguard called, "Hey!" He tweeted his whistle and said, "Mr. Crampton!"

My father walked over to the boy, looking worried for his suit.

"You can't leave her here without an adult," he said. "She's too young."

Pop took my hand again and we started to leave.

"But I want to swim," I told him, and he pulled harder.

When we got to the gate, a familiar voice called after my father.

"Allen, wait," said Bernice, wrapping a towel around her waist. "I can watch her."

She had not been to our house for many months—and there had been other women's voices in his bedroom since. My father put his hands in his pockets, and Bernice scrunched a handful of the towel in her fist, her face tight. Finally, because my father needed to get back to the body sitting unrefrigerated in our basement, he let her take my hand.

"How are you, dear?" she asked.

I looked at her painted toenails and the little silver chain around one ankle.

"Fine."

"How was your first year of school?"

I felt too shy to answer. It still hurt that she had come over almost daily and then not at all. It wasn't until she was gone that I realized how comforting I found the sound of her clomping through the house in my father's boots.

Kids splashed in the water, calling, "Marco. Polo."

I let my towel drop and walked toward the water, stood at the pebbly edge, wanting to jump in as other kids did. Perhaps the whispering had already begun, but I was aware only of a swirling, woozy fear that made me choose the stairs. I held the handrail and went down one step, water barely covering my toes.

The sun forced a dribble of sweat from underneath my hair and down my back. One more step and the water, much colder, came to my shins. It seemed that those soaked heads were all waiting for me. I held my nose, squeezed my eyes shut, and jumped.

When I came up, my eyes still closed, I heard the whispers distinctly, "She lives with dead people. She'll infect the water."

My eyes, stinging from chlorine, refused to open. I heard splashing and kicking all around me, and when I could manage to squint, I saw the blurred scrambling of children from the pool. And I was alone, bobbing in their wake.

"That's enough," Bernice shouted to the other children. "Where are your manners?"

She stood near the stairs with my towel. It was a very long time pushing against the resistance of the water to reach her, my ears clogged so that I mostly heard my heartbeat and an occasional tweep of the lifeguard's whistle.

"Let me get you home," Bernice said in a faraway voice as I walked up the steps.

She draped the towel over my shoulders, and my hands clutched it from inside. When we walked past the other children, the girl mouthed the word, *weirdo*.

That was the first stone.

Bernice kept her hand on my back, her voice soothing though I couldn't hear the words. We walked slowly, both of us in bare feet. I felt every nub in the road. She took me to the back door of my house, where she used to find my father's mucking boots set out on the mat. She knocked hard. He took his time coming up from the basement and answered the door in a soiled apron.

"Sit here at the table," she told me after we entered the kitchen. "I'm just going to talk to your father in the other room."

I felt slippery on the wooden chair.

In the parlor, Bernice said, "Ask yourself if you could put away your work once in a while and be there to guide Mary."

"What happened?"

"Ask your daughter," she said. "You need to start having conversations with her."

Bernice touched the top of my head before leaving. I hoped she might stay.

"Did something happen at the pool?" Pop asked me as the door clicked shut.

"I just want to play at home," I said.

He looked quizzically toward the door.

"All right," he said. "Play at home if that's what you'd like."

When he returned to his work, I went out back to the tiny lean-to I'd claimed as a fort. But I wasn't in the mood to play. I kept thinking of the day I sat beside the older kids on the railroad track, sharing stories about Dead Eddie. For the rest of that summer and into the fall, we played our game in the dark among the rats and sour grain.

I trusted them, particularly the girl. By the end of the summer, I'd told her about my home, and how my father kept dead people in our refrigerator and how I touched one. I told her that his job was to put makeup on dead people, and if she came to my house, we could open the giant tackle box and color our cheeks peach and salmon.

But so much had changed since that summer. Something had hardened about our town. Though the accident rarely came up in games or conversations anymore, those who had lost their jobs had become meaner, and their children absorbed that meanness.

The shade of my fort felt good, and so did being hidden. I

opened the empty coffee can, where I stored objects I found around the house—paper clips, arrowheads, dressmaker pins, an old spoon, and a horseshoe.

Pete was in town that day, visiting and doing patrols, when someone told him about the commotion at the pool. It was the first time he'd learned of what would soon become routine for me—kids afraid to touch anything after I did, and adults whispering, *The poor strange girl without a mother. What it must do to her to be around the dead all day long.*

He didn't seem to see me in the fort as he knocked on our back door and waited for my father. He removed his hat before he stepped inside. They spoke for some time and then Pop called my name. The two stuck their heads outside, where I was caught in an activity that seemed perfectly normal until others witnessed it. I'd spent much of the afternoon sticking pins through the outermost layer of my skin, and I'd done this on all five fingers of my left hand and had great plans to accomplish the same on the other. The idea was that I could clap the metal tips together, like finger cymbals, which Pop's calling my name had interrupted.

I still wore my mustard-yellow suit, my hair in chlorine-scented ropes, one hand loaded with pins. Pete took me by the unpinned hand and walked me up the steps and into the kitchen. He had a solemn look on his face and asked how my day was, how I was making friends, questions that seemed to beg the answer, "Fine." And he held my head tight between the palms of his hands and called me Button.

He and my father asked me a number of questions. Did I like school? Did I want to invite some girls over to play? Did I want a special haircut at the Agate beauty salon? During the shrugs and silences, my father and Pete glanced at each other and at me. None of us knew how to do this. We had started this idea of talking things out too late. Eventually, my father made a long speech about sadness, about how some push the hurt down and down and down. He made a gesture emphasizing how one could run out of space.

"Like eating too many hot dogs at a picnic," he said.

My father hugged me for too long, and the word *hot dogs* hung in the air between us, dumb and heavy.

Later, I sat by the window in my room, my pinned fingers on the glass as I watched the other kids run and ride bikes and walk through town with wet hair and towels around their necks. I don't remember when it became night or when I changed into my pajamas. I just remember lying on my pillow, my hand mysteriously free of pins, and hearing the comforting voices of Pete and my father one floor below. My guardians. My adoring, floundering guardians.

Until that day, my father had heard only inklings that I was coming out odd. People would mention how strange it must be to raise a child in a funeral home or to raise a girl without a mother figure. But, until then, he hadn't reached that conclusion himself. I could feel the change in my father, how he began to study me, reading every oddity as his own failure. His parenting became tentative, and the old sorrow returned, that it was my mother he trusted to make the right decisions, and now what was he supposed to do?

He tried briefly to become a different kind of father, calling the parents of girls in my class to invite them to play at our house. I stood beside him as he said into the phone, "I understand. I understand." When he hung up, I already knew the answer.

Their parents, my father explained many years later, were

afraid of the chemicals, the sharp instruments. They worried my father wouldn't be attentive enough. I could play at their homes, he explained at the time. Or meet down the street at the rusted stove, where lots of little girls played pretend kitchen while mothers looked on.

But I was no longer anxious to make friends. In fact, I was anxious to keep to myself. All my life, I have learned the lesson that closeness is tangled up with rejection and shame. I should know better.

I kick one leg out of the covers and look to the open closet door, the row of flannel shirts on hangers, reminding me I should get dressed. But what if I didn't get up just yet? Because I have found my way back to the lake. I smell the dark musk of Robert's jacket, feel his fingers place a good flat rock in my hand. Though I dread the prospect of being rejected, I can't help the wanting.

14

WHEN HE'S NOT DRIVING the school bus, Slim takes a number of odd jobs. This morning, just after he drops off the kids, he changes into knee-high rubber boots and thick gloves and sets equipment around the hole in the empty lot by the church. Funnel trap, hardware cloth, shovels, oil drum, various bottles of chemicals, and a gun. One way or another he's going to get rid of that den of snakes.

From my window, as I watch him fidget with the funnel trap, I see Martha duck into the alley where the Dumpsters are stowed and emptied once a month. She cuts behind our house and knocks softly on the back door. I watch the whole journey, window to window.

All morning Pop's been trying to convince me to get out of the house. "They've got a whole batch of fresh-baked muffins at the Pipeline," he says. "And I think there's an open game of pinochle up there pretty soon. I know that's one you like."

Pop and Martha have become more reckless about their time

together. I've found cups in the sink with lipstick on them. I've heard them laugh in the dark driveway and at the kitchen table after midnight when I've peered down the stairs. He pours them both a drink and they spend maybe forty-five minutes whispering, Martha with her bosom so big and low that she needs to push her glass forward so she can rest the whole of it on the table.

I guess the plus side to my father dating a married woman is that she doesn't have to get comfortable with the idea of moving into a funeral home or sharing space with the daughter who won't leave her childhood room.

I creep to the top of the steps and hear the whistle of the teakettle, the clink of teacups and saucers we save for special occasions. I hear soft laughter, then too much quiet. Clearly Pop believes I've left the house, and now I'm stuck. Who knows how long I'll be trapped up here, tiptoeing around.

I pace the hall—in sock-feet, close to the wall so the floor doesn't creak—and nearly trip over Pop's dirty suit, balled up on the floor. It's somehow become my job to wash his suits. Not because I think it's my responsibility but because he's not careful. If he washed them, they'd shrink and wrinkle, or they'd sour, forgotten in the washing machine. He doesn't have the patience to wash them by hand.

I would really like to wash this now, while I have nothing else to do, but that would require walking past the lovebirds in the kitchen. I've spent so much time pretending I don't know about their affair that I don't know what to do other than wait this out. I'm even afraid to use the bathroom because the noise will give me away.

I can feel myself getting agitated. And when the flirty laughter begins again, I've had it. I grab a stack of towels and walk down the stairs with the suit. Halfway, I cough to give them warning. I hear shuffling. Chairs scoot in and out. When I walk into the kitchen, I pretend to be surprised.

"Martha," I say.

She hurriedly buttons a cardigan over a very snug top, no bra.

"I thought you were playing pinochle," my father says.

"I never said I was playing pinochle."

I find the stain remover and Woolite under the sink. I squirt the stain, collar, cuffs, underarms. I'm the only one making noise in this room.

My father takes a gulp of whatever's in his teacup, and I can guess what it is because he's left the cupboard open where he keeps his whiskey. He's combed his hair to the side like a little boy dressing up. I wonder how he feels having a date at this age with all the folds and swells and sags. When you marry young, you grow into these changes as a couple. But what must it be like to start at this age? What does Martha think when he pushes up his sleeves, the way he does now, and his forearms are the texture of salami?

I fill the sink with cold water and a capful of soap and catch him looking at Martha with those sad eyes. I think he may actually be in love this time.

Love for my father is something guarded, something anticipating loss. I just wish the two of us would stop pretending his relationship with Martha is a secret. And I wish he would stop pretending first because he's the dad.

"Maybe you should tell her the news, Allen. About Mr. Purvis."

"Right," he says. "Mary, did you hear Mr. Purvis is in the hospital?"

"No," I say. "You know I don't hear things."

"That's why I came by," Martha says, as a rash of pink spreads across her throat and the lobes of her ears. "To give your family the news."

It's a clever lie. I don't doubt Mr. Purvis is in the hospital but it's not why she's here.

"Bad?" I ask, turning the suit inside out.

"At his age it's never good."

What looms between us, what we would never dare to say, is the implied new customer, the income.

I plunge the suit under the water, massaging and turning the fabric through my hands.

Does Martha know the man my father tries to keep private? Does she know this drink in his hand in the middle of the afternoon is not unusual? There are clues to his secret battles right in this room. If she looks at the cupboard he's left open, she'll see the disarray, for one thing: coffee cups, batteries, lightbulbs, and items that must have been my mother's—a coin purse, a small gold chain with a knot in it, and the rosehips tea bag we will never use.

I wring out the jacket, then the pants. After, I press them a little drier between a towel.

Martha wears a permanent smile, but Pop looks horrified that I'm still here. No one speaks or drinks from their fancy cups.

Look in the cupboard again, inside the door. Right on the painted wood, he's scribbled phone numbers in marker, and sometimes random thoughts—*eggs,* for example, and *fix board on porch.* A man whose mind is filled to overflowing, but he won't complain. I'm tempted to straighten up and categorize that cupboard—because I get twitchy with messes—but that would be like removing one of the truest things he's revealed.

"I hear you've had kind of an unsavory visitor," Martha says in a friendly, let's-be-girlfriends way.

"Sorry, what are you talking about?" I ask because I know exactly what she's talking about.

"The younger brother," she says, all cute like we're gossiping.

I hang the suit meticulously on a wooden hanger.

"What's he done to you?" I ask.

"Oh, I don't have issues with him personally," she says. "It's just that there's a lot of tension in town since he came back."

"And that's his fault?"

I hadn't intended to stick up for Robert, but this feels personal. The town's unwillingness to forgive him proves the opinion they've formed about me is not likely to change either.

"I'm just saying he makes people uncomfortable."

There were people in town who lost their jobs after the accident, and they've had to settle for sporadic, demeaning work ever since. I understand their bitterness. But there were plenty of others, two of them in this room, who had always taken the stance that tragedies happen, that the town and whole world are changing, and what's done is done. When did they turn bitter?

Pop chimes in, "The Sweet Adelines aren't happy, that's for sure."

This is our town's female barbershop quartet. Doris used to sing baritone.

"One of the girls stopped by to see Doris," Martha says. "And he sent her away."

"Girls?" I ask, because she's talking about sixty- and seventy-year-olds. I grab another towel and lay it beneath the suit to catch drips.

"Her singing partners," Martha clarifies.

Pop stares at me as if to say, *Stop it, Mary.*

I plug in the clothing steamer, and Martha moves her chair away from the cord.

"Later," Pop says. His tone is sharp. "That can wait."

I pull the cord from the outlet and begin to coil it when I hear screams and laughter outside. I leave the steamer on a chair and hurry out the front door and onto the porch. Slim has reached the rattlesnakes. People in almost every home and business have been checking on his project all day, but now, many gather closer. Five men watch from the bed of a pickup, parked right on the grass near that hole, shotguns ready.

Pop slips his suit jacket on, the clean one, before coming out to the porch. Neighbors narrate Slim's final attempts—how he's blocked off all but one opening and tried the funnel trap, become impatient with it, then decided to just start digging. I notice only now that Martha has not come out on the porch with us. I follow my father's gaze as her blue coat disappears around a corner. She must have snuck out the back door, and she will not get to see this, the giant ball of sleepy snakes dropping into the oil drum.

Shouts and applause seem to come from every window and porch, while Slim fights to get that lid on the barrel. Soon, he rolls it out of the lot while a few men, giddy as kids, stay back at the hole, pouring in the contents of different bottles.

What pride as Slim marches down the center of the street in those tall boots, rolling the oil drum, students and teachers saluting him from the school playground. Kids who've quit school run after him, and the pickup follows, too.

"Good number?" Pop asks as he goes by.

"Probably sixty or more," Slim says. "Most of 'em rattlers. Couple garters and rat snakes mixed in. Want to see?"

"Sure don't," Pop says. "Keep that lid on."

The barrel buzzes from inside. I imagine the great, wriggling ball, how one by one the snakes free themselves and strike at the sides.

"Where are you going to release them?" a boy asks, riding alongside on his bike.

"Gonna blow 'em up? Light 'em on fire?" another asks.

Slim just keeps rolling the large barrel down the road. He's like the pied piper. A kid runs over with a stick.

"That lid on tight?" he asks, then bangs the stick against the drum.

I bet, never in his life, will that kid smile so big except when he's retelling the story of this day. Children and adults cheer rather than work on a morning when the sky is an endless blue. You can make all kinds of cracks about Petroleum, but right now, who would trade this moment for anything?

15

WHEN WORK IS SLOW, I struggle with ways to spend my time. I've pulled the shoe box from under my bed to run my fingers through the collection of buttons. They fill the bottom of the box, two or three buttons deep.

Everyone I've ever embalmed is here, even a man I'd kissed, a onetime thing, and to be honest, our second encounter, when he came to my workroom, was nicer. I pick out one button at a time, feeling the details under my fingertips. The clear, nicked button from Mr. Mosley's flannel shirt, a thread still attached; the rose-shaped button from Charlotte Taylor, whose pink blouse and padded bra covered thick tracks of mastectomy scars; the anchor-shaped button from small Daniel Keller's blue-and-white sailor's outfit. He had the smallest-sized casket we sell, and still, he hardly filled it, his body curled at one end of the box as in sleep, wrists touching.

Sometimes I take out two or three buttons and put them in my pocket for the day. I don't know why. It's dumb, but I do it.

I head downstairs into the mess our house has become. Pop and I have nothing to do and yet dishes pile in the sink because I'm no good when I'm not working, and this is my father's state of being when I don't step in.

I check his office and he is there, staring at the bills as if some solution will come to him that stretches our income.

"Numbers tough?" I ask.

He looks only at the papers and grimaces.

"Fridge is kind of empty," I say. "Do we have enough in the account for groceries?"

"Maybe just get eggs and an onion," he says.

"Potatoes?" I ask.

"Okay," he says. "Nothing more, though."

Outside the school bell rings, though it's not time for school to let out. It is the wind grabbing the rope.

My feet scrape across the dirt road, kicking up dust. As I pass the Goldens' house, I watch Doris, at the window, painting what might be a clown. The sound of women laughing makes me look up. One wears her curly hair tied back with a white headband. The other wears a pink hat with a pom-pom. This view I know well—the backs of neighbors, mostly at funerals—a world so near but out of reach. My father always nudges me—*Go on, talk with them*. But why? Someone can say, *Hello*, but mean, *Oh, it's you*. Someone can say, *Join us after the service*, but mean, *Please don't*.

These women live the kinds of lives my father wishes I had. Married with children and friends.

One of the women reaches into her purse, applies Chap-Stick, and then holds it out for the other, who takes it. This simple gesture is so touching, so painfully unfamiliar, that I ache. When I was in school, I longed to be invited into these circles, wondering what girls whispered to each other that sent them into giggles. I feel for the buttons in my pocket, roll them between my fingers.

The three of us hear something speeding down the road and turn to watch a truck as it swishes by, too close, slowing alongside the women. The one with curls leans toward the driver's window.

The driver is not from Petroleum. You can tell by the license plate. The first numbers tell what county you're from. There are more- and less-trusted counties, some so different from us, it's like they're from a different state.

The women look at each other, then there is a quick change of expression.

"Maybe you should just move on out of here," the one with curly hair says, and they walk on, ignoring the driver, who now seems to be waiting for me.

"Excuse me," he calls out the window.

I look to the women, who pause to see how this will go.

"Excuse me," the man says again.

He holds out a business card.

"I own a wrecking crew," he says. "Know who I can talk to about that gray tower by the highway?"

This happens every now and then. A stranger stops in the diner and asks if someone would like to hire him to knock down the central monument of our town. The women stop to watch my response.

"There's no one for you to talk to," I say.

"I could take down that old structure," he says. "Make it a nice clean piece of land there."

"Go on," I say. "We don't need your help."

I'm just copying the words of the curly-haired woman,

really. I wouldn't have thought to say anything so bold if I hadn't heard her first. The man gives me his card nonetheless. When he pulls away, I scrunch it up.

We hear the criticism all the time—how Petroleum needs to join the modern world or else die away, chained to the past. What this stranger considers an eyesore is a link to our history. No need to scold our people for trying to hold on a little while longer to something they've loved. The tower may collapse on its own, but no out-of-towner's going to kick it down like something only good for scrap wood.

We watch the truck pull up to the deserted VFW, then the deserted pool hall, then the barbershop, still in operation, but closed today. Finally, the driver reaches the Pipeline, and the three of us smirk. He'll get an earful in there.

"That's telling him, Mary," the woman with the pom-pom says. And I know her.

"You showed him," the curly-haired woman says, but I watch the one in the pom-pom who sometimes held my hand as we played the game Eddie so many years ago and, later, scrambled out of the pool because I'd fouled the water.

The stones push against my rib cage. My hand wants to reach for the pain, but I would rather pretend the hurt has faded, like their names. The door opens at the diner, and the stranger storms out. When his truck flies past, the woman with curls grabs the scrunched business card from my hand and hurls it after him.

"Get out of here," she shouts.

They break into laughter, and then, timidly, I do too. I feel a touch on my back, the hand of someone I believed would always reject me. I begin to laugh so uncontrollably, I inhale dust from the road.

"You can walk with us if you're headed to the school," says the one with curly hair.

"What's happening at the school?" I ask, my voice froggy.

"Final band rehearsal," says the one with the pom-pom.

I am in tears. I wish I could stop, but I am in tears, laughing and sobbing.

"Oh, this dust," the women say together as I bend over, trying to cough it up.

This hand on my back. This moment of sorority. I can't stop choking, no matter how many times I try to swallow or clear my throat. We are nearly to the entrance of the grocery. I'm tempted to continue on to the school with them.

"Mary."

All three of us turn to see who has called my name.

"Mary," Robert calls again and holds his hand up in hello. He has just come out of Vinter's.

I'm coughing, shaking my head to show I can't talk.

I feel the hand release. The price I pay for this hello fills me with grief and resentment.

"We're going to be late," says the one with the pom-pom. "Are you sure you're all right? Because we have to go."

And I know I cannot continue on to the school, where I'd sit awkwardly in the gymnasium bleachers with mothers watching their children, wondering why I was there. They'd only invited me to be polite, certain I'd say no. I wave and nod my head, my throat still spasming. *Yes, go. Go.*

Robert reaches into his grocery bag as the women continue on toward the school.

"Here," he says.

He opens a can of orange Shasta and hands it to me. I drink a long sip, cough again, drink another.

"Every time I cough or blow my nose," he says, trying to joke, "I find some of this town has snuck its way inside."

From the moment he offered me a drink, I've felt a relaxing in my rib cage. I want to fit in with the others, but with Robert, I can just be.

"You know, we should grab coffee sometime," he says.

I almost let myself laugh again. It sounds like the kind of thing people say in big cities.

"How 'bout Thursday morning?" he asks.

"You're serious?"

"Sure I am," he says. "I hear there's a great diner in town."

I rub my pointer finger under each eye to wipe away any smudged mascara.

"Would ten work?" he asks.

"I don't know. Maybe."

"Is that a yes?"

"Okay. Yes," I say.

A tiny smile, but genuine.

"I almost forgot," he says, looking toward his bag of groceries, "I've got ice cream for my ma in here. I better get it in the freezer."

Once he's on his way, I open the door to Vinter's. Advertisements flutter against the bulletin board just inside, and I notice announcements for the Blizzard Festival and winter concert. I have agreed to have coffee with Robert on the same day as our town's biggest festival. All of Petroleum will have the day off to witness our date.

16

THE SHIFT IN WEATHER is distinct—grass hardening, creeks freezing, Brine Lake thickening with slush. Along Main Street, children in crimson jerseys decorate shop windows with snowflakes and snowmen. Many adults wear their old crimson basketball or cheerleading uniforms, whichever half still fits. The high school band sets up their music stands in front of Vinter's grocery, and a clarinet player squeaks out a scale.

I watch from the house as families set up stalls and unfold tables on Crooked Hill Road and Main Street. The closest fill up with canned goods, sausage, fudge, food that'll save. Others hold crocheted blankets, sweaters, and even a selection of Doris's paintings. I wonder how long they will live in Petroleum homes after she's gone.

Neighbors load still more tables with secondhand supplies: hand-crank lights and hand-crank radios, shovels for the front and back doors, flashlights, weather seal tape for drafts, portable power generators and extra gas, chain saws, bags of salt and sand, gas-powered snow throwers, matches. Another table displays hand-me-downs: skates, snow pants, parkas, bedding. There's even a fix-it corner where you can bring busted snow-blowers, televisions, anything at all, and someone will get it working for you again. The festival is less a celebration than a day to prepare for the upcoming snowstorms. Today neighbors will weatherproof homes, share tools, supplies, and labor.

Under light flurries, Slim climbs a ladder, carrying a large artificial snowflake. Several of the students who ride his bus mill below, looking up as he attaches the ornament to the top of a pole. They have a love-hate relationship with Slim, spending so many hours ogling the back of his strange head, and yet he is the man who rolled an oil drum full of rattlers through town, the man who safely delivers them to school and home each day. You see all of this in their hesitant waves good-bye.

Because this is the other reason for the annual Blizzard Festival. It's the move-in date for students who live on the outlying ranches. These children, like generations before them, will stay in what has become known as the winter dorm until the school bus can be certain of making the journey to and from their homes again.

Their families move through the crowd toward the hotel with suitcases and boxes full of bedding. Each year, the Blizzard Festival falls on a different date. This year's is fortunate. Because of the mild beginning to winter, families could be together over the holidays.

Fritz stands at the entrance, ready to receive his new boarders. They will now be under his care except for when they're in school. To look at his stooped, wiry frame, you wouldn't think he could control the kids, but they fear his temper and his cane, so they keep their rooms clean, study (or at least stay quiet) for two hours after dinner, and are in bed by nine o'clock.

He lines the kids up in front of the hotel as they arrive, and I step on the front porch to count.

"One more," Fritz shouts. "Don't dawdle."

I recognize the long periwinkle coat I've seen draped over the back of our kitchen chair. Without it, I might not have recognized Martha, her face appearing older without the flirtatious smile or the cheeks red with passion and shame. Her husband, in jeans, oilskin jacket, and felt Stetson carries a suitcase, and Minnow carries a basketball and a pillow.

"Line up," Fritz tells her.

In years past, every room would have been filled to capacity with cots lining the walls, but this year there are only sixteen boarders: five girls, eleven boys. Martha reaches out to squeeze her daughter's shoulder and Minnow shrugs it away, joining the line of students.

I pay special attention to this girl named for the wine-stain birthmark near her forehead. I've overheard Martha talking about this stain quite a lot, sharing how she and her husband decided it looked like a small fish, and fishing was the one thing that each of their families had in common. Thinking up fish-themed names was something she and her husband bonded over, a mercy, since they had struggled for most of their marriage to remember what they liked about each other.

Minnow sweeps her hair over the birthmark and holds it in place with her hand. And I've heard Martha talk about this too, how she cut bangs for her daughter when she was teased by classmates, and later tried to help her feel more confident so that when the wind tossed her hair aside and exposed the mark, she was not ashamed.

I wonder if Minnow knows our parents are having an affair, if she sees her mother's red truck left too long in the school parking lot, her mother sneaking through the back alley to our house. For a moment, I catch the teenager's eye, and she scowls in a way that seems to indicate she knows.

Pete's white Ford pulls into our driveway, and by the time I head inside, he's already come through the back door.

"You missed some excitement outside the Pipeline," Pete says, nodding hello as I step into the kitchen.

"What's happening?" Pop asks.

"Larry Rogers—you know, with the long beard," he says for my benefit. "He lost a finger working yesterday. This morning he's walking around, giving everyone a look."

"Did he bring it in a jar or something?" I ask.

"Nope," he says. "He unwrapped the bandages and showed off the stump."

"They couldn't reattach it?" Pop asks, setting his toolbox on the kitchen table.

"By the time he got to Agate, all they could do was tidy it up and make sure it didn't get infected."

"That's a shame," Pop says, checking through his tools.

"Oh, he's all right," Pete says. "Probably never had so much attention."

"Let me grab a tape measure," Pop says, "and then I'm ready to get to work."

He and Pete have a big day of labor ahead of them, helping to prepare the Purvis's home for storm season while Mrs. Purvis spends the day at the hospital with her husband.

"You're welcome to join us, Mary," Pete says.

"I'll probably just wander around," I say, as if I'm not watching the clock for my coffee date with Robert. I'm dressed in the same flannel and jeans as a normal day, but I've slipped on a silver bracelet that was my mother's, which I turn round and round at the cuff of my shirt.

My father returns with the tape measure and a knit cap.

"No crimson pride, Allen?" Pete asks, offering my father his choice of the scarf he's wearing or the school flag jammed into the band of his sheriff's hat.

"I'll have the flag," Pop says.

Pete takes off his hat, his hair pressed flat and a pink indentation circling his forehead. He detaches the flag with Petroleum School written on it, and my father looks for a place to pin it on his blue suit. Finally, he lets it peek out of his breast pocket.

"All right," Pop says and grabs his equipment.

Pete places the hat back on his head and it settles into the pink groove. Once they leave, I shut the door and watch from the front window again as they emerge from around the corner, arms full of tools and a couple of sawhorses. I'll bet that crimson flag has fallen out of my father's pocket already.

I slip on my parka and gloves, ready to head to the diner for coffee. Do I dare call it a date? I weave my way into the crowd. Most of my neighbors roam about the displays, sipping hot chocolate and chatting, when I spot something out of place. Black in a throng of crimson. Clipped pace when everyone else saunters. Staring ahead while others socialize. Empty hands when others are working, carrying, purchasing.

The high school band plays "Let It Snow," while the mascot for the Petroleum Oilers, wearing a hand-sewn oil drip suit that many say looks a lot like a Hershey's Kiss, mingles with the crowd. Whenever the oil drip turns toward me, trying to shake my hand, I change direction.

Greetings between neighbors are enthusiastic. For many who live farther out of town, the festival is the last guaranteed day before spring thaw to see friends. But an enthusiasm of a different nature is also building. It's the children who voice it first. "Is that him? Is that the younger brother?" These kids weren't even born when Robert lived in town, and still they watch with a sense of suspicion. "Why's he come?"

Neighbors who are perfectly decent on other days scowl and refuse to step aside so he can pass. There are taunts and bumps, and I'm reminded of our game inside the grain elevator, the joy of pointing our fingers at whoever played Robert. I'm afraid to approach him.

Down the road, my father unpacks tools. Pete senses the tension—I know this because he seems to follow the black jacket through the crowd. He measures a wooden board, then looks up again.

What makes Pete so popular in this town is that he has an instinct about when to step in and when to let things go. Marital and parenting disputes. The scrape running across Robert's truck. This is the kind of business he avoids. He famously turns a blind eye to thirteen- and fourteen-year-olds taking a practice drive through town. It's how most of us learned. And he doesn't take a hard stance against what residents set on fire during open burn season. He understands how hard it is to get rid of trash—from dried Christmas trees to construction waste to animal carcasses—and he doesn't harp on choices made by practical folks on tight budgets. Pete steps in only when he thinks someone's actions hurt the safety or dignity of the community.

"Look at that," someone says loud enough to call attention. "Leaves his mother alone while he goes to the festival."

Several turn toward Robert, and others toward Doris, painting in her window.

"Can't even take his mother out for hot chocolate."

I'm close enough to call hello to Robert, but not with everyone watching. I pause at a booth about fire safety and carbon monoxide poisoning. I pretend to study a child-made poster as Robert tries to cut a path to the diner. He seems to find an opening, when a large man clips his shoulder.

"Watch it," Robert snaps.

He is tangling with the wrong man.

Years ago, on that fateful day at the elevator, three boys stood in front of our house sharing details of the accident. The one with the camera, the one talking to Robert right now, isn't someone you want to mess with.

I'm sorry for Robert, but I need to leave, turning quickly into a back alley. I wind through backyards until I'm near the Purvises' house. Pete measures and marks one board while my father saws at another. They talk and laugh, though it seems impossible that they'd be able to hear each other over the electric buzz.

I walk closer until my shadow crosses over Pete's work. He looks up and motions to my father to shut off the saw.

"Hey there, Button," he says. "Nice to see you out and about."

"What are you working on?"

"Right now? Making storage shelves for their basement," Pete says. "Later? Stabilizing a column on the porch, changing lightbulbs, checking smoke detectors."

"A ways to go, I guess." I turn back toward the crowd. "People are getting kind of worked up near Vinter's. Did you see?"

"Well, the guy's wearing a getup that makes himself a target," Pete says.

"It seemed like all he was doing was walking."

"Best to just let him be," Pete says. "He'll leave town soon enough."

"Ask Mary about her mystery man," my father says, lifting his safety goggles. "I can't get more than a couple words out of her."

"Pop, don't."

"Just a name," he says. "Or the town he's from."

"You don't need to tell anything you don't want to tell," Pete says and grins at my father. "If she gave you one piece of information, you'd still want another."

"Fair enough," Pop says, smiling hard.

It hurts how a lie is the happiest I can make him.

My father lowers his goggles and starts the saw again, and I watch Robert open the door to the diner and go inside. I feel sick that I'm breaking my promise to meet him, and he doesn't even know it yet.

Teachers and elementary students begin to march through the streets, dinging musical triangles and tapping wooden blocks. Martha, who tutors remedial readers after school, marches among them, chin lifted with the day's pride.

"Parade's coming," I say, as if I needed to announce it. "I better cross while I still can."

My father and Pete put down their tools. They stand tall. A show of respect. Behind the musicians, older students carry a large wooden board with "The Wall of Heroes" painted in large letters across the top. Just before the procession passes, I slip back to my side of the street. I turn to wave to my father, but his eyes have wandered toward Martha.

17

EVERY YEAR AT THE Blizzard Festival, students solemnly carry the Wall of Heroes through the streets. The Wall is a painted piece of plywood with laminated photos and tributes attached. It's a celebration of those who helped save Petroleum from the Great Rimrock Fire, when the town, with no fire department, no hydrants, could have burned to the ground. The children carry the Wall to the front of Vinter's grocery store, where they decorate it with red, white, and blue ribbons, in remembrance of the heroes' courage and sacrifice.

Now that Doctor Fischer has passed on, the only surviving hero is Albert Purvis, who would normally dress in a button-up shirt and bolo tie and stand when his name is called. Today, he's in a hospital bed, his wife at his side. I watch Pop sawing, sanding, passing the tape measure back and forth with Pete. I know how important it is to them to provide for Mrs. Purvis, as her husband would have.

It was the fire that forged their friendship when Pete and my father were both eleven years old. I know the story well; I've overheard it enough when they're drinking late at night.

Young Pete, with his lopsided walk, was a sickly child, partly due to the birth defect—how it made him delicate with chronic pains in the hip, knee, back, ankle, foot—and partly due to his mother's overprotectiveness, how she ensured that he'd stay delicate. She warned boys who came by to play that there must be no teasing or roughhousing, rules boys could not abide. My father had no interest in a kid of that sort. And so, more often, Pete was left to play with a houseful of sisters.

During the great fire, when a wall of flames trapped a number of homes between the blaze and the rimrocks, Pete and my father were the only young boys on that deadly side. Their one escape was to put the fire out.

The sky was red, flames surging from the Mackeys' barn roof, and inside, dry grass and hay caught quickly. Jim Mackey, his face flushed from the heat, raced from stall to stall, pulling out pins so his horses could escape. The fire roared, and the panicked animals' high-pitched squealing was a sound the boys had never heard before.

Everyone was in motion. Men moved livestock and as much combustible machinery as they could, then began to dig a wide trench around the fire with plows and bulldozers. Pete and my father were among the handful of neighbors, mostly teenage boys, standing in a line, sweating, lungs burning, as they passed buckets of water toward the flames. Their mothers stood at the edges of the fire, beating back embers with wet feed sacks, everyone waiting for the Agate fire trucks to arrive.

The boys struggled to lift and pass buckets until they slipped out of the line and over to Pete's house. There they played cards while Mrs. Petersen, relieved to see them away from the flames, made peanut butter sandwiches. But my father could only play cards for so long, and soon he convinced Pete to sneak out the side porch, passing through the thick air that dried their lips and the backs of their throats. They trekked up to the rimrocks, above the smoke, black flecks twisting through the air, frenzied families on either side of the firewall calling to one another and shouting instructions.

My father learned from the top of the butte that day how young Pete snuck out on a regular basis, not quite the mama's boy everyone figured him to be. On evenings when Mr. Mackey let his horses run free, Pete would slip out of bed, pull jeans over his pajamas, and step into his rubber mucking boots. With a rope hackamore in hand, he'd hop the fence to Mr. Mackey's.

Guided by moonlight, Pete could feel the dry, stunted brush and grassy tufts of manure beneath his boots, breathing in the good smell of hay and horse and night. The horses watched him warily as he approached, some snorting, stamping, throwing their heads back, or stepping sideways. His favorite, though, a chestnut gelding named Nelson, always seemed to welcome him.

Nelson had a white mark the shape of Brazil on his forehead that seemed to light up at night. Pete would pet that mark and sometimes offer a sugar cube or a peppermint, the horse still warm from the sun. Then he'd gently slip the rope over his nose, tie and loop it, and pull himself onto Nelson's back, looking over his shoulder, making sure no lights suddenly turned on at the Mackeys' or at his own home.

Sitting high up in the dark, he was afraid of falling off, afraid he couldn't handle a good tumble—his mother's fears and doubts always a voice inside his head. But he'd ride, the bugs and dust swirling about his face, Nelson moving across the open land with beautiful, even steps. The horse's breathing drummed beneath Pete's hand. He'd cluck his tongue and slap Nelson's side, *go, go,* galloping bareback until all the fear of getting caught and the loneliness and the feeling of being cooped up and odd footed drained out of him.

Amid all the shouting and rushing around, the boys felt an ease and a distance from the emergency that could only be attributed to youth. Up on the rims, they climbed to the giant letter *P* and carved their names into the sandstone, then ran across its craggy top, trying to dodge the smoke, which stung their eyes. My father ran hard and wouldn't wait for Pete; he had to keep up. For hours, the boys climbed and jumped, they lifted rocks and kicked at gopher holes.

The firefighters, when they finally arrived from Agate, climbed into local tractors to help finish making fire lines. They used big cutters to open up fences so they could drive closer with their reserve tanks. In the end, the wind, which rules this land, was on their side, blowing the flames toward the trench and the hoses.

After nearly twelve hours, they had it surrounded. This brought no comfort to Mrs. Petersen, hysterical since the boys had gone missing. What if they were overcome by smoke or, out of fright, had wandered so far that they became prey for a bobcat? She paced back and forth at the bottom of the rims, muttering her fears.

Mr. Purvis, old even then, refused to come down from that hill until he found the missing boys. Pete and my father were huddled beside an intriguing hole in the ground when the old man extended a hand to them. Breath whistling and face full of soot, he was too tired to say anything, but walked in front of them as a shield from the embers that floated through the air. One stung him good on the cheek.

When the boys emerged through the scorched brush and gray ash and into the mud created by the hoses, their mothers ran anxiously toward them. And while their end of town still smoldered and those who'd fought the fire stood hunched and silent, the mothers stroked their sons' hair and humiliated faces.

The boys learned from their frantic and soot-covered parents about the day's toll. Every member of the Flint family who lived in the house between the barn and the rims had died—both parents, three girls, and the family pets. The other casualty was Mr. Mackey's young quarter horse, Nelson, his charred body covered with blankets and rolled out of the barn on a trailer. With nothing left of the fire but its aftershock, the two new friends felt the shame of having spent a day playing like children when they were old enough to help like men.

Mr. Mackey never recovered from that day, not his lungs or his spirit. He never rebuilt the burnt skeleton of his barn that crumbled a little more each year. His surviving horses went to another ranch, and he died a few years afterward. He had never forgiven himself for having saved money by not installing a sprinkler system, or for the unnecessary cause of the fire—an uncleaned lint screen in the barn's dryer, which smoldered until it ignited hundreds of hay bales.

Pete was different from then on. Sturdier. Someone the other boys could hang out with. Someone tough enough not to cry when they imitated his limp, which, of course, they did. But he and my father carried a private agony about that day, tormented by the faces of those who'd worked to exhaustion, wheezing and coughing up black phlegm, their eyebrows singed. And though Pete had assured his parents he was fine, he told my father that he often dreamed of Nelson running from window to window, unable to find a way out of the barn. He has always believed, if he'd paid better attention, he could have freed Nelson himself.

Each time the fire is mentioned, each time the Wall of Heroes is carried through Main Street and decorated with ribbons, you can see Pete and my father still trying to separate themselves from the idle boys they were that day.

From my bedroom, I watch the Wall of Heroes travel back down the street, toward the school, where it will be stored until next year. I kneel near the window and watch until Robert, who stayed at the diner for almost an hour, walks back to his mother's house. I sink lower, shoulders curled forward, head down. Sometimes you don't know what you believe until you feel the awful sickness of getting it wrong.

18

INTO THE NIGHT, MY father and Pete work until you can see nothing more than the narrow beam of a flashlight. The tables and stalls from the festival have all been packed away, the crowd dispersed. Many continue the festivities at the Pipeline, its strings of colored lights blinking behind steamed windows. When the door opens, you hear laughter and loud, drunken conversations.

I pace from window to window with a cup of soup, unsettled, ashamed, moving as if I might leave the feeling behind me in another room.

The top floor of the hotel glows yellow. The children, settled into their rooms by now, have claimed their cots and crammed their few belongings inside shared closets or dressers. They must have left much behind, Christmas presents they'd hardly gotten to know—creaky saddles, music boxes, rifles that will have to stay in their cases until spring. I imagine those who haven't boarded before are jittery with memories of their mothers' lips against the tops of their heads, and yet there is the excitement of sleeping side by side with other children, no parents hovering. Whenever there is a large gust of wind, faces appear at the windows to see what floats through the sky. I wonder which face is Minnow's and how direct a view she'll have of our house and her mother's visits.

My next spoonful of soup is cold. When I set the cup beside the sink, men's voices trail up the driveway. I meet my father and Pete outside, take the toolbox from Pop so he can carry the sawhorse with both hands.

"There's a lot happening at the Pipeline," my father says. "Sure you don't want to join in?"

"I'm good," I say. "Want me to make you some dinner?"

"No," Pete says. "People have been feeding us all day. Your pop still has some sauce on his face."

My father sets down the sawhorse and wipes a hand across his mouth. Down the road, the door to the diner opens.

"Take it outside!" a woman shouts.

Pop smiles at the sound of Martha's voice.

Out the door and down the steps they go, the unemployed, the underemployed, men so close to losing it all. They shove and provoke and circle each other.

"They're going to fight," I tell Pete.

"Sometimes alphas need to knock horns," he says. "Don't worry about them."

Lights blink off at the hotel, but shadows cluster near the glass. We all want to see what will happen.

"Hey, look who we have here," a drunken voice calls out. "It's the younger brother."

Heads turn toward Robert, who does not change his path, but walks more cautiously.

Pete clicks a button on his key chain and unlocks his truck. "I have to get back to Agate," he says.

"You're going to leave now?" I ask.

"These things work themselves out," he says.

He gets in his white Ford and drives down the road, no police lights on. I walk to the edge of our driveway, watch as the growing pack surrounds Robert. Just the sight of his black leather and strange hair seems to have set them off.

"Beautiful locks, miss," says one, looping a curl with his finger.

Robert shakes his head hard to show his disgust. "Excuse me," he says.

Pop taps my arm. "Let's go inside, Mary."

He heads into the house, but I hurry toward the fray, no idea why I'm running.

"Excuse me," Robert says again, but they've given him no room to move.

"Come back to collect your mom's money?" someone asks Robert.

"I'm here to take care of her, asshole."

Someone shouts from the back, furious, high-pitched. "You lie!"

Voices thunder with agreement.

It's as if they don't even see Robert. He is a fiction they've invented, some terrible force that threatens their traditions, their livelihoods. He is a release for frustrated men who are tired of the promise that life will get easier when it never does. The crowd tightens around Robert as he takes a clumsy swing.

"Ooh, look at those delicate hands!"

I elbow closer as punches fly. The wind joins in, slapping faces as we squint in anticipation.

The man Robert tangled with earlier steps forward and grabs the leather collar.

"Maybe we should drag him to the elevator," he says. "Throw him down the empty bin."

"And then what?" Robert shouts.

"Then I'll feel better," he says and hits him hard.

Robert falls to the ground, holding his jaw.

"See," the man says. "I feel better already."

The mob seems to hum with anger. So do I as I move closer. And I am frightened. Frightened of this side of me because I don't know it well. Because I worry what I might do.

"Mary, come back to the house," Pop calls.

Robert sits up, woozy. He catches my eye as he gets on his feet. Another punch is thrown and down he goes.

"What's happened to us?" I shout.

I turn in a circle, looking at each familiar face.

"When did we become enemies instead of neighbors?"

I hear laughter and feel a shove from behind.

"Stop it!" I yell, still turning. "We are better than this!"

I want to say more but I can't think. I look into the faces that sneered when I stood in the pool alone.

"Freak!" a voice shouts.

"Mary, come on home." I hear my father but can't see him.

"Go on home, Mary," someone calls.

More laughter.

"It was a good festival, everyone," my father says as he finds his way to me. "Probably time to call it a night."

He keeps pushing through bodies until he's in front of Robert.

"Do you need help getting home?" he asks, bending down.

"No," Robert says. He looks briefly at me and then away.

"Let me give you a hand up then," Pop says.

Robert stands on his own.

"Okay," my father calls out to the crowd. "Good night, all. Get home safely."

He leads me home, a hand on my back.

"I'm not a child," I say.

He removes his hand but leans close to my ear. His whisper is stern.

"Getting in the middle of all that," he says. "That's not a good way to keep our customers."

"Why are you making it seem like I was out of line?" I ask.

All through the dark of Main Street to the pure black of Crooked Hill Road, I wrestle for words. I felt like I had so much to say.

My father sees my tears and says, "It's all right."

He must not understand that these tears are not the frustration that I'd said too much but that I didn't say more.

19

I'M OFF TO AGATE," I tell Pop as I take my plate to the sink and toss half my sandwich. "I want to get the engine looked at before the big snow."

He nods. He must know my main goal is to spend the day far from our neighbors. I took no punches last night, but today I feel beat up. Pop looks beat up, too.

"No more trouble today, okay?" he says as if to lighten the mood.

"I didn't start any trouble, Pop."

"All I'm trying to say. . . ." He inhales in a way that lets me know he is editing his words. "There's no sense in getting your reputation tangled up with Robert Golden. That's what you're not understanding."

So that's the real problem. He's worried about my popularity. He knows that anyone Robert interacts with is marked by the town. And I'm marked in so many ways already. The worry is always the same, that I'm odd and ought to hide the fact as best I can.

I clutch the keys in my fist and swallow my fury into the dark of my belly. I don't say good-bye.

The sky is gray and full, blizzard season ever nearer. It's not until I unlock my van that I notice the cigarette butts stubbed out beside it. I remember my neighbors' taunting faces, how certain they were of their own truth. My hand shakes so much I can hardly open the door or latch my seat belt. I have something to say. I just can't find the words.

After several tries, the engine starts. As I drive past the Pipeline, the man who punched Robert last night stands with the unemployed, hoping for work today. He lifts his head and watches me go by.

The stones are hot in my belly, clattering over the pitted roads.

I am grateful for the smooth highway, a chance to speed away. The plains have faded to the palest beige, the sky dotted with small flakes. Elk cross the hillside in heavy coats, and I slow to watch a bull, pale except for the dark brown of his powerful neck and head. He lifts his stately horns to sniff at the sky, and even through the closed window, I hear his great, high-pitched bugling.

When I approach the old rodeo stands, I see a man in black sitting alone under the swirling snow. It could only be Robert. If I thought about it more, I'd talk myself out of stopping. But— what can I do?—I've already turned into the dirt parking lot.

I'm slow to get out of the van, trying to think up excuses for how I behaved.

"I thought that was you," I say, walking across patches of

snow toward the old wooden risers. "I'm sorry about our coffee."

He doesn't speak but raises a flask my way.

His hair blows about in the dust and flurries. One eye opens smaller than the other, and a bluish bruise stretches along his jaw.

"You're welcome to join me if you'd like to spend some quality time with a drunk," he says.

I climb into the stands. The wooden plank bows underneath my boots.

"I'm taking a break from town," he says and gives a tight, unhappy grin.

"I'm sorry," I try again.

"So is my mother," he says. "So much for coming here to make her last days easier."

I've stopped a few rows below. He angles his head toward the ample space beside him while shrugging a shoulder as if to say, *I don't know why you'd want to sit here, but the seat's free.*

And so I climb higher. I've missed him. When I listen to my instincts and not the town's, this is what I hear. I sit down, and we both look out at the rodeo ring. He passes the flask, and I touch my mouth to the place where his has just been.

"How is Doris?" I ask. "Minus the shock of seeing you like this?"

A sweet sting of warmth travels down my throat while Robert takes a long breath, as if considering whether he wants to answer.

"Everything about my mother is quiet now, the way she walks around in socks and whispers like she's in a library." He reaches for the flask. "Our time together can feel, I don't know, formal, like she's trying to entertain a stranger. We sit on the sofa she's had all my life with stains from a Coke my brother spilled and muddy paw prints from a dog we owned decades ago. We sit, making polite conversation about nothing at all. Most days it doesn't get to me."

"I saw her at the window beside her easel the other day," I say. "She was painting a clown."

"Weary Willie," he says. "The hobo clown. She paints that one a lot, and a dancing dog in a sweater. There are only so many kits." He shields his eyes as dust blows toward us. "My mother is, to me, what she is to you, to everyone in town— the woman in the window, but you can't quite see in, and she doesn't notice that you're on the street watching."

"Is it the medication she's taking?" I ask.

He shakes his head.

"This is a woman who can only be so happy," he says. "I did this to her."

For a long time it's absolutely quiet except for the wind and some very distant mooing.

"I still remember her clearing our cereal bowls as Eddie and I left the house that morning," he says, looking out beyond the rodeo ring. "She was so excited that we were working together for the summer, as if it proved we'd become close."

And he tells the story of the grain elevator but leaves out the details I know from the game. He talks, instead, about the darkness, the dusty air, the iron gears, and the smell of mildew and creosote. He remembers how their voices echoed inside and the whisper of grain beneath their boots until they turned the knobs and pulled the levers that made the whole place chug and quake like some giant washing machine filled with towels. He describes the narrow stairwells, vibrating ladders, and tiny wooden hatchways leading to wooden bins. You could take a manlift, pulling hand over hand on a rope, all the way to the top of the tower, where you'd walk through a dark passage, narrow as the width of your shoulders. Turn one more corner, and you could stand in a blast of light and wind at that top window, swaying above the town like you were sitting on a cloud.

"It would have been a normal day for my mother," he says. "She was always in motion, washing the breakfast dishes, wiping spills from the table, snipping beans in the garden, drying slices of fruit in the oven, walking the dog along the rims. You almost never saw her sit. She liked tending to us and the house, like our comfort and pleasure was her reward."

"What went wrong?" I ask.

I expect to hear the story of the boy kicking lazily at the grain, impatient for his shift to end. But the story he remembers moves at a much faster speed.

"The boss stormed up the stairs, asking why the grain had stopped flowing," he says. "I'd tied my harness to a ladder and was already out on the grain, but Eddie was shouting about what a weakling I was. He jumped through the hatch straightaway because he just had to show me how to do it right."

This is where most of the game takes place. But within seconds, Robert felt a huge pull from above and pressure on all the harness straps.

"There wasn't time to understand what was happening," he says. "I was hanging halfway down the bin. Eddie must have stepped where there was a pocket of air because he just disappeared."

Robert flailed, helplessly, legs dangling as if in a swing, while grain funneled toward the base. He tried to grab hold of anything he could use to climb back up to the hatchway so he could unstrap himself and run down to find his brother, but his arms felt like jelly.

"I shouted Eddie's name. I shouted the names of anyone I thought could help," he says. "My legs tingled, and there was ringing in my ears. But after a while, I heard blades cutting through our storage bin. I figured, since no one came to help me, it was because they thought they could save him."

I see his embarrassment that he would have had such blind hope. We all read about these kinds of accidents in the paper. No one ever survives.

"I hung there for a long time," he says. "My voice was hoarse. I kicked and pedaled my legs to keep them from going numb. I hadn't shouted or said a word for some time because I understood then that I was being, I don't know, punished, I guess."

"How did you get down?" I ask.

"Someone dragged me up from the bin and through the hatchway, and I landed hard on the floor."

"Who was it?"

"My boss."

"Mr. Purvis."

He nods.

"When I looked up at his face, he said, 'You killed him. I suppose you know you killed him, and here you are crying all this time for yourself.'"

"I'm so sorry," I say.

"I walked down the stairs, shaky and drenched in sweat. When I was outside, I didn't even turn my head to look for Eddie. Didn't feel I deserved to look. I just walked home."

"No one spoke to you as you were leaving?" I ask.

"Oh, someone did," he says. "I walked outside in a blood-stained T-shirt, walking funny because the harness had cut off the circulation to my legs for so long. Doctor Fischer stood near the opening."

"The Wall of Heroes," I say.

"He shook his head and said, 'Look what you've done, you sissy.'"

Sissy, sissy, look what you've done. This is what we chanted during the game as the one playing Eddie spun down to the ground with his tongue out to the side. This is what we chanted as we pulled Dead Eddie from the grain, plucking pretend kernels from his face, gouging our nails into flesh if we could.

"When I got home," Robert says, "my mother was at our dining room table with her head down. She didn't greet me. I sat next to her and neither of us made a noise. Sound returned to our house with my father, slamming things and telling my mother how she better not defend me or he'd absolutely go off. I didn't say a word or even look up. When your brother's dead and everyone thinks it's your fault, the last thing you're going to say is that you might need a doctor."

"Where were you hurt?" I ask.

Robert lifts his shirt, his skin becoming goose pimpled, to show thick scars where the straps had cut across his chest. The wounds disappear behind the fabric again as he slips his shirt back down.

"You can't really blame my dad," he says. "We both know it was my fault, what happened that day."

"Your brother could have put on his harness," I say.

"And I could have reminded him. Or shouted for him not to come out on the grain."

"You were kids," I say.

"I know when he stepped out on that grain, it was to put me

down. But it's also true that he needed my help and I didn't exactly try. We were both jerks to each other in our last moment together. It's something I have to live with."

Robert screws the cap on and then off again. I pull my arms around my legs to keep from touching him.

"When I see it in my mind," he says, "when I see it slowed down, I have a chance to reach out for him, but I'm too angry."

I've seen my father do this same thing. He thinks of all the things he could have done the day my mother died to make it turn out differently.

"Every time I sit with my ma," he says, "it's still there—what I've done. The quiet house, my mother hardly my mother anymore."

We've passed the flask back and forth too many times to keep track. As he speaks, our knees almost touching, I hear what he doesn't actually put into words. That he believes the things they say about him. Fourteen-year-old Robert—and not poor supervision or child labor violations or even bad luck—is what killed Eddie and stripped this town of its grain elevator and its train.

"Want to hear something funny?" he asks.

"What?"

"When you didn't make it for coffee yesterday, I sat at a table and watched how much the simple act of me eating a meal there upset the regulars," he says. "I admit it, I ate as slow as I could and even ordered a second and third cup of coffee, just to make them uncomfortable."

He laughs so hard that, for a moment, he can't speak.

"Years ago, when I left here, I had one goal—to become a success as a way to stick it to this town," he says. "Show them they'd misjudged me. I wanted them to feel small for all they assumed about that kid, who was actually smarter than them and going to do big things with his life. But the truth is, I struggled to get work just like the rest of them. We're all sitting at our tables hating each other like there's some big difference between us."

"I feel so terrible about not showing."

He laughs again, but this time, just a short ha-ha.

"Serves me right for thinking I was so cool," he says. "Because, wouldn't you know, I left my keys there at the diner. Had to go back for them later, like a real jerk."

We stretch our legs on the lower wooden seats and finish the last drops in the flask.

"When I came here tonight," Robert says, "I thought I wanted to be alone, but I'm glad it didn't work out that way."

20

ROBERT WALKS ME TO my van, where I have an intense desire to steady myself by slipping my fingers through his belt loops. He opens the door for me.

"This doesn't count as our coffee date," he says.

I think of Robert's scar, how it disappeared into his shirt, and my lips want to touch something. I am not breathing. I feel his hand stroke my hair as I lower into the seat. He watches my feet until they're safely inside and closes my door. At the window, he waves good night but does not leave. There is a look. Slow. Present. His lips part as if to speak, but there are no words. Just this look. And right before he turns to leave, he mouths, *Mary*.

I place my hand on the dirt-flecked glass, hold it there as he walks back to his truck.

I'm too drunk to drive so I only pretend I'm about to take off, waving to Robert as he heads back to town.

I toss my keys onto the dark and cluttered floor of the passenger side, a trick Pete taught my senior class to keep us from making bad judgments on the road. I lay my face against the steering wheel and watch the shadows of the bleachers stretch long and crooked into the dirt.

If I hadn't sat down in the driver's seat, Robert might have kissed me.

My fingers trace the braided edge of leather along the steering wheel, and I hum the song from the old game. I always thought the kids invented it. But maybe we only echoed the feelings and judgments of the men we've honored as heroes.

With our song, with our finger-pointing, we ran Robert out of Petroleum. All of us. I remember my own voice singing, *Sissy, sissy,* and the glee of belonging. I can't take it back. Not that and not leaving him alone for our coffee date. It sits here like a mass caught in my throat.

But he made a space for me to sit beside him. We sat, knowing each other's flaws—some of them, anyway—and let down our guards. Usually I'm more cautious, trying not to upset people, trying not to be noticed at all.

It felt good to be seen.

The last bit of sun slips behind the rims. There's a light snowfall, just a tease for what's to come. I pull my hat lower, pull my hands inside my coat sleeves, pull my feet up to the seat, ready for a nap.

He might have kissed me.

The bleachers where we sat together are now completely black, like a construction paper cutout against a canvas of watercolors—a brush of pink, a moody purple, a splash of white. I feel an ache deep-in, as if only beginning to notice that something vital has been curled up in hiding. The girl who skated in socks, who ran to meet the train with a penny, who sat in the back of the art room hunched over a drawing and forgetting time—all buried under those stones.

Night draws its shade. Coyotes call, and another day comes to an end. It's funny how time goes so slow one day, sometimes for a whole season or a whole year, and then it's like a fast-forward button is pressed, and where did time go? How could you move no closer to the life you dreamed for yourself? How could you go so long without a kiss?

21

I WAKE COLD AND QUEASY, throw open the door to my van and vomit, for the most part, outside. What's left on the footrest freezes by the time I reach home. When I enter the house through the kitchen, Pop pretends to look busy, as if he's washing something at the sink, though there is nothing in it. I know he's been fretting, trying not to call Pete for backup, trying to show he trusts that I'm an adult. But he doesn't trust me. He's been wondering where I am and who I'm with and, if I'm late, he thinks I've been in an accident. It always shows on his face, the poorly disguised worry and the hesitation to say anything.

"Did you get your van looked at?"

"Almost," I say.

I'm certain he smells the whiskey but he won't mention it. There are things we don't know how to talk about.

At my place mat sits a helping of elk—made into a meat-loaf this time—and peas shriveled beside it, mashed potatoes crusted with film. It's a message. It says, *This is how long I waited for you. Obviously my feelings don't concern you or you would have called. I'm sad for this distance, this habit we have, this habit I'm certain I taught you.*

I sit, determined to eat the shriveled peas and show him that his statement about my being late for dinner didn't work.

"I hope he's good to you, this man who has all your attention," he says. But I hear his irritation.

I don't speak.

"I'm happy you have someone to spend time with," he says, sitting now. "I just wish you'd let me know if you're going to be late."

I look at the clock. It's only eleven.

"Pop, do you have to know everything about my life?"

We are here. Again. In this small room. At this small table. The windows covered in tinfoil. Snow sprinkling down, but who would know unless you'd been outside?

"I want to know you," he whispers.

I set down my fork.

"Whenever you see the real me," I say, "you're disappointed."

I head upstairs to brush my teeth. The bathroom has been ravaged by the man without his suit. Towels and clothes dropped behind the door. A sticky tumbler on the back of the toilet. Another on the windowsill. The sink stained with coffee and the dried gunk he spits up each morning.

Pop follows me and lingers in the hallway, his reflection in the mirror. I can see him thinking of things he won't say. *How did we get here again?* his face seems to ask. *Are we better off if I stay quiet?*

Paint curls along the ceiling in the shape of dangling leaves. Some have dropped to the bathmat, ground up by our feet.

How many bills away from collapse is our business? I spit out the toothpaste, wash my face, then the sink, including his mess. I dry off with a towel. And still he waits, even as I pass him, as though he might say something. But, of course, he doesn't.

I walk, still woozy, to my room, and close the door. With only the bedside lamp on, my room glows pink like the inside of a seashell I held once at school. Someone had purchased it during a vacation to Florida and we all put it to our ears and listened to the ocean most of us would never see. I sit on my bed, mice tunneling through the walls behind me, one more fix-it project my father plans to get to when the weather warms up again.

I can hear him, still in the hallway, wondering if he should knock or leave me alone. Decades ago, I felt so close to him when he read storybooks to me here, and to make me laugh, he'd slap the wall with the palm of his hand to wake the mice. We came up with names for them and welcomed their return year after year. I can't imagine Pop laughing like that anymore. Or me.

I lay my head on the pillow and watch the shadow of Pop's feet outside my door. I can tell it will be a long while before I'm able to sleep. The bed feels like it's swaying, sloshing the peas and meatloaf.

Finally, the shadow of his feet moves back down the hall, and a door clicks shut. I'm sorry it's this way with Pop. I don't remember how to be close. We don't know how to be grown-ups together. We set aside the children's books but what goes in their place? All night, I imagine the conversations that might bring us closer, if we only knew how to begin.

22

THE TV BLASTS IN the den, Pop out cold in the recliner. Soon he'll hear the morning news program, its opening theme always jolting him like an alarm clock. I'm already dressed for the day, needing a long walk. I just have to find my warmer gloves.

"You headed somewhere?" my father asks in a ragged voice that hasn't yet coughed up the morning phlegm.

"I thought I'd hike up to the rims," I say. "I didn't mean to wake you."

"Mind if I tag along?"

"If you can keep up," I say.

I'm trying to pretend last night didn't happen so today doesn't have to feel so serious. I wait for him to change out of his pajamas.

"Trying to find a clean shirt," he calls from behind a half-closed door. "Give me a couple more minutes."

When we're both bundled up, we head into the crisp morning.

"This cold sure wakes you up," he says, adjusting his cap so it covers more of his ears. His words come out as white clouds.

We pass Doris at her window. Pop waves, but she is busy dipping her brush into the next color. I open my mouth to say something about Robert and realize that I had only wanted to say his name.

"Well, that's worth getting up early for," Pop says as a small herd of mule deer run across Main Street and into the open space below the rims.

"Maybe we'll see them again when we get to the top," I say.

Our carefree talk becomes a long silence. I notice our breath, the crunch of frozen stubble beneath our boots, specks of sunlight dancing along the hill we're about to climb.

"I didn't mean to upset you last night," Pop says, breathing harder.

"It's okay," I say.

It's easier making peace with our eyes facing the rimrocks rather than each other.

"Forgive me for what feels like prying about your mystery man," he says. "It's just that I'd love to know what he's like."

I don't mean to answer but can't help myself.

"I don't know," I say. "He has a funny little smile that turns up on only one side of his mouth. He's interested in my thoughts. And he likes to spend his afternoons out in nature when he can."

I stop there. If I say more, I may give away some detail that identifies Robert.

"And he has a good job?" Pop asks.

He seems to be worried that my mystery man might be unemployed. For now, that's a level of disapproval I can live with. Also, I never thought to ask what kind of work Robert does.

"Now you're prying," I say.

"Well, I'm glad you have someone," he says and pulls me close.

My father is not a natural hugger. No one in his family hugged when he was growing up. He and his parents and siblings shook hands when they greeted, but even that looked uncomfortable.

He learned this skill for me, the way he learned to put my hair in clips and check under my bed for monsters. Every time he places an arm around me or gently tugs at my ponytail, I know he is reaching beyond all he's been taught, beyond all levels of comfort.

His arm drops back down to his side as we walk past rusted corrals and a sagging barn. There is only one road up to the rims but soon we cut our own path, closer to the giant letter *P,* our footsteps swishing through tufts of grass and stunted yucca plants with their thorny leaves. We breathe harder, making the last push to the flat top of the butte.

The wind is a low hum in my ear as we walk across the powdery earth, stepping over slabs of brittle sandstone, animal tracks and droppings. This land still takes my breath away, the sound of birds waking, the far-off mooing, the grass swaying, nothing ever truly still.

At the crumbling edge of the rims, we look out over the town and the broken rock below. I watch the movement of men and trucks and cattle.

"You think we'll get a big storm this year?" I ask, kicking at a coyote track.

"I think it's a good thing we got all our canning done this summer," he says. "Did you get it all labeled?"

"And alphabetized."

He palms the top of my head. It feels like he's saying, *Thank you,* and also, *Oh dear, what did I do wrong that made you this way?*

In the distance, children leave the hotel in hats and gloves and scarves, walking quietly with good posture, hands to themselves unless they're in charge of younger children. Minnow scuffles behind them in a too-small coat, all legs.

"We should do this more often," Pop says. "Spend time like this."

"I'm always happy to hike up here," I say.

"Maybe we could catch a basketball game together," he says, looking right at Minnow. "Next home game. Does that sound good?"

I don't want to ruin this attempt he's making to smooth things over. I want to say yes to something.

"If I'm free," I say.

"Your schedule should be pretty light now that everything's sorted out with the Goldens."

I put my hands deep into my pockets and push till the fabric strains.

"Pop," I say. "I didn't give him those original papers."

"But you told me you had," he says.

"I dropped off blank paperwork, same as I would for anyone else. Robert doesn't even know the others exist."

"Well, this is a real mess."

"I couldn't make sense of giving him paperwork you filled out," I say. "He's next of kin."

"Mary, there are a lot of people expecting to be involved in Doris's service."

"I know."

"Her old singing group's been preparing hymns," he says. "They're going to be very upset."

"They might," I say.

"What if someone's already prepared a speech?"

"Pop, you put those plans together when there was no next of kin. Now there's next of kin."

"You don't understand, Mary. This is the kind of thing that makes people choose a different place to do their business."

"Pop."

"If we hurry," he says, "we can make this right."

"His mother's dying," I say, reaching out to a nearby juniper shrub to pluck a seed. "People might be mad, but you always tell me that planning a funeral helps a person to grieve and let go."

"Show him the plans I came up with," he says. "I can't think he wouldn't like them. I've organized singers, a speaker, casket bearers. This saves him a lot of work. He probably doesn't even know these people who've been so important in Doris's life."

I split the juniper seed open with my thumbnail to release its piney scent.

"I'm comfortable with my decision, Pop."

"Mary, I don't want to fight."

"Then let it go," I say. "You made plans and they aren't needed anymore."

We stare over the rims at the town, back to where we started. Children continue on to school, some hurrying to get there before the late bell. A group of boys playfully pushes and shouts as they cross into the schoolyard.

"Do you hear that?" Pop asks.

"It's just some boys horsing around before school."

"No. Down the highway," he says.

Now I hear it, too. A radio, maybe? We see a number of our neighbors come out of their homes and businesses, their heads also turned toward the highway. Soon I see Pete's white Ford way in the distance, heading toward Petroleum, lights flashing. On TV shows, sirens are common, but not here.

"What's going on, do you think?" I ask, but Pop only shakes his head.

The siren moves closer, and we hurry down the hill, taking long side steps.

23

I KEEP MY EYE ON the white Ford as it turns from the high-way onto Main Street, then drives slowly, block by block, siren blaring. Pop and I have rushed down from the rims and cut through the back alleys toward the flashing lights. The people of Petroleum—the busy, the unemployed, the curious—come out of their homes and businesses, caps pulled down over their faces. A cramp forms beneath my ribs, and Pop is breathing too hard.

Pete turns onto Crooked Hill Road, and many are now walking behind his truck, shielding their faces from the dust. Something big is happening and they want to be part of it. Some of the ranchers have also followed the noise, driving pickups and tractors down the highway and back into town. I don't know why we're running, only that it feels as if we must.

"I think he's going to our house," I say.

We take the quickest route. I'm beginning to sweat, though I can see my breath in the cold.

Pete has pulled into our driveway, and most of the others have gathered there, too. My father and I are out of breath. Pop maneuvers between neighbors to greet his friend. They talk privately for a moment and then Pete opens the back of his truck. My father, still winded, takes over, sliding the draped body out. Every face in the crowd is solemn, stoic.

"God bless Albert Purvis," Pete says to those assembled, and the men take off their hats and hold them to their chests.

I look at the bowed heads, still trying to slow my breath. I touch the white sheet. The man on the Wall of Heroes. The man who let a fourteen-year-old boy hang in a harness for hours.

My father and Pete carry Mr. Purvis down to the basement, and I follow. The way they keep the sheet from slipping off, the way Pete gently puts his hand on the old man's shoulder as they set him on the metal table, says what they think of him.

I slip on a plastic apron, grab latex gloves from a box. Slowly I pull back the sheet, revealing hair that is thin and coarse, a color neither brown nor gray; eyelids opening like faulty shades; cracked lips set in a relaxed frown. This body, still dressed in the hospital gown that I will mail back, has held all his prominence and all his secrets. In the end, he is not a hero so much as a man. It is the case with all who come here—flawed, vulnerable, human when they hoped to be so much more.

I fold the sheet down only as far as his collarbone. That's enough when I have company. And even this may be too much for Pete before I've done my work. But it is the scar on Mr. Purvis's cheek that he and Pop need to see—a bluish-white indentation left by that ember from the Great Rimrock Fire. A final reminder of his sacrifice and their shame.

Pete looks more at the sheet than the man, his weight resting on the stronger leg, his hands retreating to his pockets. Soon, Pop leaves, then returns with a large plastic bag containing Mr. Purvis's glasses, a photo, and a neatly folded blue suit. He puts his hand on my arm, a gesture, it seems, of warmth, of words we couldn't find on the rims or last night.

"Take good care of him," Pete says.

I wait until the men have gone to the kitchen, where they speak in solemn voices. I hear the sound of dishes being taken from the cupboard, the jar of pickled eggs being opened, metal tongs reaching inside.

Alone now, I remove the sheet. Mr. Purvis is yellow and dry like crepe paper, purple veins running beneath his sharp shoulders and hips. The white hair on his chest is sparse, his belly distended, eyes yellow where they ought to be white, milky where they ought to be brown. I close them gently with my thumb, but slowly they open again as if he's curious to see what happens next.

I sit with him for some time, just holding his hand.

Mr. Purvis was the oldest resident of Petroleum. Though he was not much of a talker, he could, if pressed, tell you about the earliest homesteaders in this area. He could tell you what it was like when there was a bank and a filling station. He could tell you about shooting wolves back when the law still allowed it. He was the last of a generation, and now there is a sense that the town is turning over to a new era—if it survives—in which its people did not build the homes they live in and do not remember the reason their families sought out this untamed land in the first place.

My fingers trace his small, dry veins. The backs of his arms are mottled with spots and gristly nubs. I smooth my thumb over his wrist as if releasing the sting of the hospital's needles and tubes. The palms of his hands are blotchy, bruises under his nails. I untie and remove the hospital gown. My eye goes to the liver, bulging, as I expected, under the right rib cage. If I open the belly, I know I'll find walls of scar tissue and the hard liver, covered with what look like Rice Krispies.

I flick a switch and the machine chugs and pulses in the background while I run a wet sponge over the loose skin of his arm, the discoloration on the back of his hand from the hospital IV. I bathe his concave chest and his tight, pregnantlike middle. By the time of his viewing, when he is dressed in the blue suit his family supplied, there will be no more sunken eyes and cheeks, no trace of jaundice or the sores from his intense itching, his cirrhosis a secret between his widow, his doctor, and now me.

I turn off the machines, and when they have quieted, I study the photograph. In it, Mr. Purvis holds a true whopper of a fish. Pop would know what kind. I study his smile—mouth closed, laugh lines on the outer corners of his eyes and something about his mouth looks as if he's holding in a joke. I'm determined to capture this happiness, as I pull the wax string tighter, then pad his mouth with bits of cotton to get the expression right. I will make him the man his wife wants the town to remember, going back and forth with the photo, adjusting the cotton and the tension in the string until I can almost see a smirk.

Finished with Mr. Purvis for now, I wheel him into the fridge, then wash my hands and start a load of wash. I find my father and Pete at the kitchen table. They have eaten a good number of eggs, one still on my father's plate, drips of pickling juice speckled across the table. They had been talking rather intensely as I came up the stairs; I know by the sudden hush that my father has already told Pete about our talk on the rimrocks.

"He's looking better," I say and sit with them at the table.

There is no sound, except for the scrape of the chair leg against the linoleum tile as I pull my seat closer. And then the sound of the chair leg scraping again after, realizing I feel too close to the table, I move myself back. Pete sweeps crumbs into his hand and claps them onto his plate. Finally we sit still—the last egg uneaten, the last word unsaid.

24

I SPEND MUCH OF THE night with Mr. Purvis, inserting the spearlike trocar into an incision just above his navel. Then I puncture each organ. It's the only embalming step, after all these years, when I still need to hold my breath. But I also find it incredibly satisfying to vacuum out the gases, juices, food, and sperm until only loose sacks are left.

Somehow, seeing the stringy, rancid contents move out of his body makes me feel as if I've freed him. Helped him let go of cravings, worries, earthly desires. The pressures he tried to drink away, the years of underemployment, the changes in Petroleum and the world beyond it, all of that, in whatever form it was held by the body, can now slip out of the incision and disappear down the drain. When I pump the empty cavity full of formaldehyde, fill it with cotton, and suture it closed, it's like I've made him clean.

Sometimes I imagine myself on the stainless steel table. Fingers without rings. Skin without the damage or pleasure of sun.

You think a life is built of dreams when, really, a life is made up of daily to-do lists. Take out the trash. Wash your hands. Make breakfast. Go to work. Wonder what to make for dinner and if you have all the ingredients you need. Eat. Wash again. Try to sleep, or maybe just go back to work.

How you spend your day is how you spend your life. Dreams, at least for me, are those things at the bottom of the to-do list. After: Fix engine. After: Make dentist appointment. And who ever gets to the last thing on the list?

I feel like I have, only now, looked up from my chores to discover I've become a woman without dreams. Heavy with stones. Perhaps the embalmer who looks after my body will read the words written on those stones as she removes them. *Strange, nervous, loner.* She may even understand that many of the words have come from those who love me best.

My eyes are blurry from making small, careful stitches. I rub them as I walk up the stairs from my workroom. Near the top, I sense a shadow, breath. Pete sits alone at our kitchen table.

"Careful with the late hours," he says.

"I learned from Pop," I say, hearing the tremble in my voice.

"That's what I mean," he says. "You see the toll it takes."

Though I rinsed my hands in the basement, I rinse them again at the kitchen sink because something about Pete's face, the force in his jaw, makes me want some distance.

"You weren't waiting for me, were you?" I ask, eyes toward the faucet.

"I wouldn't mind a little chat," he says.

I pull the chair far from the table, sit with my back touching a cupboard.

"I was under the impression that we were all on the same

page regarding Doris's service," he says. "I notarized those original forms myself."

"The problem," I say, drying my hands on my pants and speaking cautiously, "is that her son wants to do this himself."

"He's being difficult," Pete says.

"Is he the one being difficult?" I ask. "People just stare at him when he walks by. And someone's been leaving cigarette butts in his driveway."

"There's no law about where you put out your cigarettes," he says.

"It's like someone's trying to send him a message," I say. "Let him know he's not wanted here."

"It's not model behavior, but I'm not going to run a DNA test on the stubs."

"You can't do anything?"

"When this guy's on his way, everything will settle down again," he says.

"Well, planning the service is in his hands," I say. "He's next of kin."

"I'd hate for you to do something that turns customers away," Pete says. "Your father works hard to make this business one that really stands for the community."

"Robert Golden is the one caring for Doris and watching her die," I say, my words stronger than my voice. "I think it might be good for them to work through some of those questions together."

"It's kind of late to start a relationship when you take off for decades."

"It's not my job to decide who's earned the right to grieve," I say.

"Here's the thing, Button," he says, angling his chair so his shoulders are squared with mine. "Making new plans will upset a lot of people. Imagine how those nice ladies, who just want to sing for Doris, will feel if they're suddenly told they're no longer a part of the service."

"I understand," I say, my voice even smaller. "But it's not my job to worry about the town's feelings."

He leans in.

"But it's my job to worry about them," he says. "I have to be committed to the people who will be staying, Mary. Not someone here for a visit."

My chest tightens.

"You can make a suggestion," he says. "You can tell him it won't just make it easier on the town but it'll make it easier on him, too. Can you do that?"

I swallow.

"Help him see it's in everyone's best interest," Pete says.

I don't speak.

"Hey," he says, his voice softening. "Haven't I always been there for you?"

He gets up from his chair, walks over to me, and palms my head in his hands. I feel like the little girl in the swimsuit, my fingers stuck with pins.

"Don't you trust me to look after this town?" he asks.

He's still holding my head and I try to nod.

"I'll talk to him," I say in a whisper.

"I appreciate that," he says.

He lets go, puts on his hat, which helps to balance out his large jaw. I stand and we walk together toward the door.

"I've been meaning to ask," he says, stopping to push in his chair. "Are you still seeing your secret fella?"

"I'm not seeing anyone," I say. "We just talk sometimes."

"Well, taking it slow is good," he says, turning back toward me. "Love is complicated, Mary. Hearts, if you look at real ones, are not so pretty."

"I've seen real ones," I say.

"Yes," he says. "Yes, you have."

Pete kisses the top of my head and says his last words into my scalp. "Make this happen, all right?"

My hands stay against the door after he leaves. My heart—through loyalty, love, and fear, one small choice at a time, swallow by swallow—cowers, pale and shriveled, beneath the stones.

I watch from our front window. Pete's white Ford flies through town, and when it's dark again, a flame flickers at the end of the Goldens' driveway. The flare of a cigarette reveals a shape, then two, then three.

What's suddenly clear is that no one's going to protect Robert. The law isn't for everyone.

I imagine the men's hard, red faces, their feeling that something at the heart of them has been stolen. They're out of money, out of patience. But they have fight. Standing there, all puffed up and menacing, they still have their pride.

I'm almost sad for them. How they can't adjust to the fact that things have changed. That it's not going to be like it was. Just because you love something, just because you hold on tight, doesn't mean it will last. Sometimes you can only watch helplessly as it slips from your grasp. You say good-bye before you're ready. You may even refuse to say good-bye at all. Still, it slips away.

The shadows gather there for many minutes. Each long draw burns hot like rage and then rushes back into the air we all breathe.

25

POP CALLS DOWN THE stairs, "Do I have a clean suit any-where?"

I start the coffee, then check the hallway closet.

"Right here," I say. "Cleaned and pressed."

"Good," he says, walking downstairs.

I need to wash the pajamas he's wearing. They're stained with food and whiskey, and I know he'll just put them on again.

He enters the kitchen, rubbing a hand down his face, and pulls a chair from the table.

"Is Mr. Purvis ready for his viewing?"

"He will be by ten," I say. "Are you going to be ready?"

"If I get some coffee, yes."

I hand him his cup.

"Pete stayed late last night," I say.

"Oh?"

"Pop, I thought you dropped it. About the paperwork. I thought you finally decided to treat me like an adult."

"I only told him about our talk."

"Well, that's why I'm about to head over to the Goldens'," I say. "I don't need you and Pete handling things for me."

"Let me get the original paperwork for you," Pop says, groaning that he has to stand so soon.

I follow him as far as the office door. Let him navigate all the crap on the floor. He opens the file cabinet.

"Show him the service I planned," he says. "I'm no slouch at this."

"No, you aren't," I say.

"Remember, it's a win for everyone," he says. "Those already expecting to be involved in the service will be happy, and this makes less work for Robert."

"Do you need me to clean your office before the service?" I ask.

He shuts the door and heads back to his coffee.

I stand on our porch as I button my coat, watching Doris at her front window.

I wonder if having her son home, after more than two decades, is a comfort in her last days. I wonder what she would choose if she had my dilemma—peace for the town or peace for her son.

We have all been watching her die for the past two years. This is what no one likes to talk about: dying takes longer than people think. In movies, family gathers around, sharing expressions of love and forgiveness, often never voiced before. The dying person closes his eyes, feeling at peace as he takes one last breath.

Except in real life, it's not so easy. You get impatient. Because the dying goes on and on. You can't seem to make them comfortable. The loving talk turns cranky, or sometimes the talk is just mundane and you end up watching TV.

I cross the street and spot Robert in the backyard, taking down poultry netting that was stapled to the old wooden pen. Jacket open and wearing gardening gloves, he rolls the wire mesh like a sleeping bag, pressing his knee on the roll to keep it tight.

"Damnit," he says and stops to pull something from his knee, causing the netting to unfold.

When I laugh, he looks up in surprise.

"Well, my day just got a little better," he says.

I see that same smile he showed me the other night.

"Want to borrow some gloves and get in on the fun?" he asks. "Or is this a business call?"

"Business, actually."

He slowly winds his way through a tangle of wire and framing.

"So there's a small complication with the paperwork I gave you," I say. "Actually, it's more of an un-complication."

I give a hopeful smile and reach into my bag for my father's papers.

"It turns out my father had already completed papers for your mom's service some time ago," I say.

"I don't understand."

He moves a stack of posts aside, then stands close, reading.

"When Doris got sick," I say, repeating the arguments Pete and my father have made so forcefully, "there was no family here."

Robert breathes heavily into the paper.

"You can't blame my pop for assuming he had to look after your mom. He had no reason to believe you'd come back."

The words feel sharp in my mouth, as if they might puncture.

"The good news," I say, because I'm just going to talk through his silence, "is there's nothing you have to do."

"Can you turn to the next page?" he asks, careful not to put his muddy gloves on them.

I turn to the second page, watching his mouth tighten.

"Mr. Purvis is listed as someone who planned to speak at the service," he says. "Really, Mary? Even if he weren't dead . . . Mr. Purvis?"

"What?"

I quickly read the page.

"Your father thought Mr. Purvis would be a great addition to my ma's service?" he asks in disbelief.

"We'll change that," I say. "The rest is pretty standard."

I haven't actually looked at the papers, but I know Pop always goes traditional. Robert continues reading.

"I don't know any of these casket bearers," he says, his shoulders rising. "Can you turn to the next?"

I flip to the last page, staring at the words because I can't bear to look at Robert.

"The Sweet Adelines?" he asks.

"They're the singing group your mom was a part of."

"I know who they are," he says. "A couple of them have been coming to the house and my ma keeps asking me to send them away."

"They've been preparing hymns for the service," I say. "It would upset them if . . ."

"They've been upsetting my mother," he says. "And frankly, they've been pretty rude to me."

I look for the man I sat with in the rodeo stands.

"You can make this easy for everyone," I say.

He takes off a glove and snatches the papers.

"These plans don't look a thing like the service I want to give her," he says, gripping them so hard they crinkle. "God, Mary, I'm surprised you'd do this!"

"Do what?"

"Let your dad talk you into this."

His glove slips to the ground.

"Actually, I'm not surprised," he says. "I don't know why you let people boss you around like a child."

"You have both sets of papers," I say, my voice quivering. "Do what you want with them."

I don't wait to hear another word because I'm already crossing the street.

26

WHEN I GET TO the basement, I'm furious. My jaw aches where my teeth have been clamped together. I slip on a double pair of latex gloves and rush to get Mr. Purvis ready. The wheel of the gurney catches on the door frame as I roll the body out of the cooler. Tears squeeze out the corners of my eyes.

I turn on the water and wash Mr. Purvis's hair with baby shampoo. I'm careful not to press my fingers in with too much force. Sometimes the head is soft like an overripe melon and I have learned from past mistakes. *Concentrate,* I think. The familiar movement helps me relax, and I'm gentle with his thin, brittle hair, careful not to get shampoo in his eyes.

I like the smile I've given him. I look through Mr. Purvis's belongings to find the photo his family brought. I study the way he styles his thinning hair. After I comb it to one side, I trim his yellowed and crumbling nails and paint them the palest pink to create a look of health.

Normally I love the finishing work, the final touches where I feel most like I'm creating a work of art. This morning, though, my hands shake and I can't focus. How could Robert turn on me so quickly when I'm the only one in this town who's stuck up for him?

I tie a plastic bib around Mr. Purvis's neck and pick up a syringe filled with pink gel that I can insert into the tip of his nose, cheeks, ears, and eyebrows to add a little plumpness. I can't stop thinking of the conversation with Robert and wish I hadn't gotten in the middle of it. I don't like how this morning's stress has invaded my workspace. I should be thinking about Mr. Purvis, who I've just plumped up so much he doesn't look at all like his photo.

I set down the syringe and try to see what I've done. It's something about the eyes, about the crease on the one side of his mouth. Or maybe I used too much filler in that line between the eyebrows. I'd meant to make him look less haggard, and frankly, less dead, but I've lost something about his natural expression. I push on the skin to let some of the fixer escape, thin his face out a bit. It feels good to push down hard with my thumb.

I squeeze a ball of shaving cream into my palm, rub the foam between my hands, and let out a long breath. I spread the shaving cream about his beard area, dabbing carefully above the lip.

"Are you talking to yourself?"

Shaving cream slips into Mr. Purvis's nostrils. "God, Pop, could you knock? What if I'd had the razor in my hand?"

"You were far away."

"It's called working."

"Your talk with Robert didn't go well?"

"No."

I rest my hand beneath Mr. Purvis's chin, turning his head and gently pressing his skin flat before I stroke with the razor.

"Did he agree to go with the original plans?"

"I don't know," I say. "He's going to do what he's going to do."

I shave the other side, then work carefully around his mouth and chin where the skin isn't as smooth.

"I'm surprised he wouldn't want to make things easier for himself," Pop says.

"I don't want to talk about it."

"He'll come through. You'll see."

"Pass me that hand towel, would you?" I say.

I dab Mr. Purvis's face dry.

"I should have handled this myself," Pop says.

"Can we stop talking about this?"

I pinch off some mortuary wax and roll it between my fingers, warming it until it's malleable. With a thin spatula, I cover any signs of suturing. I fill in cuts and an abrasion on the back of Mr. Purvis's hand and some others along his arms. He was a scab picker. After, I smooth the wax and create featherlike lines to give the appearance of natural skin.

"Should be a big turnout today," Pop says.

I search through the makeup box, find the moisturizer and apply it to Mr. Purvis's hands and face. I open various jars of pancake foundation, mixing colors together to match his skin tone. I dab with a brush over the bruising where an IV had been inserted, smooth the color around his face and receding hairline.

"The last of our town's heroes," he says.

"Don't block my light, Pop," I say, adding lip balm and then just a touch of pink. *No one wants Grandpa to look like Liberace,* a phrase Pop taught me when I first began this work. I look up.

"My light, Pop?"

He steps aside.

I turn back to Mr. Purvis, adding warmer colors to his cheeks, chin, knuckles, and eyelids. It gives the impression that there's still blood circulating. I add brown to the eyelids, just enough to make them pop. A little red, a little dark tan, some rouge on the forehead, cheeks, and nose. It almost looks like he's come back to life. This is the sign that lets me know I'm done, the fear that he'll sneeze or open his eyes or rub a hand across his face and ruin my work.

I brush baby powder over his skin to set the final look and help with the odor. There is no more sign of his yellow skin, yellow eyes, bruises, or scratch marks. I look once again at the photo, impressed at the similarity.

"Pop, you're hovering."

"Mentoring."

"Come on. I can feel your breath on my neck. That's hovering."

And then in a softer voice he says, "You're very good at restoration, Mary. An artist."

"I guess this one came out okay," I say, untying the bib. I set the makeup box aside and remove my gloves. "Do you like what I did with the mouth?"

"It's very Mona Lisa," he says. "Maybe a little too much expression."

"I kind of like it," I say. "Anyway, too late for changes. I already used Super Glue."

Pop checks his watch. "About time to get him dressed," he says.

We stuff his soft, fluid-filled limbs into sleeves and leg holes, even the underclothes, though no one would notice the difference. My father loops and straightens the tie while I prepare his jacket.

I cut a slit in the back of it so I can dress him without a lot of lifting. And then I secretly snip off a single button, the spare sewn to the inside breast pocket. It seems fitting to remember him with something so deeply hidden.

Together, we transfer Mr. Purvis into the casket, arrange his head on the pillow. I take his wedding ring from the bag where I've kept his photo and glasses, shine it up and place it back on his finger. My father then arranges the hands, left over right at his waist. We stand back and admire our work. By the time of the viewing, no one will see the gaunt and yellow man I've spent these last days with, nor will they see that these vulnerabilities are what I like most about him.

We slide the casket onto the gurney and my father begins to roll it up the ramp to our parlor.

"Wait just a sec," I say and give the man one last touch of blush. "Okay. Ready."

And we move him together from the basement to the first floor. This is probably the first time in Mr. Purvis's life that he's worn makeup, but then again you don't know. People carry so many secrets.

27

My FATHER AND I wheel Mr. Purvis into the parlor with its faded rose carpeting and two floral couches. Pop finds this room comforting, but I think it's stale, like a club you don't want to join.

We set up the casket under pink lighting to give Mr. Purvis a healthier complexion. Often we have music playing—either from a portable CD player or the upright piano—though everyone knows we don't keep it tuned. Mrs. Purvis, however, has requested that there be no music. She says the people coming today won't be able to hear one another if there's background noise.

As my father puts Mr. Purvis's name on the placard outside the room, I set up bouquets near the casket—fragrant carnations, mums, lilies, all designed to mask the smell of death, an illusion we can only continue for so long. After the funeral, what were once favorite flowers of the dead or bereaved will become reminders of the sorrow and the vague smell of formaldehyde and rot.

Little things bother me today: a picture on the wall tilts to the left, but when I try to straighten it, it tilts to the right. The casket is also off center but too heavy to move. I keep feeling like I'm hearing the phone, hoping it's Robert so we can clear things up.

The room is chilly but my father is careful about our heating bills. I call to him as he arranges rows of folding chairs in front of the casket.

"Pop, do you really want it as cold as the prep room up here?"

"The room will heat up when it fills with people."

"You can't try to squeeze pennies everywhere."

"When it's your business," he says, "you can run it any way you like."

Such a comment used to send me into a panic. I never wanted to inherit the funeral business, or even be a part of it for this long. But like most who stay in Petroleum, my vision of the future has narrowed. Pop and I each grab an end of a metal table, move it to the corner of the room, and unfold the legs.

He passes me one end of a peach-colored cloth, and together, we spread it over the table. Then we set items on top—a framed photo of Mr. Purvis, a guest book, and a brief biography of the man, as written in his obituary. There are bereavement pamphlets, prayer cards, and details concerning the burial this afternoon. There is also a platter filled with small chocolate bars, always the most popular feature of our services.

Soon, we see a hand with a pocketbook hanging from its wrist reaching through the velvet drapes we use to partition off the parlor. The viewing isn't to begin for another twenty minutes, but the widow has come early. She is so slight, the curtains seem to push back against her.

Pop weaves through the chairs.

"Mrs. Purvis," he says in a way that expresses everything he's learned about grief and comfort and welcoming guests into this space.

He takes her gloved hand so very gently.

"Are you ready to see him?" he asks.

They walk in short, slow steps toward the casket. As she gets closer to her husband, she begins to tremble. Pop stays only a moment before giving her time alone.

He's told me how he likes finding the balance each customer desires between consoling and offering privacy. And he knows the only pain he can take away is the overwhelming demands of those first few days; the rest has to run its course, and often its course is a lifetime.

Mrs. Purvis touches her husband's hand, withdraws, then gingerly returns. As Pop finds the tie he's tossed on the parlor couch, I walk over to him with a carnation to put in his button-hole. After I pin it, I pat my hand against his chest—this is how I apologize for being cranky with him earlier—and he nods, approving of the flower's color.

Another elderly woman squeezes through the heavy velvet, complaining of the chill.

"I told you," I whisper to Pop.

As he greets her, I part the drapes and tie them at the sides of the doorway.

The widow is still beside the casket, holding her husband's hand. The second woman holds the widow at the crook of her arm. Together they look at Mr. Purvis.

"Is he smiling?" the second woman asks. "Oh, dear Lord, he's smiling."

Guests file in. I direct them toward the registry book and let them know they can leave a message for the family there.

I've laid out a number of ballpoint pens with our funeral home's name and number stamped on them in large, gold letters, hoping some will disappear into purses and breast pockets. Every gathering is an opportunity to advertise. Our only real competition is the funeral home forty-five minutes east. Even though their embalmer often leaves people looking badly taxidermied, their business offers cheaper rates, and we can't afford for them to take away potential customers.

My father greets the guests at the back of the room, but mostly it's a silent affair, brief whispers and hands touching, offers of condolence, some sitting and praying. Several cluster around the chocolates. Mr. Purvis's smile is the talk of the room.

The doorbell rings, and Pop discreetly leaves the service to answer it. I poke my head into the hallway and see Robert. He looks weary, rattled.

I listen to hear if he asks for me.

"It feels like it might be soon," he tells Pop. "I don't know what I'm supposed to do."

"Sometimes there's nothing to do."

"She's not afraid of dying," Robert says, looking embarrassed but desperate to be sharing this. "She's afraid of suffocating."

My father, who can still surprise me, invites him in, presses his hand to Robert's, and says how sorry he is.

"She doesn't want to go to the hospital," he says, "but it's the only thing I can think to do."

"Yes, I understand," Pop says. "How about I stop by after the service? I've let too many days go by without a visit to Doris."

I hear in his suggestion the need to get back to Mr. Purvis's viewing. Robert finally notices me and looks only briefly. The force he displayed earlier is gone, but I'm still hurting too much to approach him.

My father looks at me as well, then over my shoulder at the curious guests. When he turns back, there are quiet words between them and then Robert is on his way.

"What did he want?" I ask, as if I hadn't been listening.

"It's not an easy thing to watch someone's last days," he says, walking back to the parlor.

Most of the guests, if they're not in the hallway, are gathered by the velvet drapes. The widow, however, holds a vigil beside her husband. She has taken out her hearing aids, set neatly on the casket, so that nothing else interrupts their final moments together.

28

I LEAVE EARLY FOR THE cemetery, to set up before others arrive. My van is filled with folding chairs, rolled-up plastic carpeting, and flowers, most left over from the viewing, to arrange around the burial site. Robert is at the back of his mother's driveway, stacking rolls of wire mesh. I drive past slowly. He sees me but turns back to his work.

What I'm beginning to understand is how lonely I've been, a loneliness I'd gotten used to, a way of living that—after this brief glimpse into the possibility of a different life—I can no longer bear.

I cross the highway, then a dried-up creek, and finally, two cattle guards. The burial ground is filled with a hodgepodge of markers—large headstones with professional etching ordered through our catalogs, but mostly a variety of cheaper, more creative markers from when the town had just come into being. There are crosses made of two-by-fours, license plates, and even sections of the highway's guardrail with names scored into them.

I have always loved the near-perfect square Pop and I have made of this space, marked by a chain-link fence to keep out the cattle. When I try to get out of my van, the wind leans against the door. I push too hard, and the door slaps into the fence. A mule deer, spooked by the noise, scurries over a hill.

Cold nips at my neck, and I wish I'd worn a hat. I can smell the snowstorm on its way. Since I was a little girl I used to come here regularly in high boots, my father nearby with a shovel and a shotgun, to clear the field of sagebrush and rattlesnakes. He used to shoot the snakes and hang them, still twitching, over the fence. Later, when he was finished with his work, he'd cut off the rattles, which I would save in an old cigar box. I still keep that box full of rattles in a kitchen drawer, behind the matches.

What always struck me about clearing out the sage, rabbitbrush, and greasewood was how the silvery green of new growth would return so quickly. It's as if the land can't sustain a human imprint for long and any evidence is gone in a season.

Across the cemetery, there are unmelted mounds from the last snowfall and taller drifts at the windiest corner. Pop and I should have come yesterday with our shovels to clear a level path for the elderly, who can lose their footing.

In this field, you can see the history of our town—the poor man's burials, the many graves for stillborn and young children, the entire Flint family who died in the Great Rimrock Fire, and the tattered basketball jersey above Eddie Golden's headstone.

Has Robert visited his brother's grave? Has he ever sat here and talked helplessly to a stone? I wonder if I will ever know, if we'll speak again.

I pick up pieces of trash and straighten the faded plastic wreaths. On the western corner, the only place in this field that isn't flat, the stones of the Heesacker brothers—Charlie and

Sam—slip closer and closer together with each rain as if, even after death, they need to lean their heads together and gossip. I pluck a weed from their shared plot.

I am procrastinating, always shy about visiting my mother.

We keep her grave nice, a rare bush planted and watered beside it, the overgrowth cut back. The stone's inscription, LOVING WIFE AND MOTHER, feels like Pop's fantasy since she only knew me as something fat in her belly.

When I was younger, teachers tried to comfort me on the days mothers were invited to class to help make gingerbread houses or other holiday projects. And I tried to tell them I was fine. That I didn't grow up without. My father taught me so much, how to be self-sufficient and unafraid of hard work. "If you think for a minute that I missed out on a woman's touch," I once told a teacher, "look how I spend entire days playing makeup and dress-up."

I wanted so badly for a teacher to laugh at my funeral humor. I wanted to push back against pity, against the idea that I'd turned out stunted and strange.

But the truth is, I always felt the empty space when I saw girls browsing through their mother's pocketbooks, reaching for scented lotions and compacts that opened up to little mirrors and pressed powder. And I do wonder, though I insist to Pop that I don't, how our family might have been different if she'd remained with us. If I'd had memories of my mother telling me about menstrual cycles, lending me her sweater or earrings, waiting up till I got home safe. I wonder if I would be better at making friends, at finding love. I wonder what she'd say if I told her about Robert.

Sometimes I try to imagine my mother's hands on me through her belly, the sound and vibration of her voice when I floated inside her womb, wondering if anything about that brief time we had together is still with me.

I tuck my hands into my armpits. I always feel silly after visiting my mother's grave, wishing we weren't strangers. Wishing I had a single memory of her instead of standing here, dumb.

29

PASTOR LUNDY WAVES HELLO as he opens the double-wide gate at the back of the chain-link fence. We quietly get to work. He moves out the machinery he used to dig the grave, and I unroll the grasslike carpet to define the space for our service. Together we arrange flowers and folding chairs until we see the procession of cars and trucks with their headlights on. Led by my father's black pickup and the giant flag blowing in the wind, they travel under the speed limit, the number of vehicles a sign of the respect Mr. Purvis holds in our town. In that line of mourners, I see Slim's school bus, nearly gray with dried mud and empty of children. Though I don't guess he was a close friend, some come to funerals for their own reasons—a reminder of the brevity of life, a chance to socialize, the promise of coffee and baked goods after the service.

The vehicles wind along the outside fence, and I walk out to greet the mourners, signaling where they should stop, and making sure there's room to get the casket out of the hearse.

When Pop steps out, he reminds the drivers to turn off their headlights, or the end of the service becomes all about dead batteries and jumper cables.

"You look good, Pop," I say.

"I used soap," he says and winks.

The first few snowflakes begin to fall as Pop helps to round up the casket bearers—old men with curved backs and carnation boutonnieres, who can only lift the casket but for pride and their feelings, likely never shared, for the man inside of it. They carry the plain box with careful, labored steps.

I help the widow out of the car, trying not to rush her.

"A blizzard's coming," she says. "These low clouds, the ache in my knees."

She is out of breath and struggles two-handed to hold a heavy bouquet of lilies, finally letting me take them from her. Her children and grandchildren follow, and the line of mourners grows, many wearing sheepskin coats, itchy wool pants, and Scotch caps with the earflaps down. I set the lilies at the altar.

"Such a nice touch," Mrs. Purvis says about the carpet as I help her to a chair in front.

It always dawns on me, just about now, as the heavy casket is maneuvered from truck to carriers to gravesite, that I was the last to see the person who has passed. I was the last to see the secret items tucked into the casket—a lucky penny, a pack of Marlboros, a bundle of racy photos, a fishing rod, and for Mr. Purvis, his old, black lunch bucket. I saw the widow slide it beside her husband's leg shortly before we closed the casket.

Guests are occupied with talk of snow. *Got chains on your tires yet? Shovels at the front and back doors? Sacks of oats and salt tied up and stored? Have you filled up with extra gas and planned a pathway to the livestock?*

Winter is serious business here. Last year, the snowdrifts were as high as the eaves of most houses. Once neighbors dug out, they had to trundle in waist-high snow to reach the livestock. Many had cattle stepping right over fences as if they weren't there, and some smothered in the deep drifts, ranchers unsure of their losses until the melting snow uncovered the carcasses.

People talk more about the weather than the loss of Mr. Purvis, not because he didn't matter to them but because those are feelings most around here keep to themselves. Pop and I take our places in back, behind the chairs, watching for anyone or anything that needs attention. I see Pete pull his white Ford beside the fence. Every guest turns to greet him. He acknowledges each with a look or a handshake, and me by raising his gloved fingers and one eyebrow. I take it as a reminder of the pressure I'm under to do things his way.

The guests stand inside what appears to be a fallen cloud. White sky, white winter skin, white exhaled breath as Pastor Lundy welcomes everyone, naming each of the relatives. He bends before their chairs, pressing his gloved hands into theirs, and saving his warmest greeting for the widow.

The pastor has tried hard to build a congregation, but many in this community don't feel God's presence in the confined space of a building, or in the hands of a pastor, just a man. Instead, they experience God in the magnificent earth and sky, in the first sunlight over the rimrocks, in the blue, blue snow at twilight, in the care they invest in this land and its creatures— never a guarantee of a return for their labor, forever at the mercy of a force greater than themselves.

Funerals, then, are Pastor Lundy's biggest audience. He

stands before the casket now and looks out at the snow-dusted guests. "The man we honor today was quite a handyman," he says. "I think everyone here has had something fixed by him."

The widow's shoulders rise. I don't think she or her husband thought of him as the man taking odd jobs. That was only to keep his family going. But he was not that. A handyman. Even though he did that work for two decades.

Pastor Lundy opens his Bible and reads from Ecclesiastes. "To every thing there is a season, and a time to every purpose under the heaven; a time to be born, and a time to die; a time to plant, and a time to pluck up that which is planted."

There are no tears. This death is not a surprise. It's the kind of death people prefer—expected after a long life with many friends, a blessing to be free from illness and pain.

"Let us pray."

Heads bow. Some close their eyes, but most use this time to see who's here and who isn't. Children kick at stray piles of snow. Pete tries again to catch my eye, but I pretend not to notice. Instead I watch my father's wind-chapped face and clouds of breath as he says, "Amen."

And now the pastor calls on Mrs. Purvis to say some words about her husband. She stands before the guests in a funny hat, clear she rarely wears one as she's constantly touching and adjusting it. She unfolds something from her pocket, shoulders slumped, no words. Snow dusts the piece of notebook paper, and still she says nothing, but pulls her shoulders straight, her mouth tight. Whatever emotion she had when she wrote on this piece of paper, she will not show it now.

"Me and Al have only left Petroleum once in our lives. We went to a wedding in a big city that lit up at night. We saw all we were without—malls, neon lights, stylish clothes. People teased us about our lot, and when we came home we saw, in comparison, what a small house we live in, the mismatched furniture and dishes, the wind showing us where all the leaks and cracks are. I was glad to be home. The truth is we don't need as much as people tell us we need."

A small child tugs at his mother's coat.

"Albert, like a number of you, spent many winters at the hotel. He used to call it boarding school, and he referred to his room as his dorm, where he made lifelong friends. The Petroleum Hotel is where he learned to blow bubbles with gum, how to whistle with two fingers, and how to do back handsprings down the hallway after bedtime, for which he was rightly whipped. This town made him who he . . . was."

She fixes something under her coat and continues. "I know some of you worked with him at the grain elevator when the railroad made its last run through Petroleum. None of us knew then what would become of us or our town. And somehow we've carried on, and I know I'll find a way to carry on after this loss, too."

A snowflake melts on her nose but she refuses to wipe it dry.

"I missed Al this morning. I missed the smell of his coffee at breakfast. I don't drink the stuff—it burns a hole in my stomach—but sometimes I make it just so the house smells like he's with me.

"I miss the way he looks over the newspaper to read me the editorial and then tells me all the ways he disagrees with it because he wants me to know his opinions and he wants to know mine. I miss his little cough whenever he put his head on the pillow. Now falling asleep is too quiet. And in the spring I'll miss him coming inside after he's mown the lawn, tracking cut grass through the house. Most days are made up of simple moments, and he was a part of my sense of comfort and belonging here."

She folds her paper again, finished now, and moves back to her chair without looking up. The pastor reaches out to touch her shoulder but she's already slipped past and doesn't seem to want any more attention drawn to herself or the hat.

The pastor spreads his arms as if reaching around all of us. "We therefore commit the body of Albert Purvis to the ground, earth to earth, ashes to ashes, dust to dust; in the sure and certain hope of the Resurrection to eternal life."

The singing begins. It's a hymn I don't know—usually our customers go for "Great Is Thy Faithfulness" or "A Mighty Fortress Is Our God." The others don't seem to know this one either, not past the first verse anyway, as most are just humming. By the third verse, only the pastor is singing. Over his shoulder, I see a rattlesnake, head sliced off, hanging over the fence, and wonder who will keep the rattle.

Snow melts on the empty metal seats as it lands, and guests begin to set flowers on the casket. A small child sets a snowball there and gets smacked on the bottom—the first tears of this service.

30

AT THE CLOSE OF the service, those who carried the casket place their boutonnieres on top of it. Most have come
from work, their hair matted with dust and sweat and flecks
of hay. Larry Rogers is among them, and I look at both gloved
hands until I see an empty pocket of leather the missing finger
would have filled.

The pastor lowers Mr. Purvis into the ground with the crane.
After, Pop shakes hands with guests, while I walk inside the
chain-link fence, collecting trash, plugging divots, folding chairs,
rolling carpet. The pale sun climbs higher in the sky, though the
air is dramatically colder than only a few moments ago.

The widow, escorted at each elbow, takes small, slow steps
toward the flurry of these next few hours—all the guests and
condolences and food. But none of this is closure or even reality,
which will be much quieter, like walking through the same motions of your old life and having none of it feel familiar.

This is what I can't help but think as I see her hunched figure in the backseat of a truck. That when the flowers have wilted and the neighbors' plates of baked goods have been washed and returned, Mrs. Purvis will eat alone by her husband's empty chair, sort through mail that still comes in his name, and what does she do with all the quiet? Maybe she can't get out of her mind the stranger in the other hospital bed, forever behind the drawn curtain, the only one in the room when her husband died. Maybe she hates that she never learned his name or the name of the nurse who rubbed circles into her back until someone she knew arrived. Maybe she looks at the beautiful notes of sympathy she's received and wonders how those same, heartbroken friends can return so quickly to conversations about gas prices and basketball scores, as if the world were still the same.

"Good work today," my father calls out over the noise of the crane, waving thanks to Pastor Lundy, who gets paid extra to fill the hole.

"Can I help you with the chairs?" Pete asks, already lifting one and collapsing it flat.

I can hardly look at him.

"Did you do what you had to do?" he asks, reaching for a second chair.

My yes is as sharp as the words he asked me to speak to Robert.

"That's a girl," he says.

"Will I see you at the Purvises?" Pop asks.

"I'll stop in," he says. "Can't stay long."

He turns to me with a pleased smile, each arm passed through several flattened chairs.

"I'll leave these beside your van," Pete says.

My father, who's been rolling the carpet, tries to stand up when his knee catches. He tries again and slips on an icy patch.

"Do you need help?" I call, racing over.

"No," he says, grimacing as he stands. "Let's finish up here."

I watch him favor one leg as he helps move chairs and fake grass. Last of all, we collect the flowers Pop will deliver to Mrs. Purvis.

"How's your knee?" I ask him.

"Fine," he says. And then an admission, "It'll be just fine."

"This was a nice service," I tell Pop as he bundles lilies and mums in his arms.

"Yes," he says. "A good one."

He hands me a bouquet, the petals cold and wet against my skin.

"Why the lunchbox?" I ask as we walk toward the hearse.

He drops a flower but doesn't bend down for it.

"Albert used to keep it by the front door, ready to head out to the old job," Pop says. "I guess she wanted to remind them both that, somewhere inside, he is still that man."

You see fliers sometimes about seminars that'll retrain workers for new jobs. Mostly they want you to learn how to use a computer and relocate to a bigger town. The guys you see walking ahead of us toward their trucks, that's not who they are. Ask most of these guys what they do for a living and they'll name jobs they haven't done in over twenty years. Their bodies hold the memory of their former work, like phantom limbs.

"I hope Doris has this kind of turnout," I say, as Pop opens the back of his truck.

"Each funeral is different," he says, which is his way of saying Doris will likely pay the price for the town's feelings about Robert.

The wind tears petals from our flowers as we hurry to lay them inside. Then I follow my father's flag back to town.

I can't help but think it sometimes, how he and the pastor and I are literally burying Petroleum. Every day there's work for us at the funeral home means the community has become a little smaller. One more home gone dark. One more truck rusting in a yard.

Pop takes the road to the Purvises' house while I head home, past the unemployed, forever lingering outside the diner. One last turn to Crooked Hill Road, and I find the upper windows of the hotel lit up with one glum face looking out during what I assume is homework time. When I pull into our driveway, there are more cigarette butts.

31

THE DAY AFTER A funeral service, I scrub and vacuum and put everything in order. You'd be surprised at the state of our house after the mourners leave. Already, today, I've had to turn off bathroom faucets, throw out scraps of toilet paper, and itemize petty thefts—missing candles, floral arrangements, whole boxes of tissues, even items from the fridge.

Pop will spend the day making follow-up phone calls and visits. He's good at this, though it wears him out. Comforting stoics is not easy work.

We eat omelets for dinner, needing a break from elk. Our mealtime is quiet. A breather. I don't know what tires me out more about funerals—the bursts of activity or the long periods of waiting. But sometimes it is two or three days before I recover.

Pop pours himself a drink.

"Did you ever check on Doris?" I ask as he starts to leave the room.

He slowly nods his head.

"She was asleep on the sofa when I stopped by. I didn't want to wake her." He swirls his drink. "She's quite thin," he says.

He opens his mouth as if to say more and then closes it again, always cautious when observations cross over into gossip. He starts to walk up the stairs, anxious, I think, for that first sip.

"Robert asked if you might stop over," he says, pausing on a step. "I think he may have decided to go with my ideas for the service."

"Really?"

"He's feeling too many obligations right now," he says. "You can see he's overwhelmed."

"Let me clean up dinner first," I say. "Then I'll check in with him."

I walk casually into the kitchen and bend over in relief. He wants to talk. I'm no longer caught between him and my father. I breathe and breathe.

Once the kitchen is clean, I dress in hat, scarf, and parka.

I call upstairs, "I'm heading out, Pop."

"You have to go to the side door."

"Why?"

I put on my gloves.

"Front room's so crowded with her tarps and easels," he says, "you can't open the door."

Crossing the street, I raise my scarf over my face. Stray snowflakes whiz by here and there. I haven't knocked on the Goldens' door since my trick-or-treating days.

As I walk up the driveway, I nearly trip on chicken wire and netting that have been stacked behind the back wheel of Robert's truck. More lay by the driver's side. I have to watch my feet the whole way. At the side door, I knock lightly.

Robert answers. He's wearing an undershirt and jeans. Without the jacket, he's much thinner with unmuscular arms. He seems to have shaved in bad lighting, a strip of stubble across one cheek.

Before he can speak, Doris calls from another room. "Who's there? Robert? Has someone come to the door?"

I try to speak quietly. "My father said you wanted to talk to me?"

"Robert, is . . . ?" There's a spasm of coughs and heaves for breath.

"Oh, my God," I whisper. "Is she all right?"

"Hold on, Ma," he calls, but the coughing and wheezing continues. "Maybe you'd better come in."

He holds the door open, the memory of our angry words between us as I step inside.

We follow the sound of his mother's coughing.

The wooden floor is slanted, everything on a tilt, and spattered in so many colors of paint as if it's been stepped in, sat in, and tracked about the house. We walk into the living room and the spots of paint continue to the carpet, even the arm of the couch. Doris sits at one end, wearing a green knit cap and the housedress I have seen so often.

The room feels damp, a humidifier misting in one corner. A portable oxygen tank beside the couch sounds like the machine that fills balloons at the fair. Robert props a pillow behind his mother and adjusts a tube in her nose, taking out, then reinserting the little prongs into her nostrils, smoothing the tubes that stretch from her nose and over her ears like glasses.

"There," he says. "Wasn't your worst."

His mother tries to push him aside to see who has come into the room.

"Oh, it's you, Mary," she says in a thin voice that doesn't sound finished with its coughing fit.

Doris leans forward, moving a cup and a bottle of hand lotion to one side of the coffee table but giving up on the pile of newspapers and random clutter.

"I'm not prepared for guests," she says, leaning back into the couch again.

"Oh, I'm not staying," I say.

"Nonsense," she says. "Sit. Sit here."

I step over slippers and a magazine to reach the couch. I sit down at the far end. The fabric is sticky.

Up close, the woman I'm used to seeing through the window has a gray tint to her skin, a rattle in her breath. Her milky eyes look unusually large against such a thin face. There seems to be so little of her beneath all that fabric. But there is a charm to the paint splattered on her housedress and how her face is wiped clean of makeup the way I would see her in my workroom: honest, like the dead.

"I'm sorry for the mess," she says, seeing my fingers pick at the fabric. "I'm sloppy with my acrylics."

Finished paint-by-numbers, some still wet, lean against the baseboard.

"It's like an art gallery in here," I say.

Her smile is tentative, as if trying to decide if I'm giving a compliment or criticism.

"Would anyone like some tea?" she asks.

"Oh, no, thank you," I say.

"Ma, no. That's too much trouble."

But she gets up anyway, slowly, using the handle of a little cart that holds a canister of oxygen. She takes it with her to the kitchen.

"Mind if I make a fire?" Robert calls to her.

"Yes, do that," she says.

Her steps are so tiny it takes a long time for her to cross the room.

Robert crouches before the fireplace, arranging logs into a teepee.

"Mary," he says. "I'm sorry about . . ." He lowers his voice. "I shouldn't have spoken to you like that."

He jabs at the fire.

"I want to focus on the time I have left with my ma," he says, "I just get frustrated when anything gets in the way of that. This isn't an excuse for my temper."

I can feel the tension ease in my jaw.

"You've changed your mind?" I ask. "You want to use my father's ideas?"

"No," he says. "I'd rather come up with ideas that mean something to me. But of all the people here, I shouldn't have lashed out at you."

The fire, only smoking until now, ignites and Robert warms his hands. His hair is a mess. How can he not want to press it flat with his hand?

"I'm nearly finished with the questions," he says. "And enjoying them too. They've really helped open things up between me and my ma. She's told me stories I'd never heard, and we've been playing music together the last few days. She's trying to decide on her favorite."

"Really?" I ask as the kettle whistles in the other room. "You're listening to music together?"

"I bought her a CD in Agate the other day. I only thought of it because of a question on the form you gave me."

We turn toward the noise of Doris struggling with a tray,

cups and spoons and a sugar bowl clinking. She holds it so low it looks like it might hit her knees.

"Oh, Ma, that's more than you needed to do."

He hurries to take the tray from her.

"That's too much to carry," he says. "And what did you do? Leave your oxygen in the kitchen?"

"I'm all right," she says, but seems relieved to let go of the tray.

Robert looks for a clean space to set it down, and I notice that so much tea has sloshed from the cups, they're mostly empty.

"This is the problem with trying to take care of my mother," he says, catching my eye. "She still insists on doing all the care-taking."

I look at Robert, both of us bruised and glad for each other's company. He puts a hand on his mother's back to guide her. "Sit in this chair, Ma. I don't want you too close to the fire." As he retrieves the oxygen cart and gets his mother settled in again, I reach for a cup.

"This one's mostly full," I say, trying to make do.

Robert tries to reinsert the tubes into his mother's nose, as she fights him. "No. I'm telling you no. I don't need that right now."

Her hands bat him away.

"Stop fussing over me," she says. "We're having tea right now."

Robert picks up a cup that's all but empty and sitting in a pool of liquid. Doris only now sees what has happened, and I hear "Stupid, stupid" under her breath.

"Well, that's a relief," Robert says. "Can I admit it?" He gives a wry smile. "I kind of prefer wine at this hour."

Doris swats at him again. And, more upset, says, "We don't have wine."

"I'm going to have a look in Dad's old work area," he says, standing. "He used to stash bottles in the back corner."

Once he's gone, Doris and I sit stiff and quiet, machines gurgling, wind clawing at the house.

"I was afraid you were going to be one more person bringing over a casserole," she says.

"A casserole?"

"People like to show up with them at the end," she says. "I'd rather they didn't."

"You don't like casseroles?"

"Other times in my life I would have enjoyed so many visitors and so much food," she says. "But I get tired easily now. Poor Robert has to keep making excuses for me."

"I can leave if you're tired," I say.

"No. Stay," she says. "I suspect you're here to help Robert make arrangements."

I pick a piece of lint and a stray hair from the couch, then wish I weren't holding them.

"Don't feel uncomfortable, dear," she says.

She looks into my eyes and I sense her trusting me to see her at her most exposed. We acknowledge this silently and then look away. I cross my legs and clasp my fingers together in my lap.

"Look what I found under the workbench," Robert announces as he walks in carrying two bottles with a third tucked under his arm. "Vintage by now."

"But I don't have a corkscrew," Doris says.

"I have a ballpoint pen," I say.

And Robert, laughing, says, "I have a house key."

"Do you have a coat hanger?" I ask.

"I have a fork," Doris says.

Robert reaches into his pocket and smiles as he pulls out a jackknife.

"I'll have it open in two minutes," he says.

But Doris has passed me a pair of scissors, and we are already working on the other bottle. It's become a race with cork crumbling into our laps and onto the carpet.

"You're going to beat him," Doris says to me.

It feels good—carving, gouging, pounding. I hold up the bottle I've been working on and call out, "First!"

Robert laughs at the crumbled cork in my lap. He collects three wineglasses from a china cabinet, blows dust out of them, and pours for each of us.

"A toast," he says.

He raises his glass, stuck for words.

"To good company," Doris says.

The room fills with relieved smiles as glasses clink. Mine has a good bit of cork in it.

"Well now," Robert says. "I didn't have high hopes for this wine but it's quite good."

"A man reveals his heart," Doris says, "by where he spends his money."

Robert, hearing the lack of strength in her voice, steps beside her and attaches the oxygen. This time she doesn't fight.

The fire has faded to an orange glow and Doris stares into it, gloomy, hypnotized.

"I wish," she says and stops, oxygen buzzing.

"What do you wish?" I ask.

She takes a long sip and shakes her head.

"Tell us, Ma."

"It's not possible," she says. "It's just . . . I'd like to be with both of my boys one last time."

She covers her face with her thin hand, the veins blue and raised.

I think of Doris posing with her dead child and her living child. I wonder now if the story was true and there was actually a photo taken. My fingers pick at the painted fabric.

"I'm just babbling," she says. "Don't pay any attention to me."

She finishes her glass and holds it out for a refill. Robert opens the bottle he'd been working on with his jackknife and pours another round for each of us.

"It's snowing," I say, pointing my glass to the window.

My tongue feels thick, relaxed. Doris spits some cork into a napkin, and we both laugh.

"Want me to get the fire going again?" Robert says softly to his mother.

"That would be nice, Robbie," she says.

I smile at the name.

"I think I better use the ladies' room," Doris says, removing the nose piece. She takes her time standing, takes slow steps.

Robert goes outside to get more wood, and I rise to watch snow settle on the cottonwoods planted close to the house, and farther out, on machinery, barbed wire, and the grain elevator.

When Robert returns, he stands in the doorway, cheeks red and wet, snow clinging to his curls.

I turn toward him. "I know the West Coast has the ocean," I say, "but I'll bet not many places do snow better than Petroleum."

Robert puts another log on the fire and sorts out the kindling until the flames catch.

"There's a lot I missed about this place," he says. "The big sky, nighttime dark enough for stars, wild animals grazing right outside your door, only the sound of wind at night." He pauses, gives a sad smile. "Wind and oxygen machines."

He finds a pillow from a nearby chair and makes a seat for himself on the floor.

"When I was away," he says. "I could see how much of the town was in me. I like to eat in quiet. I like to take long walks and not know where I'm going. I'm forever searching the ground for fossils and plants. Forever searching the horizon for movement."

He removes his boots, then his socks, placing them near the heat to dry. Once the fire's burning bright again, he stretches his legs. There are dark hairs on the tops of his toes, and I think, *What a terribly intimate thing that I know how they look. I've seen a lot of bare feet but, lately, not many with blood running through them.*

"You're smiling," he says. "Why?"

"I'm not smiling."

Now he smiles, too. Fire glows against the dark walls.

"Hey, do you think I should check on your mom?"

"Yeah," he says. "If you don't mind."

32

I RUN MY HAND ALONG the wall of the dark hallway. At the end is a dim light and a mostly closed door. I'm nervous as I peek inside, not sure what it is I'm hearing. The room is lit with just a single lamp beside the bed. And I smile when I spy Doris dancing in a long red scarf. She watches herself in the mirror and hums something like a two-step.

She is tethered by a long tube attached to a much bigger oxygen machine than what she uses in the living room. It bubbles and vibrates against the floor.

In the dark, she can pretend the tubes aren't there. The dark hides her sharp shoulder blades and collarbone. Hides the clumsiness of her steps, how each sway is nearly a stumble.

She hums quick-quick, slow-slow.

I imagine the scene Doris might see in her mind—a smoky room at the old VFW before it closed down, the dance hall decorated with streamers, men leaning against the wall. Maybe

Mr. Golden when he was still someone she could love. Maybe someone she overlooked.

I find I am swaying to her song in the hallway. My body feels good, loose. For a moment, Doris interrupts the rhythm to gasp for breath. I am about to intervene when she begins to hum again, flirting with the mirror. She grabs a strand of beads and pulls them over her head, still dancing. Quick-quick, slow-slow.

I step just inside the door. The room smells sour.

"You're a beautiful dancer," I say softly.

The humming stops, and I wish I hadn't spoken.

"Too much wine," she says, removing the scarf and letting it fall to her dresser.

"Maybe we should drink wine more often," I say.

She rests on the unmade bed.

"Will you sit for a moment?" she asks.

I balance clumsily next to her. The cord that crosses from her nose to the machine is cold where it touches my skin. Her neck pulses, the two-step still moving through her.

"You'll make me look pretty, I hope," she says.

She touches the plastic beads on her necklace.

"I will," I say.

"My hair used to look better than this," she says and feels the frayed bangs sticking out the front of her knit cap. "It grew back as someone else's hair. Dark and wavy. It was never dark or wavy."

She removes the hat, which falls to her lap.

"I have curlers," I say. "Blow-dryers, hair spray. A regular beauty salon."

"You'll see my scar," she says. "I've always been ashamed of it."

I hold her knotted hand.

"I should have danced more," she says. "I should have worn my good jewelry. I kept waiting for a special occasion."

She coughs, so little wind moving in or out. She touches her chest as if to find air.

"I should have stood up more for Robert," Doris says, turning to me. "He was such a bright boy. He could have finished high school in Petroleum."

"Except he ran away," I say but regret sharing the gossip I knew.

"No," Doris says. "I didn't know how to protect him so I bought a ticket to the West Coast and drove him to Agate to board the bus. At the time it made sense."

We sit, holding hands in the dark.

"I'm afraid," she whispers.

I don't tell her that I am, too.

The machine rumbles through my socks to my knees. I watch Doris work the fingers of her other hand into the green knitted cap. The wine has turned tart in the back of my throat.

"Ma? Mary?"

Doris places her other hand on top of ours and taps softly. Then she takes the oxygen from her nose and sets the end of it on the bed, where it wheezes against the covers.

Robert's voice comes closer, down the hallway. "Is everything all right?"

"Yes," I say.

I help Doris stand and replace the warm cap, adjust it a little. I leave the beads around her neck.

"I wonder if it will be like sleep," she says.

We take slow steps through the hallway, back to the living room, my hand on her ridged spine. Out the window, snow falls like we're inside one of those toy globes.

"I wonder if I'll see the blizzard," she says settling back into the chair.

Robert helps to connect her tubes. I put a pillow behind her. We do this without speaking. Only the sound of our breath together, the fire crackling, snow patting the window.

Robert settles back on his pillow in front of the fire. His leather jacket is thrown over the couch, and I lay my head against it. Inhale. It smells pungent, like mink oil. I pretend the jacket is his chest I'm lying against, that I'm sliding my fingers gently against him, feeling for the scar.

One by one, we fall asleep, me last of all as I blink about the room filled with burnt logs, wine, wet clothes, and the dark sweet smell of a life near its end.

33

I AWAKEN TO A MESS of empty bottles and wineglasses, trails of cracker crumbs and cork. Doris on the couch and Robert on the floor in front of the fireplace stir just a bit and then settle back to sleep. I quietly gather my shoes and coat until I'm in the hallway, where I dress in a hurry.

I slip out the side door and into the white wind, trudging along the darkened street. I don't know what time it is, but it's late enough for the Pipeline to be closed for the night. I stand in the middle of the road as my town sleeps and smile at the memory of Doris dancing, of Robert's bare feet.

The wind stings but I want to feel every nerve ending. I open my mouth to the sky and laugh out loud. Laugh for the beauty of this night and the drumming I feel inside. The stars spin overhead, and I would dance but I don't know how.

I'm still smiling when I get home. I open the door and hear the TV.

"Pop?"

He's left a note on the stairs: MADE YOU DESSERT. UP FOR A MOVIE?

"Sorry I'm late," I call.

Nothing. Passed out, probably. I remove my coat, my hat, my gloves, and then slowly pull a handful of hair under my nose. It still smells of our time by the fire.

"Just getting in?" Pop asks, and I hear his slippers on the stairs.

"Yeah," I say.

"I should have warned you," he says. "If Doris invites you in, you're staying awhile."

I laugh.

"Did she show you the paintings?" he asks.

"Can't miss 'em."

"Are you hungry by any chance?"

"Depends if we're talking about pumpkin pie," I say.

"You'll have to come and see for yourself," he says, leading the way to the kitchen.

At the table, we sit with mismatched plates. Our slices are so large, if you put them together, it's half the pie. We laugh at the jagged cutting, the pie's lopsided crust, the burnt edges, the watery top.

I wish I could tell him about my time at Robert's. I want him to know something about my heart. How good it feels tonight.

"I added too much nutmeg," he says.

"I think I like it better this way."

"You know," he says. "I think I do, too."

Pop, I want to tell you something true.

This is what I really want to say.

I feel alive.

I want to laugh and cry and stay up all night remembering how this feels.

I watch him take his last bite. I wish we'd eaten more slowly. If we could talk to each other the way we talk about pie. If we could embrace change this easily, laugh so heartily at our mistakes, salute our appetites. I dab at crumbs so we might sit together a little longer.

34

I KNOCK AT THE OPENING of my father's office. He doesn't lift his gaze from the spread of bills.

"I wanted to let you know the Goldens are making other arrangements for Doris's service," I say. "They're planning it together, so the original plans you worked out won't be needed."

I practiced all morning how I'd say this, how I could get it out of my mouth without starting an argument or chickening out.

"If you want to cancel the arrangements," he says, "then you'll have to do it."

"I figured," I say. "Can you give me a list of the people I need to talk to?"

He writes on a piece of paper.

"Wouldn't you rather try changing Robert's mind one more time?" he asks as he hands it to me.

"No, Pop. This is the right thing to do. It's just no fun to do it."

"Who else is he going to choose to help with the service?" Pop asks. "And does he think any of those people will say yes?"

"I don't know," I say. "I haven't seen his plans yet."

He sighs, annoyed. "Well, go get it done, then."

I know Pop doesn't want me to upset the people on this list, but he probably realizes it will put the argument between us to rest. At least that might be a relief. As I wrap my scarf and zip my parka, Pop leans his head into the hallway.

"Before I forget," he says. "Do you know where my suits have gone? I know at least one of them needs cleaning."

"I'll find them when I get back," I say. "Let me get to this list while I still have the nerve."

As I set out for the first house, an ominous cloud hovers so close, Petroleum feels smaller. Darker. At the end of our drive-way, just behind my van, I find a cigarette butt. I kick it into the road, wanting it off our property.

I look at the list. I'll start with the easiest—those who agreed to be casket bearers—surely they'll welcome a chance to get out of any heavy lifting.

"Here it comes," Fritz calls to me.

He stands at the edge of his lawn, motioning down the block.

"That dog's been barking since dawn," he says. "Just barking at the sky. Can't settle himself down. Do you hear it?"

Now that he's pointed it out, all I hear is barking.

"It means a blizzard's on the way," he says.

We both look up to the sky.

"There's another sign," he says. "Right above us. You see?"

Hawks and a snow bunting glide in circles in the dark, morn-ing sky.

"Air pressure's changed," he says. "See how high they are? We've probably got two days, maybe three, before it hits."

"My father taught me that one," I say, crossing the street to him. "When they fly low, it'll be here."

I remove the list from my bag as if I need it.

"I'm running errands this morning," I say. "You're actually my first stop."

"I don't want to buy a plot until I need one," Fritz says.

"I'm not selling anything, don't worry," I say. "A long while back my father had asked you to be a casket bearer for Doris Golden."

"When the time comes," he says. "Good God, she's still painting. I can see her right now."

"No. I mean, you're right. This is just . . . Well . . . There's been a change in plans," I say. "We won't need you to. We don't want you to hurt your hip."

"The fellow with the hair has decided this, hasn't he?"

"He made some changes, yes."

"He's been trouble since he came back," Fritz says. "You could just look at him and know it."

"Well, I don't know if . . ."

"Go on, get on your way," he tells me. "I see you've got a whole list of people to upset before the storm hits."

I figure this is what I'm in for today. On the next street, Mr. Vinter shakes sand on the steps of his grocery while trucks park in front and for almost a block beyond it.

"Storm's coming," he says. "I was up on the rims this morning, looking at the ranches. And all the livestock had their heads turned to the sky. You should go see for yourself."

"I wish I had time," I say.

All the casket bearers I visit show immediate relief that they might avoid lifting in the cold. But that doesn't stop their rage at Robert or their pity for Doris.

The Sweet Adelines are my next stop. I've saved the hardest for last.

One of the singers lives quite a ways out of town, and Pop wasn't sure which of several women replaced Doris at baritone. But the other two live nearby. I look at my list again, but all I'm really doing is stalling in front of Minnie Dent's house.

Until I have an idea. It's so simple, I don't know why I didn't think of it before. I find a hard surface and write a heartfelt note, explaining everything to Minnie, and asking her to relay the message to the others. I don't sign my name. I sign, *Crampton Funeral Home,* so they might assume the note is from my father.

I bend down in front of Minnie's to prop the note inside the storm door when it opens.

"Now what is this you're delivering?" she asks.

"I'm afraid I have some bad news about Doris," I say, standing.

"Oh, dear, has she passed?" Minnie asks. "Here, come inside."

I stand just in the doorway, holding my note.

"No. No," I say. "She's . . . It's . . . There's been a change of plans."

"What kind of change?" she asks.

I offer her the note I've written and realize I'd better just say it.

"Doris's son has made changes to the service and won't be needing"—I take a breath, feel hot—"won't be needing the Sweet—"

"I knew it," she says. "I tried to drop in on Doris the other day and her son just stood there at the door, telling me she needed rest. He wouldn't even let me speak to her myself."

"I guess she's pretty tired."

"He's controlling his poor mother," she says. "He's keeping Doris from what she loves."

I watch my hands.

"Come here, Mary," she says and sits at the polished upright piano. "These are the songs we've practiced for so long."

She begins to play. "It Is Well with My Soul," "How Great Thou Art," "Blessed Assurance." She is obviously the soprano of the group. I hum along, leaning all my weight first on one leg, then the other.

"I'm sorry for all the work you've put into this," I say when she's finished playing. I unfold the note I'd written. "Maybe you could tell the other Adelines."

She takes the note.

"You'll need to tell Kay yourself," she says. "That's just the kind of person she is. She likes to get her information straight."

"She was my music teacher," I say.

"I think she was almost everyone's music teacher," Minnie says, smiling only briefly. "Why don't you go talk to her at the school. She's there now."

Minnie shows me out, and I walk toward the school. The gray cloud that hovered earlier has darkened, casting a shadow in my path, and the old anxiety of being in that building returns. I spent years watching my feet as I walked down one hallway and another, the roar of voices echoing off the walls. It seemed I was the only person not having a conversation between classes. I open the main door and head to the office.

"Mary. Hello," the secretary says. "Minnie called to say you were coming."

"Hello," I say. "I just need to drop off a note for . . ."

"I know who you're here to see," she says. "And you have good timing. This is Kay's planning period."

"I don't want to disturb her," I say. "I could just leave a note."

But the secretary is already calling her over the intercom. She holds up a pointer finger.

"Kay, you have a visitor on her way down to see you," she says. And then to me, "Go on, Mary. You know your way to the music room."

Most of the noise seems to come from the other end of the school, where the cafeteria is, and I'm grateful for the empty hallway. It smells of Lysol and pencil shavings. I touch the tiled walls. I pass crimson pennants, a framed photo of the first students to paint the giant letter *P*, and a mural featuring Dead Eddie's jersey.

I pause outside the door to the music room. Kay Gundersen was a teacher I feared because she demanded perfection and obedience. I feel the dampness in my armpits and behind my hair when I peek inside.

"Mrs. Gundersen?"

She sits at her desk, sprinkling pepper on a hard-boiled egg.

"Come sit here, Mary," she says, nodding to the chair beside her desk. "I've spoken with Minnie."

As she takes a bite of her egg, I turn toward the musical notes drawn on the chalkboard. And as she swallows the last bite, I study the back counter, covered with autoharps and bins filled with recorders, wood blocks, and shakers.

"I want to tell you a story about my friend Doris," she says, wrapping eggshells in a napkin. "Do you know when I first got to know her?"

"No."

"She was living alone. Her husband and her youngest son had left her, and she came here to work at the cafeteria to make a little money."

"I was a student here when she served lunch."

"Yes, that sounds right," she says. "And she asked about more work opportunities so I told her she could help in the music room. She wiped down instruments and set up chairs at first. And then I discovered she was a lovely baritone."

I put my hands in my lap as if I'm still in Mrs. Gundersen's class.

"Do you know why the Sweet Adelines are so close?" she asks. "You love music?"

"No," she says. "It's nothing special to love music. We are close because it takes work—persistence, attentiveness, and trust—to find harmony."

I wonder if she can tell how much I'm sweating.

"I'm sorry we won't have a chance to sing for Doris," she says. "I feel like I may never see her again."

"You can still come to the service," I say.

She shakes her head no, walks me to the door.

"Other way," she says, when I turn deeper into this wing of the school.

"Is it all right if I stop by the art room?" I ask.

"Yes, but your teacher moved on years ago."

"Where to?" I ask. "I always wondered."

"I'm not sure," she says. "Petroleum is not for everyone."

I don't know why I need to see the art room. I just notice that this hallway is quiet right now, and it's the direction my feet chose.

35

THE ART ROOM, WITH its long tables and wall of windows, has remained unchanged since I was a student here. Pinned up about the room, I find familiar projects: studies of hands and faces, light and shadow, still lifes, mosaics. But soon, the kinds of art I never knew existed captivate me: distorted portraits, wire sculptures, collages, and papers, still drying, layered in wax, pastel, and paint.

I wonder how long it will be before these students set their art aside?

I find my old seat—back row, nearest the counter, where empty cans with stewed tomato labels hold paintbrushes and pencils. The only light in the room comes from the soft gray out the windows. The scent of paint, charcoal, and turpentine rouses a deep-rooted longing. Sometimes when I sat back in this corner, the chime would sound, calling us to our next class, and I'd rather be late than not see my idea on paper, even though the idea was always better in my head.

My fingers glide along the huge roll of butcher paper, sparking the old thrill of the blank page—how no ideas became a jumble of vague emotions and images to sort through, how sometimes mindless scribbling lured me someplace deeper, where the hand and pencil could discover what was locked away. I tear off a sheet, touch pencils of different lengths until one feels right. My foot hooks the metal leg of a plastic chair, pulling it from under the table. I'm shaking.

Art, I had convinced myself, was a frivolous way to spend time. This disowned side of me, beaten back, hunches over the long white sheet.

I wait. I wait until the hand and pencil remember their alliance. I wait until they move together, uncoordinated at first, the lines faint. This doesn't look right. Why? I have drawn the memory of a window, flat and square. *No. Look at what you're drawing. Find the lines, the light. Don't watch the hand.* I move my chair to face real windows and try again.

The rough outlines of children huddle there. I feel them wanting to breathe. Faces, blank at first, begin to emerge—one is skeptical, the other proud, the third resigned.

Most will never meet these children who play pretend at the rusted stove, poke sticks down badger and snake holes, dare friends to eat live tadpoles. When these children travel with their parents to bigger towns—to shop for clothing or fill up with gas or sell their cattle—they discover how different they are from the larger world. They feel the press of crowds, the headache brought on by so many colors, so many choices. This strange world they glimpse makes little sense to them. Its people seem too soft, too concerned with trivia, incapable of the strain and sweat required for hard work. And yet many will be lured away by the opportunities they see on

TV, and the town will continue to shrink. It seems there's no way to stop it.

The children here at the window are the last gasp of a town that's fought so hard to hold on to its existence. They know, year to year, the population never rises. For every birth, for every marriage that brings a new spouse to Petroleum, more will die or move away. And these children must decide whether to stake their future here, a decision this community watches and judges.

The decision isn't an easy one. They know from their laptops and TV sets that there are cities where it never snows, where they can dance in nightclubs, where pizzas are delivered right to the front door. And they know their families' struggles—always hoping to dig out of debt, hoping disease and severe weather won't threaten their livestock and crops. Always hoping their equipment, their backs, their marriages last another season.

My hand cramps but refuses to let go of the pencil. I draw roads, a handful of homes and businesses, the cluster of unemployed men, the gray tower in the distance, the ranches beyond it. Then I return to the hotel and draw one more child at that window. A young girl who fears standing so close to the others. She stares from the hotel toward the funeral home, wondering, *Is this what I want?*

We are all feeling the pressure to be loyal, to treasure this inheritance, to fight for it as hard as our parents have. But is this even our fight?

I draw Robert's gnarled crabapple tree, a little house made of scrap lumber in its branches. Where is there a place in Petroleum for the academic, the artist, the dancer, the sensitive soul? I feel something about this town that I don't want to feel. It's as if there's a system in place that prefers one type of person over another, that protects some and lets others fall. Those of us who don't fit in are pressured to tamp down our true nature and desires—become something we're not, or else move along.

A three-tone chime sounds over the intercom—time to change classes. I stand up, quick, noticing how dark the room has grown. I've stayed too long. The hallway fills with the rumble of clomping feet and slamming lockers, students hollering from one end to the other. I return the dulled pencil to the can, shove my chair back under the table, and after only the slightest pause, toss my drawing in the trash. Head down, I merge into a throng of students, head down, head down, until I reach the exit.

Once outside, I gulp air, the musty, wet taste of a storm brewing. Clouds darken and bulge, while the merry-go-round turns on its own, only the wind riding it.

I feel light-headed, unmoored.

I want to talk to my father.

I'm used to puzzling out business decisions with him. What is the easiest way to take a body out of this space? Which body should I restore first? And there was one decision that felt big at the time—Should we leave the severed hand behind if we can't extract it quickly?—though that was more a matter of coming to grips with the only choice we could make. We consult each other often because the questions are unexpected, the answers unclear, and we are willing to get them wrong in order to have company with the consequences.

But can we talk deeply about more than work? Because I don't know what I think about Petroleum, or anything, really, since Robert Golden returned. It's as if this looming storm has moved inside of me—churning, swelling.

"Out of bread and meat," someone calls as he leaves Vinter's grocery. I've been watching the ground and only now notice the trucks, parked two deep, in front of the store.

"Laundry soap, too," calls another.

I'll bet most of Petroleum is in there buying up the last supplies. The clouds hang low and full as if they are touching the rimrocks. Back on Crooked Hill Road, the same dog barks at the sky.

I'm exhausted when I walk through the door. I find my father in his office, nearly hidden among the mess.

"You should see all the trucks parked outside Vinter's," I say.

"You look flushed," he says. "Are you feeling all right?"

"I don't know."

He comes close, touches my forehead when it's my heart that hurts.

"How did it go, talking to the people on the list?"

I exhale and lean against the wall.

"I thought that might be a bad idea," he says. "I got calls from two of the Sweet Adelines today, and they were very upset to be cut from the service."

"Like only their feelings matter," I say.

"Mary, where is this coming from?"

"All day," I tell him, "everyone let me know how bad they feel for themselves."

"Can you understand how people counted on being a part of Doris's tribute? The ladies put a lot of care into their selections."

"That's just it," I say. "I can understand their feelings, but Robert has feelings, too."

"He could have made a more thoughtful decision."

"He's taken time off work to be with his mother," I say. "He watches her fight for every breath. But no one gives him any sympathy. They just act mean and leave their cigarette butts in his driveway."

"Well, now they're in our driveway, too," he says.

"Are you blaming Robert for that?" I ask. "Are you blaming me because I want to treat him with respect?"

"If this is his influence on you, I don't like it."

"You don't like that I have an opinion?"

"Why don't you sit down," Pop says. "I think you might have a fever."

"Maybe this is how I've been feeling for a long time," I say.

The phone rings, and Pop turns his head.

"Don't answer it," I say. "Please don't walk away in the middle of this. I'm trying to talk to you."

"Honey, this is my job," he says. "I'm sorry."

He picks up the phone and I hear the soft, reassuring voice he uses when someone has passed.

I stomp over to the far side of his desk, spotting his wrinkled suit on the floor. I throw the jacket and pants over my arm.

Your. Suit, I mouth.

I stomp out of the office to throw his suit in the hamper.

The other one is already in there, and these will be mine to clean. I am always cleaning up after him. I pace from kitchen to parlor to foyer to kitchen and return to stare at my father until he finally says good-bye to the caller and hangs up.

He looks at me and says only, "Doris."

36

I PULL MY VAN INTO the driveway. Robert, his face thin and unshaven, waits at the side door. His hair, unattended since I last saw him, hangs flat.

"I got here as soon as I could," I say, zipping my coat to the top and opening the back of my van.

I grab the stretcher and he shuts the doors. He leads me into a house that no longer smells of burning logs but of anxiety, powerlessness, and a body that has released its fluids. The living room looks ransacked—drawers open, books and photo albums pulled off shelves. We go back to the bedroom where Doris danced in her red scarf and beads. She is on the bed, curled on her side, hands closed in fists. I lean over her, the machine rumbling beside us.

"I'm sorry for your loss," I say to Robert, then feel silly, like I've quoted from one of our pamphlets.

"Is it possible she's sleeping?" he asks.

Doctor Fischer used to give the official word, but since Petroleum has been without a doctor, that role falls to my father (who had to take a yearlong nursing program in order to sign death certificates) and, with a little fudging on the paperwork, to me.

Robert touches her nightgown, afraid, it seems, to touch her flesh. If he does, he will feel that she has left this life, her skin like a hard-boiled egg, and quickly turning the same gray as the outer covering of the yolk.

I touch her wrist, her neck. Listen. Look into the cloudy eyes. She is so thin, her body will cool quickly.

"I'm sorry," I say.

"It's just that the past many nights, I thought she'd died, the breathing seemed to stop, but then she was up again the next morning asking if I wanted toast or cereal."

Doris had probably asked this question since he was a boy.

Normally I'd put on my latex gloves and get to work removing the body. Instead, we just sit with Doris in this house, where, just upstairs, she used to tuck her boys into bed. Maybe some of their old clothes are still in the dresser drawers. Maybe after they got big, and after they were both gone from this house, she sat in their rooms and held their little T-shirts and jeans.

"It's okay to turn off the oxygen," I say.

He flips the switch. Pauses. Then, so very gently, removes the nose piece for the last time.

A life ends like that. A woman who painted and sang, who danced in secret, who held her dead and her living son, who struggled for breath is now gone from this world.

Robert pats the sheet near her arm. Like the relationship they lived, they are close and yet never quite touching. Always a lonely space between one and the other.

"I finished the paperwork," Robert says.

He reaches for a stack on the bedside table. I take the pages filled with his tight scrawl. There is more detail here than most forms I collect. Scanning quickly, I catch words and phrases that make me certain Robert was the right person to plan his mother's service.

"I looked everywhere for a photo of the three of us," he says.

"So that's what happened to the living room."

"She said she wanted to be together with me and Eddie one last time," he says. "I wanted to make that happen."

He hands me a photo.

"I couldn't find one without my father in it," he says.

I look at the small boys, their smiling parents, and the lie the photo tells of the life they will live.

After Eddie's funeral, Robert tells me, their father disappeared. If there was a note, if there were words, his mother kept them to herself.

"I can't think of a worse time for him to leave you," I say.

"I don't know," Robert says, looking only at his mother's hands.

"You weren't close? Even before?"

"Everything I did seemed to irritate him. I'd be in the tree house and he'd shout how I ought to be playing football with the others."

I touch his back, feel the soft tremor of his breathing. When he raises his head, his hair is a crazy mess. I remove my hand, and the moment I do, yearn to place it there again.

"He even hated the way I ran," Robert says. "My feet would slap too loud against the ground. My arms would flail out to the side. 'Don't run like that,' he would say. 'Jesus Christ, don't run like that!'"

He seems surprised to hear himself shouting.

"I've never told anyone this story," he says, lowering his voice again.

We say nothing for some time, the room so quiet without the gurgle of oxygen.

I tuck the papers and the photo into my bag.

"Have you picked out what you'd like your mother to wear?" I ask.

"I was hoping you'd help," he says.

He stays with Doris as I browse her dresser—hair spray, talcum powder, unscented lotion. Fake pearls, fake sapphires, fake gold. A hairbrush with thin hairs sprouting in all directions. Drugstore perfumes—lilac, freesia. And a ceramic tray loaded with change, a broken doorknob, and pins—a bird, a flower, the word *Mother* except the *R* is missing. I slip items into my bag and then move to the closet, which smells vaguely of cooked cabbage. I slide hangers of pastel greens and blues and reach to the fancier items shoved to the back. I choose a fitted navy blue dress like she might have worn to the old VFW dances.

When I return to the bed, I know it's time to take Doris with me. Her skin has grown mottled and plum colored, her lips blanching.

"Are you ready?" I ask.

Robert grabs an elastic band off the nightstand and ties his hair back in a ponytail. *We are both wearing ponytails.* Of all the thoughts to have right now.

"How do we lift her?" he asks.

"You from the shoulders," I say.

I hold her calves. Her toenails press against my rib cage.

"Now up," I say.

The fabric of her nightgown falls against my arm as I back into the hallway. I pause to readjust my grip.

"Am I being too rough?" Robert asks, trying to support her head and hold her under the shoulders at one time.

"We're almost there," I say. "Another step."

Doris passes through the doorway of her bedroom for the last time. We set her on the stretcher. I straighten her nightgown, place her arms in a comfortable position, smooth her hair.

"Do you need time?" I ask.

He shakes his head no as he turns to look at her empty room. Oxygen tank. Jewelry that was too special to wear. Carpet splattered in paint. A dip in the mattress and soiled covers we're both pretending we don't see.

I cover Doris with a sheet.

The hall and doorway are so narrow we scrape our knuckles at each turn. Wind bites at my face as I push open the door and walk backward down the steps and toward my van. Neighbors stand on their porches and stop in the street. The children boarding at the hotel watch from their lit-up frames. Robert looks at me for a moment, ponytail and unzipped jacket blowing wildly, and I wish this process were more private, more dignified.

37

I COULD NOT WORK ON Doris the day I brought her here. And after delaying even more today, Pop finally knocked on my bedroom door to tell me, "You ought to at least say hello to her."

For the first time since Robert and I carried her from the bedroom, I lift the sheet.

"Hello," I say.

The room sways. I hold the edge of the metal table and close my eyes. *Breathe. Breathe.* It's as if I've never seen a dead body and must experience the shock of looking into blank pupils, of feeling skin that does not respond to touch.

I try again. Open my eyes. Take in Doris, still and cold, her arms and hair flecked with paint. I miss her warmth. Her drunken truths. Her dancing in beads and that long, red scarf.

Through most of my childhood, I thought of Doris as the lady with the chickens. At dusk, she stood in her yard and clapped to get her hens into the coop for the night. They never went until they were ready, not a minute before.

We like to believe we have more control over our lives than we do.

We think if we don't smoke, we'll be spared of lung cancer. We think planning and hard work will bring fruitful crops and good prices for livestock. We think change will wait till we're ready for it.

I wash, slip on gloves, and tell Doris, "We knew we'd have this time together, didn't we?"

Her hands have been balled into fists since I felt for her pulse and Robert turned off the oxygen. I gently open the left, uncurling the fingers one by one, then massaging the palm, the wrist, each digit. Then the same with the right, I unfold her fingers, and out rolls a surprise. A small bottle of nail polish.

"For me?" I ask.

I check the color, Strawberry Ice, then breathe in long and slow, taking her hand in mine.

I sit with her withered lungs, the scar she was ashamed for me to see. How beautiful she is, even with hair that's coarse and bent when she wished it were soft and straight. One body, that's all any of us get. One beautiful, maddening container for all we are and hope to be.

I don't know when I grabbed her second hand. I only notice I'm standing now and holding both to my cheek. We carry so much through this life—sorrows we don't feel we can bear, apologies we can't speak, habits we can't break. But there are joys that sustain us. And I will never forget the three of us drinking wine together and sleeping in one room.

I've never been sure what I believe happens after death but find myself wondering where Doris has gone. Perhaps she is carried by the wind. Taking full breaths. Reaching low to feel the tickle of grass. And slowly lifting, lifting, until she finds an opening in the sky. A door to somewhere else.

I gently return her hands to the table and prepare her bath, choosing sponges, nailbrush, shampoo. I run the water until it's just the right temperature and then wet a cloth, load it with soap.

My hands go to work. Wash, flex, bend, apply lotion. I am gentle with the scar. I'm familiar with its shape. Two others have come to me after surgery on their lungs. It is like an *L* down her chest and under a rib. My sponge finds other, smaller marks, and I wonder what stories they tell—a spill from a bicycle, a shove from an angry hand, the constant rub of a toddler's shoe when she carried the child on that favored hip?

I fill, stitch, conceal. Day one turns to two, then three. I don't remember time passing, don't remember going up or down stairs, sleeping or eating. Her death is a physical pain in my body, a mass, here, under my rib, and here, where my breath feels crushed.

Pop moves slowly down the steps, using the rail to keep weight off the bad knee. He pauses near the door as if giving Doris some privacy.

"Have you eaten?" he asks.

"I don't know."

I haven't felt hungry or full. I've only felt the mass inside.

"Mary, come here, honey."

I stand before Pop, hands wilted at my sides.

"Do you want me to finish?" he asks.

"No." My feet feel the soles of my boots and the floor beneath them.

"Just tell me if you do."

I can only nod.

"I have errands to run before the storm really takes off," he says. "Are you still coming to the game?"

"Game?"

"It's okay," he says.

He touches my arm before he leaves and I notice snow collecting in the window wells.

I try once more to wash off the paint, though I'm fond of these stubborn flecks. Dots of yellow cling to Doris's bangs and ear and forearm on the right side, where she held her brush. I'm so deep in concentration, my whole body jerks at the sound of the doorbell.

"Can you get that, Pop?" I ask.

When he doesn't answer, I realize I have no idea how much time has passed since he was here. I hurry Doris into the fridge, then remove my gloves, wash my hands. Could it possibly be time for the viewing already? I race upstairs and reach the door as the bell rings a second time.

I find Robert, the gray clouds behind him so dark I can't tell if it's day or evening.

"What time is it?" I ask, trying to slow my breath.

"Four, I think," he says, confused. He checks his watch. "Almost four. I came over because I found a photo I'd rather use."

"Come in."

He kicks the snow off his boots and steps onto our welcome mat.

"I looked through all our photo albums today, hoping for anything without my dad in it," he says. "Went through every cabinet and drawer, and there it was."

He holds out an envelope from the Agate photo shop. I open it, and my shoulders sag.

"I didn't realize the story was true," I say. "There really was a photo taken that day."

He nods. "Actually, your father was there when we took it."

"Pop?"

"He helped bring Eddie straight to the house from the grain elevator. Ma wanted to have this picture taken. It was a bad idea, but how could anyone say no to her?"

I shut the door and invite him into the parlor. He moves with a weariness of someone who has spent many hours gathering up sheets, soiled with excrement, standing in rooms filled with silent medical equipment and pills no one will swallow. We both sink into the lopsided cushions.

"Your dad was in our back room. He helped dress Eddie in the clothes she'd chosen for him. Eddie really wasn't in shape for pictures."

He picks at the corner of the photo. The couch in it is the same one I slept on the other night. Same lamp beside it. A dog's tail shows in the lower left-hand corner. When I can stand to look closely at Doris and her sons, I notice her runny nose and tortured stare, her lips and teeth in a painful grimace. Robert's face is red with anger and disgrace as he sits rigid in a mis-buttoned shirt. And the brother he fought with earlier that day slumps between them with a horribly pitted face and eyes open, looking nowhere.

"He'd been in that hot bin for too long, and your dad was trying to pluck the grain that had lodged into his skin."

I can't move my eyes from the image.

Robert tells how his parents fought about where the camera was and about the whole idea of taking a photo at all. His ma dug frantically for the Pocket Instamatic in what they called the junk drawer, filled with everything from rubber bands to expired coupons to spare keys. The camera was a wonder when they bought it but, soon after, it became a forgotten thing.

"I went to the back room, wanting to get out of the way, and there they were, your father removing the kernels from Eddie's skin and putting them in his pocket. I guess he didn't want anyone to come across them in the trash. By then I was wearing my stupid button-up shirt, and I flopped down in a chair. I preferred that awful room to any my dad might walk through."

When it was time to take the photo, Robert propped his brother against him, the skin dimpled so hideously, he didn't want to look. His mother tried to stop herself from crying while his father paced and swore, telling them to hurry and get themselves set up. With his brother tucked in close, Robert realized that, except for occasional shoving and punching, this was the only time in nearly a decade that they'd touched, and the only time, possibly ever, that Robert had put an arm around Eddie.

They lined up on the couch, Eddie between them. Doris petted his beard with both hands, whispering, *My baby, my baby*. And then they sat and faced the camera. Just before the picture was snapped, Robert was told to remove his arm from around his brother because it pushed Eddie's head toward his lap.

"I could tell the moment my father agreed to take the picture that he would leave us."

He was leaving them already as he stood behind the camera, saying, "Goddamnit, Doris," and she begged him, "Please, please, one more. It's the last time we'll be together."

Robert remembered, as he felt his brother's weight, and watched his mother trying to smile when it was so wrong to smile, that he could see in his father's brief, hateful glances, the way he'd only address his words to Doris, that if he had to lose a son, he'd lost the wrong one.

"The package had never been opened," Robert says.

His father must have taken the film to Albertson's grocery store in Agate, where, two days after you dropped it off, you could pick up the prints, glossy or matte, three by five, or five by seven. Mr. Golden had ordered them in the smallest size.

"Did you look at the rest of the roll?" I ask.

He pulls the pictures back out. They span several years: Eddie wearing his basketball uniform; Eddie sitting with friends in the shade of a tractor; Eddie, with his big grin, biting into a raw potato. The photos of Robert are a blur, his back to the camera, heading up the tree house ladder or down the road with a broken appliance in his arms.

"I was an oddball," he says. "No one knew what to make of me."

He quiets when we come to several shots of Doris, skin and eyes still soft before the tragedy. Hair thick and straight, before aging and chemo. I look at Doris bending over in the kitchen so her nose and the dog's touch, Doris smiling as she gardens, Doris standing with arms open.

"I remember that moment," he says. "She was calling me and Eddie for a photo, and we refused."

When I flip to the next image, we are back to Doris in that awful photo with one dead and one damaged son.

"Can you get a frame for this?" I ask. "So I can set it out for the visitation?"

The town needs to see this mother and her boys not as a game but as real people struck by grief and tragedy. And maybe Robert needs to see it most of all, until he remembers how very young a fourteen-year-old boy is.

We sit a while longer. Neither of us seems able to move though we are done talking. I try to imagine my father as a part of that tragic photograph. While I had played in the yard with my dolls, he helped bring Eddie's body to the Golden residence. He could not have understood grief the way he does now. The man I know would never withhold comfort from a boy who feels he's at fault. Pop would know a boy like Robert needed his comfort most of all. But he was still young himself. Like the rest of Petroleum, no one got it right that day.

I'd like to know this man who pulled the kernels from Eddie's eyes, nose, ears, mouth. Who would have slapped his dead face to revive the dimpled skin. Who likely combed Eddie's hair, his beard, and positioned him so that his head wouldn't fall forward or back. Who chose not to comfort young Robert. Who left their home with kernels in his pockets. I want to meet this real, complicated man who disappears into the trance of TV and whiskey. I want to hear the honest state of our funeral business. I want to hear stories about my mother, and even the woman he likes to sneak into our home.

"The basketball game!"

"What?"

"I forgot," I say, standing quickly. "I promised Pop I'd meet him at the game."

I feel wrong letting him know we plan to watch basketball before Doris's service, wrong for shouting when we are feeling the devastation of his brother's death and his family's grief.

"I'm sorry," I say.

"No, it's all right." He gets up off the couch. "I'll hunt down a frame."

"Yes." I search for a dry hat in the hall closet. "I'm sorry. I . . ."

"It's all right. I'll let myself out."

"I'm glad you came by," I say.

And he is gone.

I open the hamper. No hat, but there are both the suits I'd meant to wash. The blue one smells strongly of perspiration. His happy suit is wrinkled but wearable. I find a wooden hanger for it and smooth it out, then leave without a hat.

38

I WALK TOWARD THE FLUORESCENT lights of the Petroleum
school gym, where I'll meet Pop for the basketball game.
It's a cold walk under a haloed moon, the ring thin and bright,
the inside of it ever so red. Fine granules of snow drop straight
down, the kind that will be heavy to shovel. Soon, the rimrocks will be as white as the letter *P,* the sagebrush buried under
drifts. If it's like the last blizzard, the highway will close, and we
won't see the ranchers or people from the neighboring towns
until spring thaw.

Through the hotel windows, I see a boy getting ready to go
to the basketball game, parting his hair on the side, as Fritz re-
quires. He also makes each boy tuck in his shirt and wear a belt.
These are some of the ways he keeps them from becoming like
the children on TV.

I look for Robert, inside Doris's empty house, but the curtain is drawn. I hold my chest as if the weight of him is there

and cut across the parking lot to the gymnasium, spotting my father's truck. He's still in the driver's seat, country music blaring, then silent when he cuts the engine.

"Hey," he says when he gets out. "You surprised me."

"Run your errands?" I ask.

"I had a lot of tools to return, checks to mail," he says. "Trying to get everything done before we're snowed in."

He lifts the wiper blades away from the windshield and locks the truck.

"I wasn't sure you'd remember the game," he says.

"I remembered."

I zip my coat to the top but don't feel any warmer.

"Everything ready for the visitation?" he asks.

"Getting there," I say. "I'll have to leave just after halftime."

My teeth begin to chatter. No matter how many winters I live through, my body doesn't seem to adapt.

"Here, let's get inside before you freeze," he says. "You should really wear a hat, you know."

We walk toward the school. I want to be gentle when I tell Pop what he must hear from me.

"I've seen the service Robert's planned for his mother," I say. "It's not traditional, but I think it's going to be beautiful."

Our boots creak through the snow.

"Can you make an announcement at the game?" I ask. "Remind people it's tonight?"

He hesitates.

"I don't know that this is a good place to do that," he says.

We haven't talked directly about the cigarette butts in our driveway or the ball thrown hard on our porch earlier this week. It seems that many in town want us to understand their dislike of Robert and anyone associated with him.

"I want this to be a good service for Robert," I say. "And Doris."

My father puts his arm around me.

"I've been thinking about what you said up on the rims," he says. "About this nature lover with so much free time in the afternoons."

I can already feel a tightness in my ribs.

"You were talking about Robert Golden, weren't you?"

I don't answer, which is as good as saying yes.

My father turns toward me and cups a hand over each of my shoulders.

"I don't want to take anything away from your happiness," he says.

"Don't start, Pop."

But he does.

"Mary, honey." His voice softens. "I think there are better men out there for you."

My body tenses and snow collects inside my back collar.

"Don't," I say.

"You hardly know him. And besides, soon enough, he'll be on his way to wherever it is he came from."

"Pop." My words come out only in a whisper. "I'm going to spend time with him. Don't make it so I have to lie to you."

We stand, not moving, as snowflakes dance between us.

"I'm only asking you to take it slow," he says and brushes snow from my hair.

"We'll talk later, Pop," I say, needing quiet. "We'll do some fishing together."

• • •

At the door to the gym, we stomp snow off our boots. I feel a nervous relief that Pop knows about Robert.

The bleachers are sparsely filled, the turnout always lower for the girls' games, and even more so with this storm under way. Still, there are a lot of people who can walk right over to the funeral home after the game. We move from towel to towel across the gymnasium floor.

"I'm glad to watch a game with you," Pop says, waving to Mr. Vinter up in the stands. "It's been a long time."

I follow his elongated steps up the bleachers. He seemed to want to join Mr. Vinter, but without a handrail, his knee is too shaky, so we sit closer to the court. My heart still pounds from our conversation in the parking lot, and I wonder if this is the beginning of us becoming grownup friends and not just father and child.

Pop takes off his coat, and I notice only now that he's not wearing a suit. I can't think of a time this has happened in public. Even when he mows the lawn, he's a businessman mowing the lawn. He can't seem to get comfortable on the bench, shifting in his seat, placing his coat beneath him, then changing his mind.

I notice a number of scowling faces. A Sweet Adeline looks our way and whispers to a neighbor. The men who leave their cigarette butts in our driveway are probably here, too. Pop begins to sweat from the top of his head. He jingles his keys until I cup my hand on top of them.

Slowly, a crowd trickles in, most wearing the school's colors. I remove my coat but not my gloves.

Pop, noticing, says, "I hope that's not a sign that you intend to dash off."

"It's just my hands are always cold," I say.

"It's because you're not eating and sleeping well. Your body's trying to tell you something."

Pop swings the key ring on his pointer finger, staring ahead, keys clacking against one another. I let it go. He'll quiet down for the pledge.

Most around us talk of snow and the belief that tonight's haloed moon is a beautiful but ominous sign of a storm even bigger than expected. No one talks about how we may soon be shut in, stranded either in or out of town. Thinking about it only prolongs the sense of confinement we'll all have to face. For a handful of teachers, designated to get stuck on the school side of the blizzard, this means they will become boarders of a sort, staying with families who've agreed to put them up. It also means that they are responsible for the students of any teachers who can't make it in.

I imagine spending the blizzard with Robert, shoveling a path from our door to his. Everyone around me stands, and I notice the principal has stepped to the microphone, ready to lead us in the Pledge of Allegiance. We place our hands over our hearts. Tim and Martha Rudd arrive, and both Pop and I pretend we're not watching everything about them. Tim takes off his Stetson and, standing in the middle of the court, stops to face the flag.

The room swells with a sense of reverence. Men hold their hats against their chests, hair pressed down flat. *With liberty and justice for all.* Then, the crowd is in motion again. Hats return to heads. Scarves and jackets are removed. Eyes drift to the court, where the girls set up in their positions. The Petroleum players are always the smallest on the court—in a school with only six seniors, the varsity team reaches all the way down to the freshman class for players. Homemade signs come out, and several in the crowd chant, "Maggot, maggot." The principal shakes her head to no avail.

A whistle blows and the game begins. Every time someone in crimson so much as touches the ball, the crowd erupts. My father glances too often in the direction of Martha, nervously jingling his keys, smiling, then not smiling.

The players' legs are pink with cold, but heat up fast. Minnow is the skinniest on either team, wearing a headband that covers her wine-stain birthmark and sneering as if everything about being a teenager is miserable. I wonder how much of our parents' affair she's had to witness. When I overhear my father speaking in that lovesick baby voice over the phone, and now, as he tries not to gape at her mother, I feel queasy. I know that each time he calls Martha, no matter how bad her marriage might be, he helps to cut the rope, however frayed, that holds Minnow's family together. Maybe just the last few cords, but he is sawing at them, all the same.

Sneakers squeak along the polished floor, as girls run up and down the court. Whenever the referee blows the whistle, they stop where they are, hands on hips or resting on the tops of heads or, in Minnow's case, smoothing bangs and making sure the headband stays in place. My father seems about as interested in the game as I am, regularly turning to look for Martha and pretending he's just looking around.

Suddenly Tim stands up, chest out. Other ranchers look his way, and one asks, "What's the problem, Tim?"

He does not take his eyes off my father. Martha, wearing crimson like most of the teachers here, tugs at the leg of his jeans, but he knocks her hand away.

"You have some kind of obsession with my wife?" he calls across several rows.

Pop ignores him as if he's too invested in the game to notice. The bleachers bang and wobble as Tim moves closer.

"Sit down," Martha begs. "Please, Tim, sit down."

I turn my head and see his square-toed boots march the last few steps to our seats.

"Stop," my father says. "Not here."

"Great. Let's have a little understanding outside."

"I don't know what this could be about," Pop says quietly.

Martha hurries down the bleachers carrying both their coats. Teachers and students look on. A group of older boys laugh hysterically in the upper row.

"Tim, let's go," Martha says, sidestepping toward us. "You're making a scene."

"I'm making a scene? You think I'm the one doing something wrong?"

"Sit down," someone yells from higher up. And others join in, shouting, "Sit down. We can't see."

The three of them beneath the fluorescent lights look so unattractive right now, it's hard to imagine why any of them would compete for each other.

When Pop stands, someone yells, "Take it outside."

Many in the bleachers shout this while others cheer extra loud for the players, hoping to drown out the distraction. Minnow stands in the center of the court, her face the extreme pale of winter, except for her cheeks, growing red and blotchy.

"I'll go," my father says. "There's no need for trouble here. I'm leaving."

Everyone must be watching our long walk down the bleachers and along the painted line surrounding the court. My father without his suit. Just a man, as I know him at home. He holds the door for me, a white spray blowing into the gym, the floor becoming slick again. I'm glad to leave the whispers and heckling behind us.

What a lot of snow has already fallen. This is it. This is the blizzard we've been expecting, the sidewalk white, and the trucks parked closest to the building already needing to be dug out. I hear behind us the principal over the microphone, calling off the second half due to weather, though it's more likely an excuse to defuse the tension.

I have my eye on the American flag hanging wet on the antenna of my father's hearse.

Pop starts the engine while we clear the windows with scrapers, brushes, and sleeves.

By the time we back out of our space, the parking lot is lit with headlights. The hotel boarders gather at the gymnasium door for their walk back to their rooms. The Agate players, steam rising from the tops of their heads, line up to board their bus. Blurred figures scrape windshields. Trucks take creative exits to the main road.

Our headlights pierce the black, and I stare ahead to keep from looking at any neighbors as we pass them.

"Pop?"

"It's just a misunderstanding," he says.

"Is it?"

He doesn't answer.

It feels like a long time to drive two blocks. When we approach the house, Tim Rudd is waiting on our white lawn.

"I have a simple message for you," he says when we step out of the hearse. "Keep away from my wife."

My father stands at a distance, seems to know it's best not to speak.

"I've been onto you," Tim says. "I've seen the looks you give her. No one looks at Martha like that but me."

Hearing her name, Martha steps out of the red truck. Minnow follows, shivering in a coat thrown over her basketball uniform. She looks disgusted that her game has somehow become this.

My father says nothing, but he gives Martha a look that expresses friendship, love, sorrow.

"Oh, Jesus," Tim says, seeing what he may not have believed until now. "Jesus, Martha. Him?"

It seems he'd come to defend her honor. But could she have actually fallen for this funeral director with thinning hair?

Tim clutches a handful of fabric over his heart.

"Tim, are you all right?" Martha asks, moving in.

"Wait in the truck," he tells her. "Leave us the hell alone. Leave this between the men."

"You too, Mary," Pop says.

"No. I'm staying right here."

And it takes the wind out of their fight, how three of us are cold and impatient spectators, standing awkwardly in the snow and wondering when we can get warm. It seems both Tim and Pop had hoped to throw punches so that something would find release. Even physical pain would at least move them from this balled-up tension. But now, like so many of the men in our town, their grievances become a part of the body, like plaque or tar or fat.

"I want to say good-bye to Doris," Martha says.

She says this to me. Not to the men.

"Her visitation's in an hour," I say.

"I'm getting in the truck," Tim shouts.

"I need to say good-bye to her now," she says, still only to me.

"She's not ready," I tell her.

But I lead her inside, with Minnow trailing at a distance.

"You'll have to wait here a minute," I tell them when we're inside the swinging doors of the basement.

As I pull Doris from the fridge, I feel protective of her dignity, unsure about letting anyone see her before I've done my finishing work. I cover her with a sheet up to the shoulders.

"Okay," I tell them, wheeling her to a corner of the room with no tools close by.

We stand near her head. Martha smooths her hair, and Minnow looks more at her mother than Doris, as if noticing something she'd overlooked until now.

"Good-bye, dear one," Martha says, close to her ear.

She kisses Doris and leaves the color I find on our cups.

I tell them about the outfit and the hairstyle Doris will wear tonight.

"That'll be lovely," Martha says.

It can't be good with Pop and Tim out there in the snow, with so many people to witness what my father keeps most private. But in this unlikely gathering, the three of us make space for quiet and tenderness, even as storms whirl about us.

I touch Doris's cheek before we leave. She was not ready for visitors, but I'm glad they came. We have not dishonored her.

As we exit the basement, I think how, if circumstances had been different, if Martha hadn't been married, I could say that my father had chosen well.

"Thank you," Martha tells me when we are back outside, the red truck rumbling in the snow.

"Get home safe," I tell her.

Pop, soaked in the yard, looks beat. He doesn't turn toward Martha or the red truck, just winces at the sound of the doors slamming shut, the wheels spinning before they find traction.

39

Pop hasn't moved from his spot on the lawn, though Tim and his family drove away some time ago.

"Let's get inside," I tell him, touching a shoulder to get his attention.

We track more snow inside.

"We may be in trouble," he says.

He has used *we,* which means our business.

"There's nothing we haven't come through before," I say, our habit of optimism, though I feel the distance my words have created, as if pushing his sadness out of view.

"How long before the visitation?" he asks, still distracted.

"About forty-five minutes," I say, finding the cleanest suit in the closet and handing it to him. "You might want to spruce up."

He moves so slowly up the stairs, bent with grief he brought on himself. I wonder, if he could only let one of his many girlfriends meet the man he tries so hard to hide, would his relationships work out better?

I turn for the basement as snow melts into my scalp and streams down my face. My hands, still red from the cold, itch as they warm to the temperature of the house. For all the sorrow today, I'm glad to have this time with Doris. I bring her under the light and open the tackle box filled with hair and makeup supplies. Plug in hot rollers. Then gently brush her hair, untangling the brittle and bent strands that want to reach in different directions.

Once her hair's set in curlers, I dress her without my father's help. Her body is so slight I can lift her easily. I hardly notice my tears except when they land on the ivory foundation I've chosen to cover the gray as well as the invisible threads and wax fillers. Next: eyeliner, eye shadow, blush, mascara, lipstick. And still a sadness shows through, the lines of anguish I saw in the family photo and even as she danced in the dark wearing her red scarf.

I spend longer than usual styling her hair, knowing the shame she feels about it. But she would like this, I think, how full it looks with these curls.

I finish with her feet. No one will see them, but I scrub and massage her crooked toes then paint them with Strawberry Ice. After they've dried and I've slipped on her shoes, Pop shuffles through the swinging doors in his rumpled suit.

"Do you need any more time to get yourself ready?" I ask him.

"No. I'm fine," he says. "Can I help you with Mrs. Golden?"

Doris lies on the metal table, fully dressed and wearing high heels.

"I don't think I've ever seen her so dressed up," Pop says.

He means it as a mild criticism.

"She wanted me to make her pretty," I say, remembering a few last details.

I dab perfume at her wrists, add jewelry she shouldn't have saved for a special occasion—a sapphire bracelet and a gold pin that once said *Mother*. Last, I slip the red scarf behind her neck and let the faux silk fall across her scar.

We lift Doris from the table to the casket, adjusting her head on the pillow, crossing her hands at her waist. I don't take a button from her dress. I don't want to harm her outfit in any way. And then we push, and I'm aware that we are walking through the still-wet footprints Martha left, the last trace of her here.

I wait for my father to help me guide the casket up the ramp that connects the basement to the parlor. His hands are in position but his gaze far away.

"Pop?"

He begins to push with lumbering steps. If only he knew how to cry. If only I knew how to hold him.

"The flowers didn't arrive," I say as we enter the parlor and center the casket under the pink light.

"I figured that might be the case," he says.

I set up what I can: guest book, prayer cards, CD player, a platter of miniature chocolate bars. Pop dims the overhead lights while I watch snow fall on the other side of the window.

"Did you read the obituary I wrote?" he asks.

"I did," I say to the snow. "I liked how you talked about her paintings."

His write-up was very traditional. Noncontroversial. He mentioned the grain elevator accident but in matter-of-fact terms, describing Doris as a woman who led a quiet life without vices.

"Robert was supposed to drop off some items for the service," I say.

"Maybe that paper bag by the front door?" he asks.

I hurry to the foyer.

"He must have dropped them off during the basketball game," I call out.

I walk back into the parlor, lifting two bottles of wine and a CD from the bag. When I find the framed photo at the bottom, Pop steps close and touches the edge of it. I hear an intake of breath.

You cannot look at this photo without feeling the enormity of that day. A mother in shock, trying to smile. A young man with a beard who doesn't look the least bit alive. And a boy—a boy—who won't receive a scrap of sympathy.

No one in his family or in town could have prepared for the impact of what hit us that day. No one knew how to do this, how to lose so much at once. I wonder if Pop is remembering the kernels in his pockets, the compassion he withheld.

I place the photo on the table beside the guest book, and he doesn't interfere. What a night this might be, a night of truth telling, of healing, of returning to an old trauma with the benefit of time, a chance to understand it differently.

My father and I are dressed for the visitation, and we adjust items in the room as we wait for guests to arrive. The phone rings, and Pop disappears to answer it.

I look out the window again and see Robert coming up the snowy walkway, but there are no others in sight. When I open the door, he does not come inside. He just stands there in the cold, wearing a dress shirt and tie with his leather jacket over top. His hair sprouts in all directions as if nervous fingers had raked through it. He can't seem to walk inside. Snow blows through the open door, and he just stands there.

"Guests will come before long," I say, and I pull my cardigan tighter around me.

He tucks in his lips and says nothing.

Wet flakes settle on my eyelashes, heavy, lopsided, and I blink to shake them loose. Any warmth my body had held seems to have escaped out the open door. I begin to shiver uncontrollably when Robert surprises me by opening his jacket. I pause, then my heartbeat speeds as I take a step closer and lean in. He wraps all that will reach around my arms.

"This won't win you any favors with the town," he says into my hair, his body tense.

"I know," I say and feel his unshaven chin against my forehead, his mess of curls tickling my cheek.

Our chests are touching. The toes of our shoes are touching. He holds me as if he's holding that little girl who walked home from the pool and sat at the window with her pinned fingers. I hold him as if he is the boy who was cut down from the harness, landing hard on his hands and knees.

A two-step begins in the parlor. My father must have put on the CD. I think of Doris tethered to that long tube of oxygen, dancing. I look over Robert's shoulder for anyone who might come to say their regards to his mother. The streets are silent, empty, glistening with snow. I'm cold and my back hurts from leaning in, but I know if I move, this moment is gone.

"Let's save on the heat," my father says, coming to the door.

Robert releases me, the jacket slipping off my arms and the chill moving in.

We step into the parlor and Robert takes his first steps toward Doris. His wet curls hang against the back of his jacket. How did I not notice until now that he's wearing dress pants, the cuffs wet and bunched over his snow boots. He bows his head. His mouth stretches in grotesque shapes as if he is trying very hard to hold back a swell of emotion.

"Ma," he whispers.

Pop and I move to the kitchen to give him some privacy. I can't look at my father, knowing how he disapproves of Robert, knowing how quickly his gaze will make me feel like a child and not a woman who's finally making choices that feel right. But he may understand how we have both chosen to love people we are not supposed to love.

"That was Lundy on the phone," Pop says. "Dug the hole this afternoon in case the weather gives us problems tomorrow."

"That should make things easy," I say.

"The trick might be finding where he did his digging," Pop says, looking to the front door and then his watch.

There are still no guests, and it doesn't appear there will be. Robert has taken a seat up front. Pop walks back into the parlor and opens a bottle of wine. He finds the plastic cups and pours into three of them.

"It's that kind of day," he says, handing one to each of us, and we take seats beside Robert.

I misjudged how unforgiving the town would be. I had hoped people would rise beyond their old resentments.

My father paces the parlor and the hallway, looking out various windows, sitting, then pacing again. We have all but given up believing anyone would come when the door opens and boots thump against the welcome mat. I take a sip of wine and watch Fritz enter the parlor. Soon after, the widow, the pastor, Slim, and a few teachers, including Kay Gundersen, arrive.

Pop finds his seat beside me again and stays put, as if approaching our guests might chase them away. I know he was publicly shamed tonight, but I was touched to see his heart exposed.

Gradually, the room grows warm with neighbors lingering in back until, finally, Mrs. Purvis walks down the aisle toward Doris. Slim follows, waits for her, then helps her back between the chairs, where she sits in the last row and whispers into her folded hands.

Another family walks to the casket and kneels in prayer. The teenager with them drifts over to the dish of chocolates and scoops up a handful, his eye spotting the photo. He calls his younger sibling over, and they are joined by the parents. Then more gather round.

"My God."

"All these years, I wondered."

"Oh, poor Doris."

"I can't believe he's throwing that awful time in our faces."

One woman races over to my father. "Allen, what's this about?"

"It was the family's wishes," he says.

The woman backs away from his breath. I can smell it, too—he must have refilled his cup with whiskey.

"We've always supported our local businesses," she says. "But this service tonight is a slap to our town."

The family storms out. Soon, however, more come to our house, mostly teenagers, responding to that first teen, who made calls on our kitchen phone.

"We should start the service," my father tells me.

But there is no real plan, other than drinking wine and listening to music, as if that alone might recapture the closeness we shared with Doris the other night. I was too optimistic.

And then a surprise. Kay Gundersen, her teeth purple from

wine, stands over Doris and begins to sing, just a whisper at first, like singing a lullaby at a child's bedside. "How Great Thou Art." Her warbly hymn grows louder, and those who remain, even the teenagers, join in.

When the song ends, many file out, eased just a little bit. A hand touches my shoulder, and I turn to see Bernice, Pop's girl-friend from long ago. Her new family waits in the hallway. She smiles with older eyes that dip at the corners, lines that show years of kindness and concern she gave to these other people. This visit must confirm all the reasons that made her leave us in the first place. She squeezes my shoulder and turns, leaving before I can find words. When she rejoins her family, she turns once more, and I raise my hand the way I used to in school— tentative, halfway.

"Robert," Pop says, when I return to my seat, "would you like to say anything on your mother's behalf?"

Robert has not budged in his chair, watching only what's in front of him, what he can see without turning his head. Neigh-bors sign the guest book, touch Doris's hand, our front door opening and closing, until all of them have left.

"Robert," Pop tries again.

"Sure," he says, dazed, looking around the room. "I guess, since it's just us."

He stands, then changes his mind and begins to sit again.

"Go on," Pop says. "Take the floor."

And Robert stands in front of the table, pushing his hands deep into his pockets.

"This is the story of my parents' first date," he says. "I only learned of it this month."

Damp hair falls in his eyes, and he leaves it there.

"They'd gone on a drive to the Breaks," he says, the area

out-of-towners call the badlands. "I'm not sure why. It's a funny place for a first date."

"Maybe because it's nearby," Pop says. "And private."

Robert nods as if to say, *Maybe.*

"Pop, quiet," I whisper.

"So while they're driving," Robert says, "Ma suddenly shouted, 'Pull over!' My dad was scared he'd offended her somehow but the reason she wanted him to stop was because she'd seen a single flower on a cactus."

He takes another sip of wine.

"The two of them got out to see it up close," he says.

And I can imagine them walking over the dried, rugged clay to look at those tiny, yellow petals, soft like tissue and protected by hairlike needles. In these parts, such flowers usually go an entire life cycle unseen by humans.

"Ma was in awe of this little flower. It was the only one they'd seen for miles—he wouldn't have noticed it at all," Robert says. "And she told him this flower would become the prickly pear fruit, and if she still knew him when it ripened, she would use the fruit to make him a batch of her homemade jelly."

"That's sweet," I say.

But Pop, shifting in his chair, looks as if he's thinking, *Is there a point to this story?*

"They shared their first kiss beside that tiny flower," Robert says. "And later that year, she brought him a bright red fruit and pretended it was from that same plant."

I've made this jelly before. I imagine a much stronger Doris holding that fruit with its pesky spines piercing her rubber gloves as she scrubbed and cut it. I imagine her setting the pieces in a pot to boil, along with sugar and a lemon peel, until it became a seedy pulp, the color of ripe watermelon.

"I wish I'd known my parents when they were still in love," Robert says.

He takes another sip of wine. Pop stands to look at the framed picture again, and moving closer to Robert, puts a hand on his shoulder.

I look at them both and think, *Please understand why I love this man.*

40

LAST NIGHT, AFTER THE visitation, we watched snow fall past the windows and knew getting to the cemetery would be difficult. Pete got here late and slept on the couch in our parlor.

We're all up early with coffee in thermoses, shoveling out vehicles in the driveway. I'm not sure Pete would have braved the weather for Doris's funeral if he hadn't heard all the talk about Tim Rudd or the grim family photo. I'm thankful he's only spoken about the storm in my presence.

Robert and Pastor Lundy meet at our house, snow nearly to their knees. It will only be the five of us heading to the cemetery. The men have all picked up a shovel, and without words, get to work. Men who don't want to ride together. Men who don't want to be in this weather, in suits no less, pants tucked into boots.

Pop tells me quietly, "We should go inside for Mrs. Golden."

"You haven't mentioned last night's service," I say as we walk down the cellar ramp.

"You know," he says. "It was different from the one I had planned."

Trickles of sweat and melting snow run down his head and face, wetting the floor.

"I thought more people would come," I say. "I thought they'd stay to hear Robert speak."

This time he says nothing.

I have one last look at Doris. I smooth her dress with its buttons all intact. I whisper, "Thank you," stretching my hand inside the casket to feel for the paints and brushes I'd placed within her reach. Pop helps me close the lid.

"This is a lot of snow," he says. "Might make the day tricky."

He dries his hands, and we slide the casket onto the gurney, roll it up the ramp. Pete and Robert grab opposite sides and help to hike Doris through the snow and into the back of the hearse. Then we load up with shovels, extra gloves, flares. No more small talk. Everyone just does what needs to be done, and quickly.

No one says they are afraid of driving in this weather. No one says how this trip to the cemetery may not feel like a funeral so much as a hurried burial.

One of the neighbors with a snowplow attached to the front of his truck scrapes up and down the streets. This should make it easier to get to the highway.

"Your mother was a good woman," Pete says to Robert as they close the back.

And with that we split up between the two vehicles, both well heated, with scrapers and emergency equipment inside. I ride with Pete and Pastor Lundy in the white Ford. Pop and Robert ride with Doris in the hearse. I raise my hand to Robert through the glass. He doesn't see.

"I'm going to keep my strobe lights on," Pete shouts out his window as he backs onto the street. "I'm hearing on the radio scanner that you can barely see the road, much less oncoming cars."

The chains on the tires clank and struggle along the white road. Out of habit, I look for Doris painting at her window. I will have to get used to the closed curtains.

Our ride through town is slow and hot, the wipers moving furiously. Snow falls in every direction like an explosion, telephone wires and power lines bobbing in the wind. All our canning, our weatherproofing, our belief in our will against nature is up for a test.

My father, his engine heaving behind us, goes slower and slower, eventually stopping. We stop too, seeing Pop step out to dig snow from the wheels and hubcaps. Still carrying the shovel, he walks to Pete's window and waits for him to lower it.

"My truck's not going to make it there and back," Pop says. "How 'bout yours?"

"I'm good if we hurry," Pete says.

There is only the briefest time given to frustrated sighs as they look together into the backs of both vehicles and figure out how to consolidate everything essential into Pete's Ford.

"Let's start by making room for Mrs. Golden," Pop says.

They move quickly—rearranging supplies, letting down seats, setting the casket inside.

"Two will have to stay behind," Pete says.

Pastor Lundy hands over his Bible.

"Mary," Pop says, "can you drive the pastor back in my truck?"

He has such a serious tone, I know not to argue or delay.

Pete kisses the top of my head. "I may not see you till spring thaw," he says.

For a moment I can't move, my head still bowed as the warmth of his kiss evaporates.

"Let's get to it, Mary," my father says.

"Just a minute." I walk toward Robert. "Tell your mother good-bye for me."

He places his gloved hand on my shoulder. No words. I feel the heat of our night with wine and fire, the sorrow and affection we shared. I let his hand stay there longer, even in front of men who disapprove.

"We have to go, Mary," my father says, ushering Robert inside and sliding in after him.

"The three of you are going to lift the casket?" I ask.

"We'll get it done," Pop says. "We're out of options."

I use my coat sleeve to sweep snow off the windshield, watching the others go on without us. When I get in Pop's hearse, the floor is covered with husks of sunflower seeds. He likes the kind with salt on the outer shell. Sucks on them when he drives, gets the husk good and soft.

"Turning around should be fun," I tell the pastor as he buckles in.

I can barely reach the pedals but this is no time to adjust my seat. The wheels spin in the deep snow as I try to turn us.

"Should I push?" he asks.

"No, I've got this."

And after almost ten minutes, we are facing the right direction. The road has all but disappeared, but I try my best to drive through the tracks we already made.

"Shame about Robert's truck," the pastor says.

"His truck?"

"Someone slashed his tires last night."

"God! What is wrong with people?"

I press on the gas, and the slick road reminds me to take it slow.

"Want me to drive?" he asks.

"No, I'm just . . ."

I can't even finish my thoughts I'm so mad.

Pastor Lundy begins to sing quietly in his deep, breathy voice, "Rock of ages, cleft for me." My hand rubs at the fogged glass to create a space I can peek through. The wipers, useless to keep up, squeak to the right and bang to the left, a buildup of ice beneath the blades. The hearse smells of perspiration, breath, and sunflower seeds.

Once again, I press too hard on the gas, and as the hearse slips against the growing walls on either side of us, I see the pastor's foot working an imaginary brake. I think of how we must look from the sky right now. Just a dot. A dot hoping to get home before we are buried in snow. This is the life we commit to here. That we cannot rely on others. That no one can reach us so we had better help ourselves. Our lives could end here in my father's hearse with the pastor and his songs and the swish of wipers. But there, at last, is the grain elevator.

We both exhale as we turn where our neighbor's plowing has revealed the road. This view of Petroleum is picturesque as the community, every single member, it seems, helps to shovel what they can.

My leg is tired of stretching so far for the pedals. As we pass a group of bundled-up children, I recognize Minnow's long legs sticking out beneath her too-small coat. She turns her head, and seeing the hearse, slowly sticks out her middle finger.

I hate you, she mouths. She must think it's my father behind the wheel. Her finger rises, slow motion, until her arm is fully extended toward the sky.

The pastor says nothing, but I feel the shame of what Pop has done to her family, his sneaking around, his slow dismantling of something that was already fragile, his hand in hurting Minnow, despite how fondly he speaks of her to Martha.

Her body turns as we pass, continuing her salute. Her little mouth has more pout than rage, like a girl who wants this to be her time, not her parents', to act rashly and make mistakes.

When we turn the corner, there is only the sound of the wipers and the defroster on high, neither of us wanting to speak about this. The A-frame church is just ahead, white gusts blowing from the roof.

"Why don't you let me out here," he says, meaning the middle of the road. "If you try to pull off to the side, we'll have to dig you out."

I stop the hearse and stay there as he trudges toward his front door.

"Get right home," he says, waving me on. "Don't wait. Get on your way."

I park as best as I can near the bottom of the driveway. Snow amasses against the south wall of our house. I have to shovel my way to the door. We've hoarded supplies, but are they the ones we need most? We stored peach preserves, but what about sanity, laughter, love?

41

EVERY HOUR, I SHOVEL out both doors and down the drive-way, thinking they should be back from the cemetery by now. They must be cold out in that open field, lifting the casket through deep snow, searching for the grave the pastor dug.

So many people I see shoveling their own walks could have set aside old gripes and helped clear roads, carry Doris through the snow, lay her to rest.

I don't get it, the loathing one neighbor can have for another. The same storm bears down on us all, and for days or weeks we will be trapped with whatever electricity and provisions we have at hand. Certainly, we are capable of understanding each other. It's as if we refuse our most natural instinct.

We have forgotten what we have in common. We've forgotten when we walked to school together, when we picked up trash from the same storm. All of us have worked since we were children, on ranches, at the elevator or grocery store. In summers, the fishermen of our families likely kept jars of worms in the fridge. Go into any of our homes and I bet you'll find a Charlie Russell painting and a Louis L'Amour novel. Walk outside and we hear the same cattle, feel the same wind. How strange that we find ourselves at odds with people so similar to ourselves that someone from another town could not tell us apart. Don't we all just want simple things from this life—a use for our talents and passions, a chance at love, an old wound healed, someone to hold after a hard day?

I feel the handle of the shovel in my gloves again. The sky begins to dim until I see only gray and white. But what is that smear of color? I set the shovel against the porch rail and look again. There are Pete's flashing lights turning from the highway, the wheels grinding through the buried streets. My knees nearly buckle in relief.

His truck stops in front of our house, and Pop struggles out the door and up the walk, wet and exhausted. I hurry to lend him my arm.

"I'll help you inside," I say.

His blue lips are too frozen for him to speak.

I fetch towels, a blanket, help remove the outer layers. After I serve him soup and buttered toast, I watch from behind the storm door, as Pete's truck idles outside of Doris's house, strobes flashing. Then a silhouette of Robert, blurred by snow, returns to the white Ford carrying, what, something large, and gets back inside. They are moving again. My mind churns in place, like the truck's wheels, until I understand. He was carrying luggage.

"Pop!"

I open the storm door, snow dotting my face.

"Pete and Robert understood they had to leave tonight or they wouldn't get out," he says. "Pete will drive Robert to the airport as soon as it's open again."

"Pop," I whisper. "What did you do?"

It is the slowest leaving, blue and red lighting up the snow, the house, the snow, the house as Pete's white Ford edges away with Robert in it. I grab for my heart and stand shivering at the open door.

From behind, I feel my father's hands, one on each shoulder, his grip firm. He's done this. My father, with Pete's help. Snow sprays our oriental carpet. The radiator clicks on again, my father's breath too close, and a fury boils inside, rising through my gut toward my shoulders. I shrug hard.

"Get away from me," I shout. "Call them back. Call them back right now!"

I run down the snowy steps, run to the end of the walk, shaking, not wanting to let Pete's truck out of my sight. Blue and red lights up the highway and then any sign of those lights is gone. I look at my house as if I don't know it. My footprints have already filled with snow. I look again to the barren highway and wonder if I will see Robert again, my world silent except for wind hurling snow. It is as if white sheets drape across the roads, across every structure, the town bedding down for the rest of winter, and all of us trapped underneath.

42

PETROLEUM IS WHITE AS far as you can see, the plains endless, disorienting without any markers. We have to shovel
every hour or the snow could barricade the doors shut. Snow
builds at the edges of windows, the view contracting. Soon
there will be no sky. No stars.

Sometimes during long hours with nothing to do, I imagine
Robert so fully, I believe I can touch him. One moment I feel
the rumble of the plow, but it is the shudder of Robert's skin as
I trace the scar that disappears beneath his shirt. Another moment I hear wind against the windows, but it is Robert whispering in my ear.

Shh, shh now.

He has removed his shirt. He does not have the body he
would like to have. He says this. He points to his thin shoulders,
his doughy middle, the loose flesh inside the bend at his elbows.
And I welcome him, his insecurities, his shame. I welcome
his arm that scoops beneath my back and all the way through

to the other side. We press our imperfect flesh together, his long, raised scar against my assortment of stones. He clutches my hand, once stuck with pins. He kisses what cannot be made right, but kisses all the same.

And my tears fall because I want this and because a part of me knows my arms are empty. *Don't open your eyes, don't.* I will him here, caressing, holding him gently then forcefully. I beg myself to keep believing, to keep my eyes shut so I am not alone.

I am different than I was that windy night when I first opened the door to Robert Golden. In that one volatile month, Robert had, it seemed, placed his hands against my chest and pushed hard, pushed till ribs cracked, to get my heart beating.

I thought I wanted a life that was predictable, the perfect steadiness of my sixty-five-degree world, with all my supplies lined up in order. That is no longer enough.

I leave my room and wander down the staircase that feels too narrow, the ceiling too near. Pop waits at the table. We still eat our meals together, but they are often quiet. I sit in front of my plate, not hungry. My father, unshaven, smells of whiskey though it's only lunchtime. We have given up on forced conversations. We have given up pretending we're fine.

His attempts to apologize to me are clumsy and insensitive.

"You'll fall in love again," he says. "How well did you even know him?"

But that was the wrong question. The real question is, How well do I want to know him? And my answer is that I want to know his room, what he keeps on the dresser and in the junk drawer. I want to learn the names of his closest friends. I want to watch a bad movie together and learn which of us is grumpier when we're sick. I want to sit on the toilet while he brushes his teeth. I want to make up from an all-night argument.

"Pop?" I say.

He looks up and I realize I don't have the words or the courage to speak of what's grown between us, how I feel squeezed into a little box of my father's wishes for my life.

"Never mind," I say.

And the snow falls and falls.

If I let myself think too long about this small space, I feel a sense of panic—an impulse to run without stopping. The walls are too close on all sides and the air smells too much of ourselves, our sorrow and boredom.

Through a rip in the tinfoil, I see a sliver of winter's pale sun and am left to imagine the sharp air in my nostrils. I feel desperate to be in all that untrampled space, running so long and so far that I must remove my hat and unzip my coat.

How many days have we been inside? Do I dare count them? Do I dare guess how many more are to come? And without thinking, I've stood up so fast the chair falls behind me.

"Mary, what's going . . . ?"

But I've gone, bolted out the door because I'd go mad staying inside a second longer. I flail through our shoveled path, slipping, standing up again, trying to run. Everything ahead and above is so blinding white, I can't tell where the ground ends and the sky begins. It burns when I breathe. I want to run fast and far but the dead end is just ahead, and before I can slow down, I've slammed into a wall.

Frantically, I claw at the outer shell of it, push and kick at the softer snow behind. I need to run faster and farther. I need to see color.

"It hurts!" I yell, and the wind swallows my words.

My cry is primal, raging. I feel a pounding in my ears and hair rising on the back of my neck. In the same moment I hear Pop call my name, he's wrapped his arms around the outsides of mine and tackles me, both of us falling.

"Don't you know this is dangerous?" he shouts. "Out in this cold with only a sweater."

He holds me tight, our cheeks against the snow.

"I hate you," I say, the wall crumbling into the side of my mouth.

"There will be others to help you forget," he says.

"I might have gone with him," I sob.

Pop holds on tight, and I let him—these things we don't do easily. Faces peer from windows, where towels and tinfoil have been peeled back. Faces watch from their own shoveled mazes. My skin, my eyes sting from the wind.

"We have to get you back inside," Pop says, helping me stand.

Everything feels numb as he lifts. And it ends like this, walking back without a look between us that would bring reassurance that our relationship will survive. Pop is only thinking right now about keeping us warm, and I am only thinking of my boots stepping in and out of his footprints.

Once through the door, I drag myself on wobbly legs to my room. I sit by the front window and stare at the endless white, my skin burning and itching as it warms. Now and then I hear my father come into the room. He says nothing and leaves again.

To Pop, I may always be the girl sitting here by the window, watching a world I can't seem to join, and he may always see himself as the one who couldn't give me what my mother would have.

My fingers feel the cold glass, while sound moves far away.

Wind. Mooing. Flushing. Ringing. Footsteps. Knocking. My name. My name. My name.

My fingers bend, straighten. The blurred room comes into focus.

"Mary?"

My father knocks hard on the open door.

"Mary? Phone call for you."

I move in slow motion, counting stairs until a thought crosses my mind. Speeding now, I nearly trip on the last step and turn the corner to the kitchen, where the phone sits off the hook.

"Hello?"

When I hear Robert's voice, the tears fall, salty, to my lips. He speaks before I'm fully listening—something about rain, seagulls, how long it took to catch up at work.

"Did my father ask you to call?"

"I was going to call anyway," he says.

The phone trembles in my hand as he tells me what's outside his window. The sound of tugboats. The smell of fish. The taste of salt in the air. And he tells me about the inside of his office, where he is working late and about the computer bugs he discovered.

"My life's not that interesting," he says.

"I like to hear about it."

I tell him how my windows are blocked by snow and we laugh about what we might find underneath it all—the step to the barbershop like broken piano keys, an old faded sign with three remaining letters on it, a once-shiny truck with a scrape along the length of the door and slashed tires.

"Will you come back for it?"

"Eventually," he says. "Tell me about the ranchers. What are they doing in all that snow?"

I can't see the ranches from any window, and I've been so mad at my neighbors for what I've learned about them. But old stories rise to the surface, stories I've accumulated over the years from my father or conversations I overheard at the Pipeline, and I tell Robert what I remember.

"In the mornings, and then several times a day, they crack through frozen layers at the watering hole and trough," I say. "And calves are born between now and the end of March so the cowhands stay close in case they need to get in there and pull."

"Must be tough keeping them alive in a blizzard," he says.

"They have to check on the newborns all the time," I say, "to be sure their slick coats don't turn into shells of ice. Once I saw a guy driving a newborn around on the floor of his truck, trying to keep it warm."

My ear, pressed against the phone for so long, feels bruised. Gaps steadily grow between our stories until we've run out of words.

"I should probably go," he says.

"Please stay on the line," I say.

And we listen to each other breathe.

After I've hung up, I walk down the hallway to shut off the lights before bed. My father, passed out in his office chair, must have tried his best to listen to our call. I kneel beside him, my hand on his forearm. Could I do this if he were awake—slide my fingers gently down his arm until my hand is over his?

"Good night," I whisper to this man who loves and hurts me.

I keep my hand on his a little longer.

After I go to bed, I watch the white windows and the hints of violet that show through. Gradually, they darken to black, the house exquisitely quiet. And then I feel it. A feeble stirring deep-in, beneath the stones. Desire, dreams, the soul that had curled up in hiding, trying to rise.

Robert's calls aren't predictable but they come before I fret.

"Phone for you," my father says, no longer trying to keep us apart.

He leaves the kitchen along with the dishes he promised he'd wash. I don't think he's cleaned anything since the blizzard. I put the phone to my ear and pretend we are skin to skin. I love the surprise of our conversations, hearing about a world so different from Petroleum, finding that one story leads to another I didn't see coming. As he speaks, I quietly load the dishwasher, switching ears whenever one feels too hot or sore. I wash the counters and the spills that have dripped down the cabinets to the floor.

"My father's driving me crazy," I whisper into the phone. "You wouldn't believe the mess he made of the kitchen. We've been locked in this house so long, all the stories he tells are ones he's told before."

"When he's gone," Robert says, "you'd be amazed what you'll miss."

I put down the dishrag and sit at the table as he tells me of his mother tiptoeing behind him to drop oyster crackers into his bowl of soup. Or her winded laugh whenever her favorite game show started.

"The opening was funny to her every time," he says. "I couldn't see it, what made her laugh. But the sound. The sweet, sad sound of giggling with no air behind it . . ."

I want to see his face and touch my hands to his cheeks.

"Even painting . . ." He stops speaking for a moment, swallows. "The same stupid hobo. You can even miss that."

"I'll be more patient," I say.

"He loves you," Robert says of my father.

He has said the word *love*. For the rest of the call, I memorize his whisper of that word.

More and more, when I close my eyes, I dream of a bigger world. I dream of blank pages to fill. My hands long to hold paintbrushes, sticks of charcoal, pencils. Is this fair to my father? I watch him slump over the kitchen table, over his office desk, in the recliner in front of the TV, no more secret phone calls or visits to fill his time. I feel guilty having such dreams when I see the sorrow that shows in his eyes and at the edges of his mouth. But I refuse to crawl back beneath the stones.

Epilogue

THE DAY OF DORIS'S burial it snowed twenty-nine inches. There was another storm not far behind it, seventy-six inches for the year. Ranchers scrambled to save their livestock. Many lost a quarter to half of their herds. Petroleum was such a huge stretch of white that, for weeks, it was without streets and sidewalks, and for some time, electricity.

With no shipments to the grocery store, our town managed on the goods we prepared in warmer weather or purchased during the Blizzard Festival. The doors of the abandoned homes were walled off for months. The rest of us were restricted to wherever we'd shoveled while the snow was still soft enough to move. And we milled back and forth in our outdoor mazes, trying not to count the days of our captivity.

The calendar has said for some time that it's spring, but only recently have I seen evidence—creeks flowing, snow dripping from branches, birds returning. The giant letter *P* on the rimrocks slowly reveals itself again, while homes, trailers, sheds, and stores emerge from all that white, everything leaning a little bit more.

The air smells of mud and new growth. My feet sink into the slush. Cottonwood seeds fly toward me like a surprise, warm snowfall. And I am glad for the sun.

I carry a bucket of soapy water down the driveway, toward my van. My hands fish for the sponge as windows open on the upper floor of the hotel, the sound of vacuuming inside. I soap up the hood, swirl the grime in circles.

"Do you think the rumor's true?" a voice says from across the street.

A group of boys stands in front of the Goldens' empty home, which now displays a sign saying, FOR SALE BY OWNER.

"The money's going to the school."

"No, it isn't."

"It's going to fix up the library."

"We could have band uniforms."

"My dad says, if there is any money, Petroleum won't see it."

I've asked Robert about the rumor and he still doesn't know if there are any savings. Between his work schedule and whatever remains in the locked house, there are many loose ends.

The kids move down the road and turn into a field. One picks up a stick and throws it in the direction they're walking. What the people of this town seem to crave is a different ending to their story. But a mortician knows something about death. Can sense it coming without the need to turn away. Like old age, it comes whether you fear it or not. And hits hard even when you expect it.

Still, some must hope. Others must rage and strike out.

You can't tell someone how to mourn.

You can't tell someone how to die.

Pop joins me with his own sponge and starts on the head-lights and grille. We don't talk about what happened over this last winter—I think it's how we'll always be—but that after-noon when he tackled me in the snow has weighed on each day since.

I stand on the footrest to reach the top of the windshield, and that's where I say what I've been pondering these past many weeks.

"I'm thinking I might try a different line of work," I say. "Maybe a different town."

He stops washing.

"Is this because you're angry with me?" he asks.

"I stepped into this business because it was right here. It was what I knew." I stare at the sponge in his hand, unable to meet his eyes. "I need to see what else is out there."

He nods his head as if to say, *It's because you're angry with me.*

"I've never seen the ocean, Pop." I sit on the bumper. "I want to see tall buildings and trains that run."

He drops his sponge in the bucket.

"Maybe there's a place where I'll fit in better," I say, finally looking directly at him. "Maybe there's a place where I won't have to work so hard at making friends."

"I've nagged you too much," he says.

The school bus rumbles to the front of the hotel, washed clean so it's yellow again.

My father sits beside me on the bumper as children file out of the hotel, carrying suitcases and boxes. We watch Minnow at the back of the line. I want to touch Pop's arm, but I've thought about it too long, and I clasp my hands together instead.

One by one, students board the bus. When the door squeals shut, Slim, waving good-bye to Fritz, drives the boarders back to their families. These children will find their ranches slopped in mud after all that melting snow, coating the legs and bellies of their livestock. They'll meet the new calves. And they'll also see the ugly but necessary work to be done after a harsh winter. Because there's livestock and there's deadstock, the range littered with carcasses, and the grim work of tracking down the dead. One way you find them is by looking at the sky and seeing where the birds are clustered and diving. You can see those birds even now.

Some of these kids will help, or at least look on, as ranchers get out the backhoe and drag carcasses to the far end of the property, careful not to go too close to a stream or you'll get runoff in the water supply. They'll lay out the bodies in a single line on a bed of straw or sawdust, never letting them touch, then cover them with manure. The line of deadstock will be a long one on each of the ranches this year, and it will be someone's job to turn them now and then, like any other composting job, and to keep the dogs from rolling in all that rot.

"I don't know how I'll manage without you," Pop says.

"You'll have to take better care of yourself. I won't be here to wake you up."

"Have I been a burden to you?" he asks.

"Oh, Pop," I whisper.

There is a slight lift at the corner of his mouth, but not a smile, as if he understands that his best effort left some bruising.

The prairie has shed its winter brown, and the quiet palette of colors I know so well has returned—orange stems of scrub willow, the blue gray of new sagebrush, and grass finally, though only briefly, green again. Rattlers slide from their dens, and buds grow plump and ready to burst.

I stand at the back of my van, doors open. Pop carries my duffel bag, the last of what I've packed. He's wearing his happy suit. And it sits in my throat, all my feelings of love and sorrow and anger and aloneness and belonging that I don't know how to express except by doing this.

I am leaving Petroleum. I am leaving to preserve a part of me that can't flourish here. For too long, I've made choices based on the opinions of others, ignoring my own impulses and dreams. I'm not even sure what those dreams are or whether they're fully formed. All I know is I've lived a cautious life, and it hasn't made me happy.

"You're sure your van can survive a long drive?" he asks.

"I had a mechanic—the bartender—look at the engine," I say. "He told me, 'You can't call this thing good as new, but you can call it good enough.'"

Pop looks over my shoulder. I look to my feet.

"You'll be okay here? With the business?" I ask.

"Yep," he says. "Are you having second thoughts?"

I want to reach out, but I slip my hands into my pockets instead.

"No, Pop. I have to go."

I step closer to him, and he grabs me in an embrace so tight I know he understands I will only come back as a visitor, that this is his home now, and not ours. What I don't say is how proud I am that he's my father, even with our secrets and our silences.

When he releases me, he says only, "Drive safe."

And I say, "I'll send you my address when I have one."

I get inside and close the door. The engine starts right away.

I sit here awhile and take a long look at the only home I've known. The house that began with my mother and father dreaming a life together and planting the two burnt rosebushes that he will not dig up.

"Van working okay?" he calls through the glass.

I roll down the window but can't speak. When he rests his arm on the frame, I grab his wrist. It is my desperate need to be close though we don't really know how.

We stay here, awkwardly pressing each other into the rim of glass until the need to hold on increasingly becomes the need to break free. I let his hand go, put the car in reverse, and Pop steps back from the van. I roll slowly away, not daring to look. Only when I reach the road and shift into drive do I turn to him.

Pop, in his green suit, holds his hand up in good-bye. I think he may stay here as long as there is a town. If the town's forgiven him, and it seems that the warm breeze is all that's needed to make it so, he may even see its end, ensuring that it comes to a close with the dignity and ceremony a life deserves.

I pass the Goldens' home and wonder how long it will be before the kids find a way in. What I am certain of is that they will walk through the rooms of Dead Eddie and the Younger Brother. They will open drawers and claim all that was left behind. I'm sure they will turn on the oxygen tank, aiming the tube at each other so that Doris can breathe on them, as if from the grave.

I drive from Crooked Hill Road through the ever-expanding potholes of Main Street. I pass the unemployed who've claimed their spots for the day along the wall of the Pipeline. A couple of them watch me leave. A boy walks in the road without a shirt—it's half tucked into a back pocket—his chest sunken and shoulder blades sharp, but his strut says that today he is a man. On the next block, children bake mud pies at the rusted stove that may sit forever in that vacant lot. I breathe in the dust that sprays through the window.

I thought I would shout "Good riddance" when I finally drove away, but I can hardly see the road for my tears, can hardly take a full breath for the space these people take up inside me.

I thought I'd feel disdain for those I'm leaving behind, but all I feel right now is admiration. There are not many left like these folks. The child who, without malls, fast food, or movie theaters, spends his free time exploring abandoned buildings, sometimes falling through collapsed boards, surviving such falls with glee. The rancher who wakes up at five in the morning, and before he's had anything to eat, steps into his mucking boots and feeds the stock. The grandmother who must get out of her truck at every cattle guard, opening the gate in rain and snow and subzero temperatures. These are people with hands rough from labor, and faces creased from a life lived outdoors, from worry over loved ones and making ends meet. There is a spirit here of durability, of hard, physical work, of sacrifice and survival.

No matter where I go, I will always think of a year in terms of a rancher's four seasons, and the weather in terms of how it will impact lives here—*This rain will be good for the crops. This dampness will bring out the rats. This freeze may put the calves in danger.*

Outside the grain elevator, bikes are thrown on their sides but there is no singing. I wonder if there will be new songs this year, or if the story of Dead Eddie is one this town will always need to tell.

When I reach the turn for the highway, I stop and get out, hair blowing across my face. My father still stands in the driveway. I will miss the simplicity of our time at the kitchen table—the smell of burnt muffins, the paper opened between us, newsprint on Pop's fingers. I'll miss hearing his plans for the day. Maybe he'll finally fix that creaky board on the front porch or move the rusted hotel sign off our lawn.

Nowhere will ever feel more like home than this place. It's in my genes, sometimes feeling more like a cleft palate or a clubfoot, but just as much a part of me. With my leaving, there are 178 residents here, and as another high school commencement approaches, six more graduates will decide whether to stay or go. Most, I'm guessing, will move away, chasing opportunities and lifestyles they see on TV. The empty buildings in Petroleum will stay empty, roof tiles and shutters will work loose and fly away bit by bit with each storm, and the walls will tip still farther from the wind.

I won't be here for branding season—ranchers wrestling down calves to tag and vaccinate and mark them with hot pokers, the little fellas (as Pop likes to call them) bawling and smelling of burnt hide. I won't see high school students up on the rimrocks, touching up the white paint on the giant letter *P*. I won't be a part of how this story ends because it belongs to those who stay.

I get back in the van and turn left on Highway 200, the town, the gray tower disappearing behind me, elk, still in threadbare winter coats, zigzagging and then gone. There is no guarantee for what I'll find on the other end of this journey. But in a way, it's the thrill of not knowing that excites me. After living so long in my basement world, I crave the far more unpredictable emotions of the beating heart. I long to do more and see more, to be a part of the gloriously flawed and chaotic world of the living.

Farther out, there and there and there, plumes of smoke rise. It's burn season so you might smell anything at all burning. I'll miss even this. But my foot stays on the gas. Something beyond this town is drawing me. I dream of places I only know in my imagination, built of Robert's words. I want to taste foods made of spices I can't pronounce, hear languages that aren't taught in school. I try to imagine air with salt in it. What does that even mean? I only know I must find out.

When I start my life someplace new, I will not be cautious. I will buy rolls of paper and art supplies. Perhaps I will learn to dance and wear my best jewelry, even when there's no occasion. I don't know if my future will include Robert in it, or if I even need that, but Seattle will be my first stop. We will at least, at long last, share a cup of coffee. And then I, or we, may go anywhere at all.

Soon the home I've known all my life will be a place I go in my sleep, a story I tell to strangers. Petroleum, I will tell them, is a town you won't likely drive past, and if you blink, you might not see it at all. It's a story of wind and the havoc it wreaks, of the outside world encroaching and time encroaching, and yet, its people, beat up like the tilted monument beside the highway, defiantly persist. They don't ask a lot from life, just a two-fingered wave when they pass each other on the road, a game of pinochle or a beer on the weekend, and a chance to look out and up and see nothing in the way for miles.

Tonight when the sun drops low, when the tractors and machines are shut off, the hot engines smoking and clicking as they cool, when the cattle have been fed and are left to their mysterious chattering, the remaining people of this town will head toward their lighted homes, the air pungent with sagebrush, jackrabbits coming out of their burrows to forage, the brown remnants from winter blowing away with the wind. They will untie their worn and dirty work boots and set them outside the door.

For those who stay, Petroleum is home. This is what they know—this life, this land—it is not only where they live; it is who they are. They may be a dying breed, but if they are dying, they would like to die here. For however many days or years remain, they'll choose to end their evenings looking up from their battered porches, wrapped in stars.

Acknowledgments

THIS BOOK WOULD NOT be possible without my beloved agent, *my star*, Gail Hochman; my fearless editor and wine buddy, Sara Nelson; the whole brilliant team at HarperCollins, with special shout-outs to Amanda Pelletier and Mary Sasso; and to these inspiring souls: Ron Carlson, Kim Chinquee, Bridgett Davis, Juliet DeWal, Jessica Keener, Dylan Landis, Caroline Leavitt, Wayétu Moore, Helen Simonson, Jim Tomlinson, David Ulin, and Amy Wallen. You were absolute lifelines for me and for this book. Thank you for your sharp editorial eye, for lending me confidence when mine had run out, for giving nudges and asking questions that plunged me deeper into the work, for encouraging me to let go of the handrail and be bold on the page and in the world.

The warmest appreciation to the people of Winnett, who invited me into their homes, gave me tours of ranches, told me their stories, and understood I would breathe a whole lot of make-believe into their world; to Marty Lee Moses for answering all my mortician questions; and to these authors, whose books taught me so much about the dead, the dying, and consequently, the living: Mary Roach, *Stiff*; Richard Selzer, *Mortal Lessons: Notes on the Art of Surgery*; and Kenneth Iserson, *Death to Dust: What Happens to Dead Bodies?*

Gratitude to the editors of these fine literary magazines, where portions of this book first appeared: *The Coachella Review* ("Our Little Angel"), *Elm Leaves Journal* ("Dead Eddie"), and *New World Writing* ("Cold Hands," "The White Sheet," "The Embalmer's Threads," "The Blue Hour," and "The Last Thing").

Finally, to the three who mean the world to me—David, Trevor, and Dylan—thank you for being so deliriously and fantastically you.

There are more I'd like to acknowledge, but when I started to write a list of names it felt wrong. The list went on and on, and I was tormented by people I might have left out. The list included everyone who ever touched a single page of my work, including the fifty-four chapters I eventually threw away. It included anyone who ever inspired me, reminded me to take a break, gave me a shoulder to cry on or a place to stay and write. The list included plenty who don't even know I exist, just those I stalk online and learn from their work ethic, perseverance, or the balance they've brought to their lives. Many others on the list were long-dead, mighty voices from the past, talking about craft or simply teaching through the literature they left behind.

I think of this giant body of writers as *my tribe*. We are a community of avid readers, of misfits and introverts, of observers and deep thinkers. Many of us work in a near constant state of doubt, consumed with the ways our ideas seem so big when we dream them and so small when we translate them to the page. We know what it is to write through a fog, to write into a dead end. We share the scars of rejection, of "help" from people who may have meant well as they wrote notes in the margins of our stories that read like hate letters. We face the same, hounding questions that make us feel like failures: *Have you finished your book yet? Oh, still? When do you think it will be done?*

We've all been in this game longer than our résumés would indicate. Many times, we've considered giving up, the experience too discouraging. Our drawers and hard drives are filled with stories that didn't work or didn't sell. Many in our lives wonder when we will get a real job, encouraging us to move along to something more reasonable and lucrative. But we keep on, writing with no guarantee of success, because something inside speaks louder than logic or fear.

And so, it's to you, this beautiful and bruised body of writers, that I must thank for creating the paths I've followed, for opening the doors I've walked through, for teaching me how to fight the self-doubt, for being generous with your time and your heart. I thank you if you ever held one of my terrible drafts and taught me to nurture rather than strike out against that wrinkled and trembling life. I thank you for providing company on this long, strange journey. We are in this together.

About the Author

SUSAN HENDERSON is the author of *Up from the Blue*, a five-time Pushcart Prize nominee, and the recipient of an Academy of American Poets award. Her work has been published in books such as *The Future Dictionary of America*, *The Best American Nonrequired Reading*, and many magazines and newspapers. She blogs for the writer support group LitPark.com.

ALSO BY
SUSAN HENDERSON

UP FROM THE BLUE
A Novel
Available in Paperback, eBook, and Digital Audio

"This is not a book you'll soon forget."
—Sara Gruen, author of *Water for Elephants*

The extraordinary debut from Susan Henderson, *Up from the Blue*
is the story of an imaginative young girl struggling to make sense
of her mother's mysterious disappearance.